Lies and Old Lovers

Deb Kemper

Charlie Dawg Press

This book, or parts thereof, may not be reproduced in any form, stored in a retrieval system or transmitted in any form by any means – electronic, mechanical, photocopy, recording, or otherwise – without prior written permission of the author except as provided by United States of America copyright law and except by a reviewer who may quote brief passages in a review to be printed in a newspaper, magazine, or journal.

This book is a work of fiction. Any resemblance of the characters to people, living or dead is unintentional.
Historical facts are correct.
Nairn, Scotland, you are the most beautiful place on earth.

Cover: Ken Kemper, Charlie Dawg Press
Back Cover:
"Black Isle View" from Nairn, Scotland where the Moray Firth flows toward the North Sea

An excerpt from:

Blàr Chùil Lodair

(The Battle of Culloden)
April 16th, 1746–reputed
as a beacon, to all who hold liberty,
precious and fragile in their sturdy hands.

Hail, Scotland, brave and bold!
Never forget that day, though you've fed
your sons to bleaker conflicts.
The opportunity now is your choice
to claim your land and freedom.

No longer shedding costly blood
but rather, shed the cloak
of oppression for your children
and theirs to come.
Culloden, you were not the end of our struggle!

Prologue

Nairn, Scottish Highlands

"You're an idiot, Isabel!" Arthur Fielding roared. He turned his back to her. "I can't believe you ran off to Gretna and married *the publican's son*!" He regained a measure of control. "Minerva tells me Sinclair's abandoned his regiment, AWOL. You're a fool—and no daughter of mine."

Naomi Fielding propped in the doorway, glaring at her husband. "Arthur, you may continue to pretend this has nothing to do with your common bloodline, but the truth always tells." Her hatefulness was chilling. She lunged at Isabel, viciously pinching her arm and hissed, *"You will* have an abortion!" Her eyes flashed with malicious gleam.

The younger woman backed away.

Naomi pressed into her daughter's space, her voice softened, her mood shifting. "You have an appointment...tomorrow morning." She tucked a strand of short mahogany brown hair behind her diamond-clad ear, struggling to maintain control.

Isabel hesitated in her flight.

Naomi struck out, slapping her face. Teeth and fists clenched, she hovered before Isabel and screamed. "Are you *listening* to me?"

Isabel regarded Naomi's dark blue eyes, growling. "I heard you." She turned a glance towards her father, lightly touching her burning cheek. "Cullum's missing in action, wounded, presumed dead—not AWOL." She spun away, dashing through the door, across the marble tiled foyer.

"Return this instant, young lady!" Arthur barked. "I'll take care of your little problem." His volume increased as he hurried after her. "If you birth that child, I'll take it and have you committed!"

Isabel stopped beside a marble statue in the center of the vast hallway, whirled back, and thundered. "No!"

She ran away.

"Isabel!" Her father's bellow trailed her escape.

Through the front doors, thrown open to breezes from the North Sea, along stone steps, crossing the clipped lawn, past the startled gardener pushing a barrow, she raced.

Reaching the road, she scurried down the side of the berm to a mossy, shaded vale. *They won't follow me here.* Isabel stumbled along the rocky shoulder, away from her family estate.

Approaching the burn, she paused. Icy water tumbled over rocks and slipped past the embankment at her feet. She closed her heart and mind to the memories of Cullum at their secret rendezvous.

She swiped her face on the sleeve of her ivory wool cardigan. *Only four miles to Aunt Min's. I've walked this way a thousand times...though not feeling so weak.*

Resting on a boulder bulging from the emerald grass, she glanced around, and down. Her tightly bandaged wrist throbbed.

What was I thinking? Killing myself destroys my child, as well. Surely, just a moment of insanity. How I miss my husband! Please let Cullum be alive!

She wiped her face again. *I'll do anything to bring this small part of him into the world. Anything!*

Chapter 1

April 2013 Almost thirteen years later
Isabel

As I perused the luggage carousel in the Inverness Airport, the message Cullum left on my voice mail replayed in my head.

"Bel, Aunt Min died...this evening. Please...come home. The funeral is in a few days and...ah, well...please, darlin'."

Oh, the sound of his voice....How I've missed the sound of his laughter, his touch....

The conveyer passed a fifth time without my baggage. I felt a flash of concern before spying the lime green case toppling onto the belt.

I returned to my daydream. *Mmm, glad I saved his message to replay when my life feels bereft from his absence. Perhaps I'll see him while in Nairn. But I've hoped so hundreds of other times.*

Hot breath sent a tingle down my spine, attended by the husky voice behind me. "Hullo, lovely."

Dazed, I turned into the melody of my heart. "Cullum?"

"You don't recognize your husband?" He grinned and reached past me for the suitcase and hefted the green bag. "What'd you'd pack, rocks?" He frowned and smiled at the same time.

Some things you need to know about this man: we were married, he *is* the love of my life, and he's Ewan McGregor handsome. A glance and you think, hmm. A long look and you want to know everything.

I used to know everything. We'd been friends since we were six years old.

"I like your beard." He's always been stylishly well-groomed. I smiled. "I can carry my luggage." Reaching out my hand made it accessible to his.

He snagged my fingers and started for the door. "I can too, Bel."

Another note: he loves to walk in the rain, hold hands and lip kiss. I turned my cheek for a peck once, and he pouted for a week.

"How did you know when I'd arrive?" Touching him made me feel fluttery inside. It's been almost thirteen long, hard years without him at my side.

"Called your office. Spoke to Joann. She told me your flight number and ETA."

I laughed. "You called Edinburgh Metropolitan Police Department and our unit secretary gave out information? You're still a charmer." I tugged back and he stopped, gripping harder and smiled.

"Just told her I was your husband. She was a little surprised but...." He shrugged. "Let's go." He steered us to the parking lot.

"We need to talk, Cullum."

He paused to open the boot of his pristine twenty year old red Mercedes convertible with a remote. "Plenty of time for tha' later, darlin'. We're going to Minerva's cottage. You need to ken what's happenin' with the local investigation. Then, we'll have a bit o' tea and meet the solicitor." He laid my case inside, placed his hand in the small of my back, and efficiently guided me to the passenger's side.

I climbed into the red leather interior and glanced up while slipping on my sunglasses. "I was going to rent a car."

"You can have mine. I'll drive Aunt Min's beater." He closed the door, but not before I noticed he wore the wedding band that I gave him thirteen years ago.

My stomach lurched.

I'd come for our aunt's funeral.

An hour later, we arrived in Nairn.

The front of the charming bungalow, which Aunt Min moved into when Uncle David died, is a bountiful cottage garden. No lawn grows in her yard, only flowers, fruits, and vegetables. Early spring, even in the Highlands of Scotland along the coast of the Moray Firth and North Sea, is a season of wonder. More than being with Cullum, for the first time in years, took my breath away.

Edinburgh is grey in comparison. That's where I live—with our son—whom Cullum doesn't know.

He parked the car at the curb and began the tale of the accident that robbed Min's life. Turning in his seat, he rested his left arm across the back of mine.

"She fell from the steps inside the front door. Bertie, who's the constable now, thinks she was facing the door: about to answer it, maybe. She slipped, or was pushed, and tumbled down four steps and struck her head on the marble statue at the base. Trouble is, she couldn't move that statue. It was on the hearth when I was over the day before."

I gazed into his clear, pale grey eyes. "I work for the police, Cullum. That doesn't make me one. All I do is examine scientific evidence. I don't investigate afield."

"I ken that, love. But I acquired a copy of the paperwork from Bertie, for you. See if you can find somethin' he missed. That's all I'm askin'." He glanced away and took a deep breath. "I loved Min."

My eyes misted, but I managed to choke out words. "Me, too." I patted his free hand and he grasped my fingertips, raising them to his mouth for a kiss.

"Had it not been for Min, I'd *never* have had you." His wounded look prompted tears.

My heart tightened. "I feel the same, Cullum." I struggled to get a handle on my emotions. "I'll look at the facts and see if Bertie…did you tell him I was coming?"

"Nay, just told him I wanted a copy for my own peace of mind. Did you call your mother?" He didn't wait for an answer, but climbed out to open my door, then round to the boot for my bag.

I followed, glancing at the garden through the gate of the white picket fence. "She left a message on my phone about Min. I didn't call her, haven't talked to her since my father died, five years ago."

"I was at his funeral."

Surprised, I glanced back. "You were?"

"Aye, stayed on the fringe of the private club crowd." He smiled.

I melted a little more. "I looked, but didn't see you."

"I intentionally stayed outta the way. Besides, it gave me a chance to see how much your son had grown." His broad back turned to me, as he strode toward the front door.

***

I scanned the report. "Can you show me how she lay on the floor?"

"Sure." He dropped to the old oak floor and propped his legs, askew on the steps. "It's like this I think. Does it match the sketch?"

"Aye, ponderin' somethin', sorry." I stepped past him and up four tiled stairs to the small stoop and turned. "The marble statue was where?"

He signaled with his left hand to the base of the rail. "Here, her head was…bashed in…." He indicated the left side of his head above the ear. "There was blood and tissue on the statue. I'm not sayin' it couldn't happen like tha'. I'm sayin' the statue *couldn't* have been at the bottom of the steps. It weighed ten stone, at least. I moved it for her to clean, once in a while." He watched me from his position on the floor.

I sighed and frowned. "Who would she let in, while in her dressing gown, able to move a hundred-forty pound statue?"

"Exactly!" He stretched, rolled, and practically bounced onto his feet. He's in fine shape, very buff.

"The neighbor didn't see strangers or different cars in the area." I read Leah Mabry-Mitchell's statement. "Old women have a penchant for keeping track of all movement in their vicinity." I sat on the rose-covered chintz settee and crossed my trouser clad legs, pondering the situation.

He sat beside me, close enough to smell. It was nice, but far too much like all the times we'd been in Aunt Min's house, a thousand years ago, when we were best friends, lovers, and then married. He reached for me as I vaulted off the seat and escaped to the kitchen. I heard him sigh and pictured him rolling his beautiful grey eyes. He followed me.

"Who told you about Liam?" Gathering teacups and such for tea I shot a frown his way.

He lit a fire under the kettle. "Saw 'im once, when he was five, I think. Surely you don't wonder how I ken he's my son." One brow rose as he glanced at me, then turned to settle himself against the counter, crossing his ankles. "Does he not look familiar to you *at all*?"

Wincing at his sarcasm, I nodded. "He's just like you, even more so at twelve than five or seven."

"We need to sort it out, Isabel. I want to know 'im." He checked the kettle as it began to hiss. "Min finally told me the whole sordid tale of your reaction when you heard I was MIA in Bosnia. Said your father hung the suicide attempt over your head. Your mother insisted on abortion, and you ran to Aunt Min for comfort." He sighed. His voice cracked. "She helped them find the man you left me for, so you were auctioned off to the highest bidder, I suppose." He rubbed his hand over his mouth and down his trim beard.

"Cullum, it's so *awful* when you recite our history aloud and it wasn't like tha'." I carried the tray for tea to the counter beside the Aga range and poured the near boiling water over the tealeaves in the China pot. "There was never an auction for my hand, just a deal Daddy brokered with a longtime client and club chum."

He hadn't responded, but turned to gaze into the rear garden.

"Cullum?" I laid my hand on his back.

"Hmm?" He didn't trust his voice.

I rested my head against his upper arm. "Please don't be angry with me. I fought to keep our son, doing whatever I had to do. My parents would've taken him, believing they did the best thing for us all."

He spun and grasped my shoulders. "What part of us included your husband?"

"None. Aunt Min caught hell for encouraging our relationship. She scrambled to save her connection to Mother. Daddy refused to allow them communication until Min agreed to help. She suggested sending me abroad, even offering herself as my escort. They were adamant." I wiped my hand across his strong chest. "*I'm so sorry*. If I could make it up to you, I would. I'd undo all the pain if I had the power."

"I was MIA for *eight days*, Isabel. In *eight days* my life transformed from bein' the happiest man alive, having you to come home to, to pure bleedin' hell. It was torture to wake of a mornin', unbearable to close my eyes at night. For two years I barely existed before I stumbled out of tha' pit and found my way back to sanity." The raw agony of his loss darkened Min's cheery yellow kitchen.

My voice softened. "It was difficult for me, as well. The difference was I had Liam." I looked down at the space between us. Tears splattered the tile floor at my feet. I sighed. "What can I do, Cullum?"

He shrugged and pulled me into his arms, resting his face against mine with a sigh. His body quivered. "I apologize! I didn't mean to drag all the rubbish out. I came to fetch you because...I need you, Bel. I want you to help me try again, if you'll have me."

Snuggling into his hold, I smiled, wondering what on earth he meant. "For you, anything."

He pushed me back for a look and sniffed. "Let's have tea. We're to be at Damian's office in an hour, for the reading of the will. Your mother will be there, Isabel. Prepare yourself to see her." He kissed my forehead and grasped the tea tray.

Perhaps he'd given up lip kisses.

***

At Damian's office, we sat in leather bound chairs in a stylishly appointed room. The Macintosh Building is on High Street near the center of Nairn. I glanced out the second story window as gulls screeched, diving toward the water of the burn beyond the alley. Damian opened and entered a side door. He took his chair and smiled across the massive cherry desk.

Cullum caught my hand, squeezing.

"Well, look at the two o' you, like old times, eh?" He shared the smile with each of us. "We're waitin' for Naomi to arrive. Does she ken you're here, Isabel?" One elegantly sculpted brow rose.

"I haven't talked to her." I glanced back at the window. Doves pranced along the ledge, waddling like Charlie Chaplin in silent films. He and his wife owned a vacation home here.

"Cullum, is Robin comin'?"

"Nay, I'll tell Da what you say. Kyle's busy birthing lambs so he'll settle for my version as well."

"Suppose it's easier for you to get away of a day?" Damian propped on one arm of his high-backed chair.

Cullum grinned. "The brewery and pub don't run themselves. I employ good people." There was a spark of defiance in his voice.

The outer door opened. Cullum and Damian left their seats as my mother entered.

Naomi is one of the most beautiful women in the country, the whole UK for sure. Born to Scottish aristocrats, second in line for the title, masses of debt and land, but little money, she landed my father. He had heaps of cash by then. She considered herself lucky to have landed a billionaire. That was a matter of opinion.

She spotted me and paused in the middle of the large room, both hands on her face, her mouth a perfect 'O', like a delighted five year old. "Isabel, darling, I had no idea you'd be here."

Damian circled the desk, drawing a chair similar to the ones Cullum and I occupied and indicated it was for her pleasure. He glowed.

She graced him with a smile, her head tilted to one side. Glancing my way, she moistened her lips before addressing me again. "You didn't call me back, so I assumed you weren't coming. When did you get in, dear?"

"Several hours ago. Cullum was kind enough to pick me up at the airport in Inverness."

She had yet to acknowledge him.

She aimed a cool look his direction. "Hello, Cullum. How are you these days?" She pulled a pretty pout and tucked a strand of short dark hair behind her ear.

Cullum nodded to her. "Fine, thank you, Naomi. Better since having tea with...my wife." He turned back to me and perched one hand on the back of my chair.

Damian waited for my mother to indicate he was free to speak. She nodded.

9

He cleared his throat and began. "Well, since we're here about Minerva Rose-Banks' estate, we'll begin with the executorship.

"Naomi, allow me to make it clear that I was dead set against her selection. I tried my best to get your sister to hear reason, but she steadfastly refused to budge." He shared his frown with us. "Cullum and Isabel will jointly hold the position. If either of you wish to step aside, now is an excellent time to say."

Cullum looked at me and laughed. I couldn't help it. I joined him, to the point of nearly crying. Dear, sweet Aunt Min had finally found a way to make us face each other again. No doubt, in her mind, we could patch things up, let bygones be, and all would end splendidly.

"What's so funny?" My mother raised her shrill voice above the noise we caused, perching on the edge of her seat. She turned her fury onto Damian. "I demand this be contested at once."

I intervened. "Give it a rest, Mummy. The old girl didn't have so much that it'd pay for you to drop the solicitor's fee, unless...." My eye shifted to Damian's reddening face.

Cullum shook his head. "Keep reading then, man, let's be done wi' this." He chuckled again.

Damian read through the provisions of the will. "It appears that you get the cottage, Isabel, and all its contents, such as they are, and Cullum is the proprietor of a piece of art that she thought might be quite valuable. She wouldn't allow me to have it assessed, or even see it, for that matter." He produced a key and a sealed packet. "It's kept in a vault. The location and passwords are in the envelope." He read on for a moment. "Kyle inherits David's coin collection. Again, in a vault, unappraised." He handed over another package.

The solicitor turned a frown on my mother.

She laid her hand on her chest, over her expensive enhancements, and sighed. Her little girl tone took me by surprise. She'd always used it on Daddy. "What of me, Damian?"

A sad smile framed his answer. "Dearest Naomi, she leaves you the contents of this envelope." He handed over another sealed envelope, in the finest linen stationary.

"Oh, sweet, sweet Minerva." She glanced at me from the top of her eyes, long lashes framing her latest tuck up job. "She didn't forget she had a sister."

I fought a smile, having no idea what Aunt Min left. Poor Mummy needs everyone in her life consumed with the fact that she *is*. Cullum has only been polite to her, never in awe, as men should be—unforgiveable.

Damian released a similar envelope to Cullum. "This is for Robin and Genevieve Sinclair with this message, 'David wanted you two to have this. The last time I checked, it had risen considerably in value, so I left it alone. How I wish I could see your faces when you get it but it had to be held in trust to avoid exorbitant taxes. He said to tell you that the champagne's on him.'" He forced a smile, more like a grimace. "Your mother's *David's* sister isn't she?"

Cullum answered. "Aye, my Uncle David married Isabel's Aunt Minerva." He spared a look for my mother. "That's why there was no concern for our children when we married." His eyes narrowed and frost nipped the room.

Total silence reigned for a full half-minute. I had no hint what made Mummy so uncomfortable. Damian rose and cleared his throat.

Cullum answered my unasked question. "It's one of the arguments your mother used to explain your parents' disapproval of your choice of husbands."

I looked at my mother. "Really? I ken you're not as smart as Aunt Min, but there's no blood relation...." I shook my head, hoping to clear the fog of my mother's presence. "Are we finished, Damian?"

"Aye, lass, we are for the day, then." He tried to smile and remained standing as Cullum and I took our leave.

I stopped in the doorway for a last look at Mummy. "I'm so sorry I disappoint you." It was just enough fuel to detonate the fiery furnace.

"Come back here! You have no right to speak to me that way." She was on her feet, heading toward me, a hand on her hip, and one finger wagging. "You listen to me, you ungrateful brat...."

Cullum reached back and swept me through the doorway and took my place. His voice was calm. "There'll be no more, Naomi. If you've anythin' else to say, let *me* know. We won't be doing this again. It's a small village and it has to suit us all."

Mummy's teeth clenched as she poked her finger in his face and screeched. "She won't stay here, you idiot! She's leading you on, like she's always done, draggin' you around by your...."

Damian's hand clapped over her mouth, his tone sharp. "Enough, Naomi! Please come, sit." He led her back to her chair, her head against his chest. He pressed a button on his desk and ordered tea and brandy.

Mummy's a bit of a handful at times

Chapter 2

"I made reservations for dinner at The Bandstand."

The surprise I felt failed to register with Cullum. He kept his eyes straight ahead.

"One needs reservations these days?" At one time the restaurant was a café.

"Aye, if you wanna seat beside the windows to watch the tide, you do." He flashed a grin.

I melted a bit more. "Thank you for standing up to my mother."

"It should've been done long ago, Isabel. I was terrified when we were kids. Your parents frightened me. After we married, I thought someday the situation would arise to say my piece. Today was tha' day." He checked traffic and made a turn.

We drove towards the pub his father inherited from his father, and so on for about ten generations. Cullum's family also raised sheep. The farm and pub responsibilities were divided between brothers.

"Do you have any idea about the painting Aunt Min left to you?"

"I may. Have you?"

It was my turn to play coy. "Maybe." I glanced out the window as the gulls dove towards this morsel of red car and swept back into the sky, when they realized it moved too fast to be prey.

"You can drop me at the pub and go back to Min's or stay, if you like." He drove into the parking lot and pulled the brake.

"I think I'll go back and have a soak. Did you know Min kept a diary?" I watched him glance around and back to my face.

"Nay, you're thinking there may be clues?"

"Could be. I'll dig them out and read through, see if she kept company with someone new. I'd like to see what her thoughts were on...well, us. I can surmise a few things but...."

"Aye, it'd be nice to know. I ken my thoughts on us. " He climbed out and rounded the car to open my door. "Come back around seven?"

"Aye, seven it is." I thought he might kiss me as he stopped and studied my mouth, but he didn't even bother shaking hands, just turned and left. He looked back at the doorway. "'Til seven, Isabel." He disappeared inside the darkly aged portal set into well-weathered stone.

On return to Aunt Min's cottage, I entered the holy sanctum of her bedroom and checked the bookcases flanking the fireplace. There, arranged by dates on the bindings, were her journals. I pulled the most recent, then decided to check her desk for her current entries. "Tell me who has been here, Aunt Min. Smelling your fragrance in the room brings you so near, I feel I may hear your voice any moment." I closed my eyes and remembered the night of *the* parental confrontation when I'd run through woods, taking the road to skirt bogs. When I finally made it to Aunt Min's house, I was out of breath and weak as a newborn kitten from blood loss. That's a Minnieism she used infrequently.

I ran a bath and took her most recent diary with me, to soak in the large claw-footed tub. I sprinkled herbal salts, which sat on the shelf beside the tub and undressed, dropping my clothes in a pile and stepping into the hot water.

A chill swept through me, earlier, while standing outside the pub with Cullum. Wondering where his new approach to our relationship was about to lead, I slid into the fragrant water and sighed. Drying my hands, I reached for the diary and opened it to her last entry.

I've felt my age today, all my joints aching with the arthritis I inherited from Father. I'm amazed that Naomi doesn't have it as well. My sweet Isabel will, hopefully, be spared this agony. She looks so much like me, her reddish brown curls flying in the breeze, her father's dark eyes and long lashes and she has Arthur's bearing. I wished I could've mothered her, instead of Naomi.

I miss my lassie and long for the day she returns to make amends to Cullum's shattered heart. We were all very wrong to interfere with those two. I'll never forgive myself for the misery I brought on that precious lad but I cannot bring myself to encourage him. I promised Arthur to never interfere again.

Depriving Liam of his dad all these years, perhaps this pain is punishment, from my heavenly Father, to teach me to mind my own business.

Come to think of it, the arthritis never bothered me so much as it did after Isabel went away. The pain increased when Cullum returned home, to an empty hearth and vacant cradle. The years he wasted, searching for oblivion, will be my cross to bear to my grave.

Bernie's report said she wore her dressing gown when she went to the door. It had to be someone she knew. I couldn't accept that she'd open the door for a stranger in the middle of the night. It wasn't dark until after ten, this time of year, and rarely dark on this street, what with intermittent lampposts and her front lanterns.

With the diary put away, I closed my eyes for a moment, felt myself dozing, and sat up hastily. I'd been involved investigating the death of a woman who fell asleep while soaking, only to drown. I stood, toweled off, and wrapped the heavy terry cloth round me, tucking in the corner, and headed for the guest room.

A key scraped in the lock and the front door opened quietly.

I stepped behind the bedroom door and waited. Something weighty was tossed onto the coffee table. The floor squeaked in a well-known spot at the edge of the rug.

"Isabel?" Cullum's voice brought a sigh of relief.

Peeking round the door, I scolded him. "I'm hiding in here. You scared the life outta me."

"I'm sorry, lass. I had no...." His gaze drifted slowly toward the floor and back up to my face. His mouth was still open.

Remembering my attire, a blue towel, I stepped back behind the door.

"I'll wait out here for you, then." He didn't leave the spot where he stood but, through the crack between hinges, I watched him gaze at the ceiling a moment and look around as though lost. "Bloody hell," he mumbled through his teeth and scrubbed his fist over his mouth.

Closing the door softly, my heart pounded. A warm feeling crept up my belly and I knew I still loved and wanted the man in the front room, with everything in me. Those feelings lay dormant, having been suppressed after the threats my father made against his life.

I snatched a dress from the hanger and pulled it over my head. Tucking myself into its shelf bra I glanced around for a wrap or sweater. A double layer of wraps sufficed, covering the bare parts of me.

What are you thinking, enticing Cullum? He can't possibly have forgiven you. He wants to know his son. That doesn't mean you're a package deal. I considered the bed, remembering one of the times we made love there.

What am I doing? I pulled off the dress and settled into a nice pair of woolen slacks with a light cashmere jumper. It would be cold outside later. I needed to dress warmly. *And...I'm scared he feels the same way I do...or worse, he doesn't.*

When I walked out of the bedroom, Cullum hadn't moved far from the door. His hands stuffed into the pockets of his khaki trousers, he tilted his head and gave me a sideways glance. "I'm sorry I walked in on you. I called a few minutes ago, but there's no answer so I thought you might be nappin'."

"In the tub. I read parts of Min's diary that I think she wrote the night she died or some time near then." I didn't know if my words made sense. It sounded like babble to *my* ears.

A frown tainted his brow. "She may've been interrupted."

"Looks that way." I nodded but couldn't meet his eyes.

"Well done, Bel. We need to go, reservation and all tha'." He swept his hand toward the door.

Turning to leave, before I debased myself, I hopped up the steps Aunt Min had fallen down, reached for the knob, then stopped. "How many people have keys to this door?"

Cullum paused behind me, his hand on my back. His voice sounded husky. "I don't ken, love."

I whirled to face him. "I want you, Cullum."

He nodded slowly; his hand dropped by his side. "And I you, Isabel, but it's too soon. Give us time, lass."

I spun back to the door, my face burning, and leaned my head against the cold oak. "Whatever you say." My hand turned the knob and I stood aside when the door swung wide. "You go first."

Frowning, he filled the portal and I looked back to the place Aunt Min fell. "She may've surprised someone inside. She could've been pushed or fallen onto the statue, by the fireplace, when she came into the room. We've looked at it from Bernie's point of view, not what you think actually happened. "

Cullum considered the scene from the doorway. "You're right. Is there a way you can search for blood in front o' the hearth?"

"Blacklight." I breathed.

He smiled. "I have one in the brewery. We'll stop by after dinner...or... after a walk along the shore."

"It'll keep." I joined him on the stoop outside, while he secured the entrance.

Chapter 3

Tide was out again, when we walked on the tan sand and rusty slabs of shingle along Moray Firth where it feeds into the North Sea. Thick wads of seaweed clung to the ripples of coarse sand and rocks.

Tidepools hold surprises. Colorful chunks of stone, a wad of tangled sea veg, deposits of beach glass, edges worn from the grinding of surf and sand, stimulate the imagination. Who and what exists on the coast opposite? Did someone drop the bottle that made the beach glass or shatter it first, lessening the time it took to become treasure?

I pulled my wrap tighter round me. The sky became overrun with wispy clouds, an aura of a golden glow, all that remained of the sunset. That was one of our places: Cullum's and mine. I avoided the shore, whenever possible. There were too many difficult memories of our laughter and love.

He reached for my hand, standing behind me, and shouted, to be heard. "See the ships moving along the horizon? Port traffic is on the increase. Great for Scotland's commerce." His arm extended beyond my shoulder.

I studied the vessels drifting toward the North Sea. Sailboats were plentiful, embellishing the choppy grey water with brilliant color. A few late fishing vessels headed into harbor. The wind blew steady at just below gale force. It's always gusty here, regardless of the season. The sea is never calm.

I felt my body fold into Cullum's strong, sure embrace, and leaned back into his shoulder.

His face buried in my hair, my eyes closed, while he breathed into my ear. "I've missed you, Bel."

I'd dreamed of hearing those words again, for thirteen years. It really happened. I was back in my lover's arms—for the moment.

***

I found a magnifying glass on Aunt Min's desk. Cullum waited in the living room with the blacklight plugged into the outlet beside the hearth.

I hurried back to him. "If you'll shine the light this way," I indicated toward me. "I'll crawl across the rug looking for evidence. You're sure nothing was cleaned except the floor beside the hand rail?"

"Aye, I was here." He flipped on the switch and cast the purplish black glow my way.

Ahead was a blood splatter on the hearth that I didn't need the magnifier to see. I dropped to my knees and began to comb the area in front of the fireplace for hair, fibers, anything I could find. I lay flat on my belly and ran my fingers over the hand-hooked rug Aunt Min took great pride in finishing about a week before Cullum and I married. I found little at first: a hair, pink fuzz, perhaps from the cashmere throw on the settee. I skimmed the surface of the level loops. Something shiny came into view.

"What's that?" Cullum squatted in front of me, where a piece of an object nestled in between the hand tied loops.

"Looks like part of a button." I bagged the black and silver fastener and sat up. A look under the microscope was in order. "Doesn't mean it came from the killer though." I glanced up at him from my prone position. "I'll go through her clothes and see if there's a match."

He shrugged. "Aye, but it *may* have come from a stranger." He stood watching, as I continued combing the rug.

It would be too hard imagining anyone who knew Min could kill her; she was a friend, never an adversary.

An hour of perusal left me with six bags tagged with particulars and an interesting fact. There was blood on the stone hearth. The killer scoured the stone to clean it, but couldn't get all of it off. There were several small splatters on the rim of the beautiful rug, missed because of the floral pattern. That explained moving the statue to the steps.

Bernie should've called a detective inspector in to investigate, even though he thought it was an accident. His head may roll because of the oversight.

I looked up to find Cullum studying me. "Bernie's in deep trouble."

He cocked his head to one side. "Goes with the job, lass." He switched off the light and sat on the settee.

I joined him, straightening my jumper. "I'll have to find a microscope, maybe when I go back to Edinburgh…well…after the funeral when I return…."

His fingertips touched my mouth. "Shh, we don't have to talk about tha' now. I'll find a microscope for you, Isabel."

I sat closer to him and nodded. "Okay, but it needs to be a specific kind and…."

"I'll get one from the procurator fiscal's office."

"You have that kind of pull?" I leaned back against the settee.

"You might be surprised." He laid his arm behind me.

I longed to cuddle into his side and—relish being close to him. "How can you get a microscope?"

"Your curiosity held longer than I thought it would." He shifted a minute inch or so closer and leaned to my ear. "Have a bartender who works nights in the PF's office."

"Ah, that's good, then." I met his gaze. "Liam has your eyes, darker, but shaped like yours. He has my mouth, your chin, and the shape of your fingers."

"Why'd you never come back to me?"

Light diminished outside and the lampposts kicked on automatically. Corners became dim shadows, making it safe to say the hard words that needed saying.

"Have you forgiven me for stealing your son from you, for breaking your heart, and deserting you when you needed me most?" I swallowed the fear that oozed out with every word.

A moment ticked past, then another. "If I hadn't been able to let go of it, Isabel, I'd have been crazy long before now."

"Why'd you not come for us?"

"I did, a thousand times in my mind, but in reality only a few hundred. I never had the courage to approach you. I'd have gone over the edge, even last week, if you'd sent me away. I had to wait for you to come home. Min never encouraged me, as I kenned she would, if you'd be receptive." He held my hand up, peering at my fingers in the near dark.

"If I'd have known you were nearby, I'd have run to greet you."

"I checked on our son, tried to find 'Liam King' at his school a few years ago." Cullum's voice broke.

I peered through the half dark. "His name is not King, Cullum. His name is Liam David Sinclair."

He looked up. "Really? I didn't imagine…well then, thank you for that, Bel."

We sat in silence for a few minutes. The train passed in the near distance. The Flying Scotsman hurled along the tracks, rocking passengers to sleep.

"Does he ken…me?" He sounded hopeful.

"He never thought the man I married was his father. Bradley tried to…it just wasn't…he didn't have the tools to operate as a husband or father."

Cullum pulled away and stood, walking to the window to study the street through the shadows cast by trees and shrubs. "I wanted to *never* hear his name, especially not from your mouth."

"It wasn't him who stole your family, Cullum. I was as convenient to Bradley King as he was to my parents. After his father died, a few years ago, he was finally free to pursue his own life, without the baggage of a woman. We lived as prisoners sharing a common bond, the safety of our parents' social standing and political ambitions." I tried to think of something I could say that would make a positive difference to Cullum.

He rejoined me. "I ken it wasn't your fault, but you never even offered me a chance to meet our son." He earnestly felt betrayed.

He was right.

"I received a call from my father, not long after you returned from Kosovo. He'd worked up a bit of liquid courage, said that you bein' alive changed nothing. If I tried to see you or defaulted on the deal he made with Bradley's father, he'd have you killed.

He said he had a lot invested in getting me out of his way and your breaths were bein' counted."

His voice rose to the rafters. "That bloody bastad!"

I studied his scowl in the near dark. "After my father died, Liam and I discussed you. He wanted to meet his da. I'd make plans to come to Nairn, hopin' you'd be available to us, maybe meet us here, at Min's. He'd get sick the night before we were due to leave, throwing up, headache; it was like the flu every time. But I knew he was so afraid of being rejected, he made himself ill with worry."

"What about now, Bel? Why can't he come now?" His dark brows rose, his eyes narrowed.

"He can. I'll call him in the morning, before the funeral, and ask him to come up on the train. Will that suit you?" I leaned on the arm of the settee, far too aware of his proximity. This wasn't about us; it was about who we were supposed to have been, once upon a time.

He nodded. "I'll reserve his ticket on Scot Rail." He looked at me for affirmation.

"Make it two to Inverness. His au pair, Mrs. Peterson, can accompany him and get him on the train to Nairn."

"How long's she been with you?" He sighed.

"Since Liam was a few weeks old. I found work in Edinburgh before he was born. She and her husband live near our flat, but she stays on the rare occasion I need to be away. Hadn't you better get to the pub?"

He leaned back and sighed. "I don't have to go." He reached for my hand.

I swallowed fear, pride, and desire. "It's probably better if you do, though. Tongues will wag and what did you say earlier? It's too soon?"

"Aye, you're right. I don't wanna ruin your reputation." He chuckled, a low sexy sound that still warms me.

I smiled. "Too late for that, Sinclair." My voice broke. I wanted to cry and needed the time alone. "Oh, and take the snazzy ride with you, please. I'll drive Aunt Min's beater."

"You're sure?" He rose from the seat where we'd made out on a number of occasions.

"Absolutely, I wanna get into Min's persona. See if it stirs anything." I crossed my arms.

"I'll pick you up tomorrow?"

"No, you need to be with your family, Cullum."

"You're my...."

"No, I'm not. Really, go along with yourself then." I felt tears pressing. My throat tightened.

***

I read Min's journals into the night. One thing stood out above all else: the way she referred to me. I began to doubt my parentage.

I had to apologize to Naomi again today. I interfered when she disciplined Isabel. I'd promised to allow her to raise the child any way she chose, trusting she'd want the best for her, as I do. Jealousy never occurred to me in those days. Naomi underwent fertility treatments for three years. I was with her and witnessed the pain and frustration she endured.

Still, when she shrieked at my fine little girl, I lost my temper. That's a rare thing and shocked her into submission for a moment. Then the spoiled brat she's always been surfaced, to claim she was the one wronged. We'd only given her the very thing her heart desired. I'd never have agreed to Arthur's terms had I realized Naomi would turn on Isabel.

That explained a few things and left some in shadows. It wasn't the relationship with Naomi that Min had to salvage, when my parents discovered I married Cullum. It was her relationship with my father. Naomi hated that I was pregnant with Liam. Even after Min and Daddy cut a deal with Bradley's father, she'd insisted I abort the child to cut Cullum out of our lives forever.

I refused.

After all, why marry someone I didn't even know, if not to keep my son alive? A dead baby would have foiled Daddy's plans.

Chapter 4

I was up with the sun, between 4 and 4:30 a.m. for those of you who aren't blessed to be in Scotland on a fine spring morning. The wind gusted, at times, more than 40 miles per hour. I propped on a window seat with a cup of coffee and watched the sunrise.

At six-thirty I rang my son's phone. After three dancing chimes, he answered. "Hi, Mum."

"Hi, yourself. How are you this fine mornin'?"

"Okay, no exams today. School's kind of dead. Oops, sorry. For a moment, I forgot about Aunt Min."

"The funeral's today, at ten. I wonder if you'd like to come up and hang out with me for a few days."

His excitement engine revved. "Really? Sure, absolutely. Must I fly or…."

"Deep breath, Liam. Mrs. Peterson has agreed to come with you on the train to Inverness. She'll get you on the train to Nairn and return to Edinburgh. Tickets wait at the station and the train leaves at nine-thirty so you'd better hurry."

"Cool! I'll pack right now. Will you meet me there?"

"Probably." Cullum and I hadn't discussed that part. "At any rate, you shan't have to walk. If I can't be at the station, someone else will."

"Awesome! I'll see you this evening. Mum, thanks. I was wasting away here."

"You're welcome. I love you."

"I love you more."

"You can't…." The call disconnected. I smiled.

My lad was coming to meet his father and there was no time to make himself ill.

I stood apart from the crowd of family and friends of Minerva Chrisselle Rose-Banks, perusing the array of probable suspects. My mother leaned heavily on Damian's sturdy arm. Black crepe draped her sublime figure and she wore a monstrous silk hat, complete with veil.

Robin and Genny Sinclair, Cullum's parents, stood shoulder-to-shoulder with their sons. His father, bent a little with age, was a decade older than his mother. Genny was a lovely woman with her son's grey eyes and greying black hair, sporting a stylish cut. She wore little makeup and didn't need it, as she had perfect skin. She caught my eye and winked. A sad smile touched her full mouth.

She'd loved me well, but I broke her heart too.

I walked away early, toward Aunt Min's beater, parked near the church, wanting to have a moment of quiet after the service.

"Ashes to ashes, dust to dust. Our lives are but vapor, but the Word of the Lord lives forever." Vicar Angus MacBride's deep mellow voice was suited to mesmerizing small children and bereaved family. He could have announced games for St. Andrews Royal & Ancient Golf Club, had the lure of the church not engaged him.

***

I climbed the graduated steps to the front door of the police department. There's also a ramp. Handicap access is available but, in this country, the terrain and weather discourage weakness.

Opening a glass door I spotted an old acquaintance. The sergeant on the desk glanced up from his reading. "May I help ye, Ms. Fielding?" His merry blue eyes took note of my attire and the smile melted.

"You can do tha', Jimmy. I'm here to see Bernie. Is he in today?"

"Aye, I'll ring you through. Go down the hall to the right and his door is on your left. It's next to the loo."

"Convenient." I smiled and headed toward a confrontation that could have been avoided, but here we were.

Bernard Leighton, Chief Constable, the gold lettering was newly applied. I tapped on the glass and waited his summons.

"Enter!" Bernie's voice boomed.

I eased the door open a crack and peeked inside. "You sound like an ogre when you put on the monster voice, Bernie."

He threw back his great head of dark hair and laughed, jumping to his feet. "Come in, come in. Hey, I'm sorry I didn't make Minerva's funeral, lass. I was in a meeting all mornin'." He shuffled the papers, dispersed over his desk, into a neat pile.

"Thank you for your consideration. I noticed the flowers your wife sent." I took a seat so he could take his. "I'm here on business, Bernie." I gave him a moment to adjust his attitude from a harmless visit to a career-altering situation, at least for him.

"Aye, what can I do for you, Isabel?" He laced his fingers together on his desk top planner, a tolerant smile on his lips.

I removed the objects Cullum and I found in Min's living room and laid them before him. "I haven't reported my findings. It's between the two of us, alright?"

He appeared to be wary, brushing a hand to wipe away the perspiration sprouting on his upper lip. "Alright, then. Wha's this?" He waved toward the bags.

"Evidence I took from the rug in front of the fireplace at Aunt Minerva's cottage. I inspected everything under a borrowed microscope. You need to be aware of the implications, Bernie. There's evidence of blood splatter on the stone hearth. I saw that under a blacklight, but there *are* a few drops on the rug as well. It would be missed easily enough because of the pattern."

"And wha' caused you to peer so closely at *my* case?" He produced a handkerchief to wipe his brow and upper lip dry.

"Too many variables fail to align. I'm not here to bust your chops. I'm here to ask you to reopen the investigation. It will be probed. You ken I won't just shush when told to quieten. Will you send forensics to the cottage?"

He glanced out the window at the gulls swooping, their sharp voices shrieking. "And if I refuse?"

"I'll pull rank on you and you won't be sittin' behind this desk next week, Bernie. I don't want to make that phone call." I leaned back in my chair and pondered his reasons for not looking further. Then it struck me, Scotland's Socialist Party. "Bernie, are you involved with SSP?"

He flinched. "Wha'? Nay, nay, Isabel. I'm uh...well you ken, one cannot be in public office and too closely affiliated with political organizations. Get my drift?" He wiped his forehead and upper lip again.

"Aunt Min was adamantly set against the party." It made me uneasy to broach the subject. Cullum was on the board of directors of SSP and watched like a hawk by people who kept tabs on such individuals. At one time, it caused a rift in his relationship with Min and his parents, before he learned to keep his involvement under wraps.

"You best talk to Cullum, lass, if you're of a mind it's one of his pals. I got nothing to do with tha'."

"Bernie, you have to pursue this, regardless of who's involved." I perched on the edge of my seat. "Look, Cullum brought this problem to my attention. Why would he do it if he thought it was someone from the SSP? I didn't come to wreck your career. I'm offering you the opportunity to take what I've found and see if you can make an arrest. I'm here to help you, not cause difficulty."

I was almost begging him to step up to his responsibilities. I could never return to Nairn again if forced to report his lack of fervor for investigating the murder, especially if he turned out to be a member of the SSP.

He gathered my evidence bags and studied me a moment. "I'll have someone look into it but I'll not promise you a thin'."

I nodded and left my seat. "Good enough, then."

He rose and rounded the desk, offering his hand. I accepted and he pulled me close. "Isabel," he whispered near my face, "use caution." He stepped back and bobbed his head once, looking around the room. I guess he considered it wired, at least for sound.

I acknowledged his warning and left his office. *Is Cullum a suspect now? Why would he insist on examining the matter further? Bernie appeared to be impotent, just where SSP or someone else might want him.*

I waved toward the desk sergeant and made tracks to Min's old Volkswagen. I worked the choke back and forth a few times, as the ancient gal needed a bit of coaxing, and turned the key. *Click, click, click.*

"Great!" I slammed both hands on the steering wheel and climbed out, not relishing a walk to the cottage in pumps.

Cullum's fine red Mercedes pulled alongside. He called through the open window. "Hey! What's wrong?"

I leaned in to answer. "Dead battery, I think."

"Get in, I'll take you wherever your heart desires. How'd Bernie take the news?"

I slid inside the car and closed the door. "He says he's tryin' hard not to step on certain political factions, but he'll look into the case again." I watched Cullum ponder the situation, conscious I expected a reaction.

"What more could we want? Are you implying that the SSP has somethin' to hide?" He pulled into a roundabout.

"No, just curious. He said to talk to you, so I'm talking."

"Not that I'm aware of, Isabel. It doesn't matter. If it's someone from my party, I want them caught as badly as I would anyone else. We don't go around killin' little old ladies because they love the Queen, you know." He shot a look my way.

Through his sunglasses, I couldn't make out anything his eyes might reveal.

"I'll call a tow truck and have the car inspected." He parked in front of Aunt Min's cottage and opened his door. He was still dressed in the navy flannel suit and tie from the funeral.

I was out of the car by the time he'd circled. He closed the door behind me and took my arm. "Let's go inside. I need to talk to you about somethin' else." He steered me to the door, taking a look around before we entered.

"What's that?" I removed Aunt Min's ruana wrap I'd worn over my dark green dress. He took it from me and hung it on a hall tree by the steps. Watching him take off his jacket and loosen his tie gave me ideas I'd rather not have, when alone with him, as he'd turned me down once already.

"Well, Liam's on his way?"

"Aye, do you wanna fetch him from the station?"

He paled. "I do but…." He glanced round the room. "Well, do you think he'd mind if I join you when you pick him up?"

I had an idea. "Why don't you meet me there?" I edged towards the settee and lowered myself on it, kicking off my heels.

"I can do tha'. You keep the car and I'll…."

"No, I'll get a taxi or just walk up." I smiled and studied him closely. He was clearly nervous, but I assumed he would be, about to meet his almost teenage son for the first time.

"Alright then. Tea? I'll put the kettle on." He started for the kitchen before I could reply.

I slipped into the guest room and shed tights, padding back to the kitchen in bare feet. The red tile floor was chilly against my soles but welcomed over heels any day.

He prepared the tray, glancing up to watch me enter the room. The tea length hem of the dark green dress swooshed round my legs. He likes: long dresses, soft feet, and my hair down, or he used to like them.

He turned to the rear garden after lighting the eye of the cooker. "Some of Min's flowerpots may need to be watered."

"I'll tend that after tea."

"I can help you." His voice lifted at the end, hopefully.

"We can do it together then." I laid my hand on his mid back, lightly stroking. "Cullum, are you nervous about meeting Liam?" I leaned towards the sink to see his face.

"Mortified, Isabel. I was anxious to fetch you from the airport but determined to carry it through. But Liam…what if he walks away from both of us, what if he refuses to have anythin' to do wi' me? What if…?"

I touched his chin with my fingertip. "Shh, it won't happen. He may even realize, on the way, that it's likely he'll finally meet you. He'll be as awed of you as you are of him."

He grasped my shoulders and pulled me into his chest. "I hope so, darlin', I do. I want more than anythin' to know our son." He kissed the top of my head and squeezed me like a lifeline.

I patted his back. "I understand."

***

I dressed in running clothes and found a tatty old grey hooded sweatshirt of Min's. I pulled it over my bulky sweater and donned a pair of sunglasses, my hair tightly clasped at the base of my neck and covered with a knit hat. Tying on running shoes, I left by the back garden and jogged up to the rail station, careful to stay off the main streets.

I arrived ten minutes before Cullum and fifteen before the train. I hung around the eastern end where the taxis park. There's good cover in the form of flowering bushes. After his arrival, I covertly checked Cullum's position every few minutes. He's well-known in Nairn, all the surrounding small towns, and most of the Highlands. He didn't lack for conversation though he cast a glance around every minute or so. I supposed he looked for me but I had no intention of revealing myself.

He pulled out his phone. My phone vibrated. I ignored the nuisance.

The announcement from the intercom alerted Cullum to scan the crowd for me in earnest. *"The three-thirty-five from Inverness is on time."*

A few more minutes ticked past while he engaged with a lovely young woman who kept one hand poised on his arm. I felt a pang of jealousy but had no claim on him, having relented that long ago.

"The three-thirty-five from Inverness is now arriving on track one." Brakes squealed as the train pulled in front of the platform.

Reading lips is handy at times like this. He spoke to his companion, facing me. "Didn't ken you knew Aunt Min but I appreciate your concern. Thank you." Cullum politely removed the pretty brunette's hand from his wrist and glanced around the crowd again. He studied the motionless train and paled. Doors were about to open. He cast a look round, brushing his hand over his well-trimmed beard. His eyes widened in desperation. "Where are you, Isabel?"

I ducked behind the corner, pulling on the hood before easing into the crowd.

Liam was at the door to exit before the train stopped.

I scrutinized my son's expression: doubtful, hopeful, confused. He looked for me, but then his gaze landed on his father. His eyes widened and he didn't blink.

"Be alright with this, lad." I encouraged him from the safety of my disguise. "Your dad won't bite. He as scared as you are, perhaps more."

Their gazes locked as Cullum approached the door; Liam stepped out. They clasped hands, Liam's face breaking into a smile.

Cullum reached out for our son and they embraced, holding onto each other for a very long moment. Liam buried his face in Cullum's shoulder. I could see his back shudder and knew my son wept.

A chance they'd both dared dream was now real. Once a someday had become this very moment, not to be hurried, but savored.

When they parted, Cullum kept one arm around Liam while he searched the throng and mopped tears from his face. "Don't ken where your mum's got to."

The crowd began to thin. Turning away, I jogged back to Aunt Min's to change and await news of these two men I loved more than life. My phone vibrated and I ignored it for a third time. My presence would intrude upon them soon enough.

***

I heard Cullum's car door close and watched my only child heft his duffle bag to his shoulder. He looked, for all the world, just like his father had at twelve.

My heart leapt into my throat and I stuffed it down. The door opened wide to welcome them both, faces wreathed in smiles. Cullum clutched Liam's shoulder as they approached the portal. He looked up and found my eyes, though I'd stepped aside.

His voice scolded and enticed at the same time. "Where were you, Isabel?"

"I must've dozed off and lost track of time. I'm so sorry." I kissed Liam's cheek and he eyed me knowingly.

"I told...." Liam considered Cullum. "What do I call you, sir?" He lowered his bag to the floor, beside the steps.

Cullum looked at me for an answer. I shrugged. "Uh, what's comfortable for you, lad?"

Liam pondered the floor for a moment. "I'm not sure what you're expecting, but I know what I want."

"Then do wha' you want." Cullum squared his shoulders to brace for the revelation.

Liam checked with me. I nodded. We'd played 'what if' for years.

His voice was soft, terrified Cullum might refuse him. "Since you're my dad, and there's no mistaking that, I'm partial to calling you Dad, if you're willin'."

Cullum flushed bright red and nodded, choking out one word. "Aye."

Liam addressed me with a smile. "I told Dad you set us up. I know your ways, Mum." He eyed me sagely and exchanged glances with Cullum, who could only nod in agreement.

"You caught me, Liam. I *was* at the station, though. I wouldn't have missed being there for the moment you met." I smiled. "Kettle's on. Would you like tea?"

Cullum shook his head. "Need to get to the pub. Get dressed and come with us?"

"That would be delightful, but I don't want to intrude."

"Nay, Isabel, get clothes on. Tonight, we dance." He smiled as a sob escaped and he brushed his hand over his beard and took a few steps to the window to gaze into the garden, arms crossed, until his heart stopped racing.

Liam grinned. "Mum, may I stay…with Dad?"

"Certainly, I think it's a very good idea." I left them to change into denims and a jumper after running my hands under cold water to splash my face. I unclipped and shook out my hair into its normal silky disarray.

Tonight, we dance.

***

The pub buzzed with activity and discussions. When Cullum walked in the door, twenty or more hullos rang out above conversations. He threw up a hand and sauntered towards the bar with us in tow.

He seated me on a stool at the brass rail and gestured toward a stool for Liam. More than a few heads turned to inspect the lad resembling Cullum Sinclair, down to the lint on his jacket. He served us himself, his regard lingering on me. Each time he looked up from what busied his hands, I found he studied my eyes or face. Occasionally, when caught, he'd turn to Liam.

"What'll you have, lad?" He managed a hale, hearty expression, like becoming a dad happened every day.

"I think orange juice would be fine."

Cullum gripped a jug and filled Liam's mug. "And you, mo chroi?"

Mmm, my heart?

"White wine, please." I accepted the glass and sipped while observing him.

We munched pretzels, familiarizing ourselves with locals, who all had a great deal of interest in Liam.

After a few minutes, Cullum grabbed a mallet and struck the cymbal, mounted at one end of the bar. The place stilled. "Since most of you are speculating on the identity of the handsome lad wi' me tonight, I'll introduce 'im to you."

Hoots and hollers followed with a few wolf whistles thrown in for good measure, assuring the host his guests were eager.

Cullum wagged his hand at Liam. "Stand, lad, and meet your friends and family."

Liam obeyed, pivoting to face thirty or more curious strangers.

"This is my son, Liam Sinclair. Take a bow, then."

Liam gave a curt bow, blushing almost to the point of tears, sighed, and settled himself beside me. "I didn't know he'd be so popular, Mum."

"He's always been." I grasped his arm. "Are you okay with all this at once?"

He nodded, eyes damp. "I've waited for him my whole life."

I leaned my face into him and whispered. "Satisfactory, Liam. Well done."

I caught a glare from across the bar. A pretty red-haired lass not long past twenty, kept a wary eye on proceedings. Later, I learned her name—Skye Paisley. She'd prove a worthy adversary.

Glancing away, I found Cullum studying me again. I felt like a science experiment gone awry.

A guitarist arranged equipment near one end of the pub and tuned his instrument. Early diners left and night cappers joined the crowd.

A crew of four young men walked in, through a side door, and headed for the bar's empty stools beside us. The nearest swung a glance my way. His voice carried like a gong. "Well, now, lads, there's a bonnie lass." He tossed a leer my direction, as he touched my arm.

Cullum slapped the ancient oak bar with the flat of his hand and leaned into the newcomer's face. "It's my wife you're ogling, Fergus McGee. Move your hand away if you plan on keepin' it attached."

Fergus sat back and smiled. "Hey, honest mistake, Cullum. No offence meant."

"I'll take more than offence with any man who acts like a buffoon in my place. Now, order your drinks or leave."

Fergus looked at his crew. "We'll have your fine house ale, sir."

Cullum served the four of them, maintaining a stern gaze on the youngsters. He dried glasses and racked them, policing the crowd with an occasional scan.

With interest, I watched as men checked in with him at the bar, several sending fleeting looks our direction.

One, I knew quite well, David Ferrell, the head of SSP. He cut a handsome figure, a bit charismatic, but not so much he'd offend the older members. He met my eyes for a brief second and bobbed his head once. I looked away.

The other five, I guessed, were officers in the party. Cullum directed them to a back room and shook his head a lot, apparently denying them his evening. Skye Paisley was the last to join the group, entreating Cullum with a pretty pout, tugging his arm like a determined child.

I watched his mouth, reading his response like a book. "Not tonight, Skye, my wife and son are here."

He peeled her hands away from his arm, shooing her from his presence.

She turned and peeked back over her shoulder at him, but he'd moved away, serving a customer.

He returned to us and leaned towards me. I tilted my ear to hear him. "My other bartender must be at the meeting. When he's finished, I'll be free and we can grab supper."

A wispy blonde sprite joined the guitarist to sing and play flute. The music lured patrons to their feet, and onto the tiny dance floor. Liam and I watched while dancers shuffled through the steps of an old Celtic love song. I recalled the words. Min taught me Erse and Gael when I became old enough to learn. The Irish tongue was easy compared to the mixture of Scots and Gael that passes for Scotland's native language.

Cullum left the bar and rounded my seat. "May I have this dance?"

"You were serious, then? I thought you had to tend bar." I smiled, thrilled with his attention.

"Bobby can handle it alone for a few minutes. I wanna hold you and calm my tormented soul, lass." He grasped my hand and led me to the floor, drawing me into his arms.

"For that, you need your priest. I'm only good at tea and biscuits." I felt like a queen, clasped against his chest, moving to the sensuous tune of bygone love—a lot like our own.

We danced three songs in a row. A third of the patrons envied me and most were women. Half-smiles graced their lips, as they eyed me critically, no doubt wondering about the invader's identity.

Liam joined the floor when a pretty teenager agreed to be his partner. I thought then how young they looked, with promising futures ahead. In that moment, I caught a flash of impending doom.

I believed I understood what happened to Aunt Min, even if I didn't know exactly who killed her. The influence of the group in Cullum's back room brought unsettling disquiet to an otherwise perfect day.

Revelation altered my outlook; then again, I've always given myself the luxury of melancholy.

Following a quick bite at a family restaurant, Cullum and Liam dropped me at the cottage. I waved goodnight from the door, after quick kisses.

Once alone, I dove headlong into journals and read until half three the next morning. Knowing the sun would be up soon, I slumped into bed.

"Min, if there's somethin' worth finding, I'd appreciate a clue." I muttered a prayer and passed out.

Chapter 5

I woke slowly, groggy from little sleep and three glasses of wine so late at night. I listened to the screeching gulls, diving for breakfast in Min's garden. I considered what seemed to be darkness in Scotland's Socialist Party and why I felt wary to avoid contact with them.

I threw my son directly into their reach by honoring his request to stay with Cullum. *Will he learn to maintain a logical understanding of the political spectrum? Will he fall prey to the socialist agenda, because his dad's views lean that direction?*

Hoping the former, I bailed out of bed and into the shower. I needed to return to Edinburgh, to work, in a few days. I had to settle things with Cullum and Liam, giving them time to come to grips with their relationship. I'd called the school to extend Liam's absence.

When I stepped out of the bath my cell phone rang. I answered without thought of who the caller might be.

"Isabel?" It was Bernie.

"Aye, Bernie, what can I do for you?" I toweled my hair dry. We don't use blow dryers much here. The wind suffices.

His voice was upbeat. "I sent down a special request to Edinburgh for your assistance in this investigation."

That sly devil! "What was the response?" I hung my towel over the shower rod and stepped into the bedroom.

"You're out on loan to my department indefinitely." He chuckled.

"I see. Why didn't you just ask me?" *The jackass!* I wanted to punch something.

"I was afraid you'd say nay. Couldn't take tha' chance, lass." He sounded pleased with himself.

"You were right. As it is, I'll see what I can do to have the decision reversed."

"Ah, now Isabel, please don't be tha' way. I need your help on this or my nu...butt will be in a sling."

"Your problem, Bernie, not mine." I wanted to hang up, but that left the situation unresolved, and I'm into solving problems, not creating them.

"You want to find who done this terrible crime to Min, don't you?" He pleaded.

"Aye, I just don't want to be the fall guy when it blows up, tha's all." I sat on the side of the bed and pulled my gown over my lap to pretend I wasn't sitting there talking to a man on the phone, while undressed.

"You won't, I promise. I'll do all I can to keep you outta the spotlight. After all, I want all the glory when you blow this thing wide open. SSP may be in the midst of your problems, darlin'. Reckon you've figured that out, eh?"

"No, I haven't given it a minute's thought, Bernie." *Liar!* My conscience roared.

"I'll let you go for now. Report in when you get a chance. My door's always open to you."

I shouted, hoping to get his attention. "Bernie, I'm not an investigator. I'm a scientist!"

"There now, lass, don't sell yourself short. You'll do fine, then. Bye for now." He hung up.

"Jerk!" I had to let off steam before Liam arrived to spend the day touring the area. Part of me hoped Cullum would pass on the sightseeing adventure, then the part that still loved him went giddy with the thought of seeing him.

I slipped my gown over my head and called a number I knew well, my office. I punched in his extension and waited for his voice mail. He answered.

"Harry, what the devil do you think you're about, loaning me out like an old movie?"

"Good mornin', Isabel. That constable sounded desperate."

"He is, but this is a murder inquiry involving *my* aunt. I'm far too close to the deceased to have an unbiased viewpoint." I'd use any excuse to avoid this job. I couldn't leave Nairn and what if—?

"Uh, well, like I say he sounded desperate and you've already submitted evidence to his office. I figured you had the emotional end of it in hand. You know, see it through to the end."

"I'm considering resignation, Harry. Honestly, I don't need the hassle of trying to do Bernard Leighton's job for him."

"Isabel, don't be rash. Consider this an opportunity to learn more about the service you provide to your country."

"Bollox, Harry!" I hung up on my boss and wondered if that was enough for him to fire me or if I *should* resign. One small doubt nagged me.

What if we never learned what really happened to Aunt Min?

***

Dressed in denims and a light jumper, I stepped out for post. Sorting through envelopes, a postcard addressed to me, with a picturesque scene of Nairn on the front, surfaced.

I lifted the card by its edges and flipped it over. In block letters were the words 'click, click, boom'. Interesting. I bagged the card and added it to a list of items to send to the lab.

I sipped coffee while waiting for my men to arrive. I'd always wanted to have at least two, though, truth be told I could be convinced to have more children—with the right man. As Cullum's the only one I've ever loved, it narrowed the field considerably. Besides, all the wife talk he did scared me. I didn't want to be duped into thinking he really felt like that. It may have been a way of twisting the guilt knife I carried all those years, lodged deeply in my heart. Or a way to get to his son that was safe for both of them. For my part, they didn't need me as a go-between. They were comfortable with each other, something I never was with either of my parents.

My cell phone rang again. "Hullo?"

"Mum, we're almost at Aunt Min's. Dad said to be ready. We're going for breakfast."

I smiled. Dad sounded like it felt foreign to his tongue. He'd practiced, but having a live version on the receiving end made all the difference.

"Meet you at the curb." I knocked back my coffee, pocketed my phone, and snatched Min's brown ruana off a hook beside the steps. When I opened the door, a large, stocky man in a priestly frock stood just outside, hand poised to knock.

"Isabel Fielding?" His heavy jowls quivered when he spoke. His watery blue eyes blinked in the overload of a fleshy, bloodshot face given to excessive drink.

"Aye, sir, and you are...?" I frowned suspiciously. I've always mistrusted clergy, having too few reasons to find their honor dependable. The ones I knew were for sale to the highest bidder.

"Father Ralph. I apologize. I feel as though I ken you, lass. Cullum's told me so much through the years." He smiled and bobbed his head.

Now, *that* made me uncomfortable. Had he been Protestant I wouldn't have given it a thought. He's Catholic. He hears confessions. I wondered how much of our love life had been aired behind the confessional screen.

My mouth must have hung open, because he flushed.

"I said that incorrectly. Cullum and I are friends. He's filled my willing ears with tales of your childhood together, and so on."

So far, I felt more exposed. "What can I do for you, sir?"

Cullum's car parked at the curb. As soon as it stopped rolling. His door opened. He was on his feet and loped up the walkway. "Father, so good to see you this fine mornin'." He clasped the older man's broad shoulder and offered his hand, which Father Ralph accepted.

The priest began to bluster again. "Oh...Cullum, fancy meeting you here, lad."

"You've come to try and convert Isabel, sir?" Cullum's tone teased. His wonderfully full mouth smiled with amusement.

I turned away and locked the door.

"Um, well, I was out visiting and thought to drop by and pay my condolences to her on the death o' your aunt, you ken." He shuffled two prayer books and a few flyers in his pudgy hands.

"I'm stealing her away, sir, for breakfast with our son this mornin'. Perhaps you could come by again when you're in the neighborhood?" Cullum smiled and steered the priest down the path to the garden gate.

I followed at a discreet pace. Liam clambered from the car to watch his father and the priest make their way towards him and allowed me the front seat.

41

"Father Ralph, this is our son, Liam." Cullum reached behind and gestured me to his side. I stepped up.

"Ah, your son…I thought…well, then…humph." The old clergyman's dimpled hand stretched to my boy for acknowledgement. "Verra nice to meet you, young man. Well, then, you do favor your sire, yes…yes you do."

Liam gripped his hand and released it again with a frozen smile.

Cullum opened the door for me to sit. I climbed in, grateful to be away from a man who knew far too much about me, not to be related. Liam sat behind me and yanked my braid.

"Good mornin', you." I reached back one hand.

He nuzzled his face into my palm. I hope he never gets too old or stuffy for that kind of behavior. "Mum, have you been to Dad's place? It's awesome."

I shook my head. "Nay, I don't even know where it is."

"It's right on the beach. My room's windows open towards the surf. It's great. Of course the gulls are screaming at first light."

"Of course."

"He painted my room blue because he liked that color when he was my age. The quilt on my bed was *hand*made by Gram and Aunt Min. Dad said they made it just for me."

My eyes teared; I covered my mouth and blinked back the first thing that came to my mind. *He's planned this for how long?*

The driver's door opened and the love of my life entered. He glanced over with a smile. "I'm sorry about that, Isabel. The old man's not quite all there anymore. He rambles and confuses easily."

I bit my lip and didn't dare say what I was thinking in front of Liam. "It's okay."

"I'll speak to him privately. I was jokin' about the conversion thing, really. It's never mattered to me that you're Protestant." He drove away from the curb.

"Thanks so much, Cullum. I never considered your faith a threat either, until a few moments ago." I stole a look peripherally.

He grinned. "It still isn't a threat, love. The old guy's cracked, tha's all."

"We'll see," I added doubtfully.

"Thought I'd spend the day with you two: if you don't mind me tagging along."

I smiled relief. "Not at all, was hoping you would. I hate to ask, you're so busy." I plucked at imaginary lint on the dark brown ruana.

He grinned. "I'm a dad. I'll make time for the task."

We proceeded down Thurlow Road onto a short side street.

He turned into his drive and shut off the engine. "Liam and I've worked on breakfast half the mornin' so I pray it'll find favor with you."

"I'm sure it will." I felt honored they'd planned and prepared a surprise for me, but secured the walls around my heart. *Don't let this make you feel like you're part of them.*

After leaving the car, we walked a cobblestone path to the deep front porch furnished with two gliders and comfy cushions.

Cullum unlocked the door and waved us through the vestibule, into an open airy living room with a seaside view. I walked to the French doors and marveled that he'd have a ringside seat to storms rolling in across the water and Aurora Borealis through the dark winter months. Back inside, a large stone fireplace spanned one wall.

"Great view." I smiled my delight. "Breakfast smells wonderful."

Cullum and Liam exchanged glances. "Let's go to the kitchen, Mum. I'm cooking eggs. Dad gets them from a lady down the street, so these were gathered *this very* mornin'. How cool's that?"

"*Very*, Liam." I followed him into a modern kitchen with stainless appliances, except for the black Aga, and marble countertops. An island in the center was equipped with a small sink and butcher's block. I looked back at Cullum. "This is gorgeous."

He bobbed his head and looked around as though it lacked something, and it did. A woman's touch. Good.

He mumbled. "Um, it does the job."

Liam cracked eggs, while Cullum poured juice, coffee, and tea for us all. I helped him finish laying the table in the breakfast nook, but mostly felt like a third wheel.

What am I doing here?

43

I tried to enjoy the moment but that thought kept flitting through my mind, causing me to question things I didn't want to answer just yet.

Cullum slid into the booth beside me and reached for my thigh, which he patted. He turned a tired, but pleased, look my way. His voice dropped. "I wanted to bring you out here but....It's easier not to get carried away with our lad in tow."

"Aye, a child makes effective birth control for a lot of people." I grinned.

He threw back his head and laughed. "Ah, woman, I've missed your freshness in my life. Truly, I'm a very dull man these days."

"Oh, I doubt that, Cullum. I've noticed a number of young ladies hanging on your every word *and* your arm." I hoped my smile hid the jealousy churning my stomach.

He sobered, his cheeks reddened. "I only have eyes for one woman, lass."

Liam appeared with plates in each hand and a very grownup voice. "The chef's prepared to serve at table today, lady and gentleman."

"How kind of you to take notice of these hungry wretches who await your masterpiece, sir." I bowed my head reverently.

He chuckled. "Mum, that makes me sound like a prig."

"Or Bobby Flay."

Cullum reached for my thigh again and absently brushed his hand to my knee. I felt as though I'd pour into a puddle on the floor.

He sighed with a smile and glanced at me. I thought, for a split second, he might kiss me in front of our birth control. He sighed again and attacked the chef's special eggs with two rashers of bacon and a side of sausage. A half loaf of toasted bread later, we were appropriately stuffed.

***

"I want to take Liam on a drive by the estate," I suggested.

"As in dropping in to say hi or a quick that's the driveway to your inheritance?" Cullum steered his car towards my family's estate.

"I don't want to go in. I just want him to know where it is. Are you taking him to the farm?"

"Aye, today, love. Mam asked if we could visit."

"Perhaps after you drop me?" Fear crept nearer.

"Nay, she specifically asked for you. I said we'd be there for tea. Alright?" His left hand gently grasped my leg again.

I took a deep breath and looked away. *Oh my, a trip to the farm for tea with the Sinclairs.* A bit of sensory overload, but then again I expected him to want to take Liam. I just didn't expect them to include me.

"Tha's fine then." My opinion didn't really matter, at this point.

His mouth turned out a sweet, melancholy smile. "She never got over you either, darlin'."

I had no idea how to feel about his statement. I returned the look. "I'm so sorry." Unable to stop the tears, I dabbed my face, blew my nose, and swallowed the remorse coursing through me.

Cullum slowed at the entrance to the estate. "We're here."

"Turn into the lane, please." Leaning forward, I glanced back at Liam. "All of this is your domain someday."

"When did you visit last?" He asked, tilting his head to see the view from the back seat.

"Five years ago, I was here for about fifteen minutes." I opened the car door and stepped out. "I left you with Aunt Min while I picked up a few things from my old room."

"I thought this was a drive by." Cullum reminded me.

I leaned in the door. "You know if I want to put her out and into one of the other houses we own, I can do it with a phone call. She'd have to comply."

"Do you wanna go to that much trouble?" Beloved grinned.

"I think about it, sometimes." I scanned the place once more and climbed back into the car.

He reached across me and pulled the door closed, then propped his arm on my seat and studied the area. "It's a beautiful place, but rather…froufrou, isn't it?"

I chuckled. "Very froufrou, if memory serves."

Liam scanned the grounds. "I think I want to see inside."

"Not today, Liam. When the resident witch is in Europe, on one of her tours, we'll venture forth and survey our empire." I brushed a hand over his wavy hair. "You'll hate it."

"We could tear out all the froufrou and turn it into a skateboard park."

Cullum and I laughed at the image. "We might at that. I hope to transfer rights to Scotland's historic land trust."

We drove down the wrought iron fence along the road that I'd run beside, hidden in the woods, that fateful day almost thirteen years ago. All alone in the world, but for the precious cargo that now sat behind me, in his dad's car. I shuddered.

"You alright, Mum?"

"Aye, it's just the memories return and there aren't many good ones."

Cullum cut a glance at me and sighed. "I'm sorry, love."

"I wish it could have all turned out differently. If only...." I watched the wrought iron fence end and forest retake the roadside.

The ride to the farm was short and lovely. Gorse dotted the hillsides with dark green foliage and brilliant lemon yellow clusters of flowers.

When Cullum turned into the long drive to his parents' home, the scenery changed to fields of verdant grazing, full of sheep. New lambs cantered round the ewes, their smiling faces delighted with spring and the life it brings.

After he parked the car, he spent a long moment studying me with a half-smile on his lips before he climbed out and walked round the front to open my door.

Our son silently took it all in, awed. Liam released his door and gazed round the homestead, barns, and paddock.

Cullum held his hand out to me and Liam slowly rose from the back seat. "Wow! Is all of this your family's farm?"

I looked up at Cullum, when he responded. "Aye, lad, all of this is *our* family's farm." His voice broke and his eyes misted as he inhaled a shaky breath.

"What're the black dots running around out there?" Liam pointed at a herd of sheep driven towards us by two of the resident Border Collies.

46

"That's a few of this country's finest herding dogs. Your grandpa raises the very best. Shepherds come from all over the world to buy from him." Cullum raised his hand to wave toward the house.

A glance in that direction revealed Robin and Genny Sinclair, arm in arm, headed our way. Genny's hand covered her mouth, as she watched Liam. Her eyes widened as she approached.

I reached for him and steered him their direction, Cullum beside us, sniffing.

"This is your gram and grandpa." Cullum's hand rested on our son's shoulder.

Genny's arms reached for Liam and she pulled him close, her eyes shut. Liam, fully acquainted with hugs, wrapped his arms around her.

"Hi, I'm Liam." He spoke over her shoulder. At 5'6 he was a smidge taller than Genny.

"I know who you are, lad." She held him and wept.

Robin held them both and comforted his wife, weeping with her.

Cullum reached for my hand. I dabbed my face and enjoyed the scenery of this lovely family's farm. A peak in the distance sported a white cap of fresh snow.

Kyle's long stride carried him up the hill. Cullum's brother paused and rubbed both hands down his canvas pants and proceeded to the cluster of humanity on the crest. "Wha's this?" A grin brightened his weathered complexion.

Genny grasped Liam's shoulders and presented him to his uncle. "Liam, this is your dad's brother, Uncle Kyle."

Kyle extended his hand and took Liam's. "Good to finally meet you, lad. Look like your dad, you do. Guess you hear that a lot, eh?"

Liam nodded. "Aye, sir, more in the past day, though."

"Ah, good manners too, that'd be your mam's side, I reckon." Kyle glanced round at his family. "Anyone'd think we were at a funeral here. Where's tea, Mam?"

Genny laughed, still wiping tears and considered me. "Come, everyone, to the house and let's have our first tea together as family, in a long while. Lachlan should be home from school in a few minutes. Caleigh called. She's running late today, but said you'd best not leave before she's home."

My heart lightened. Caleigh and I became instant friends all those years ago, attached forever through our love for the young men who became our husbands.

Robin reached for my arm. My first instinct was to run. He dragged me into a bear hug. "Daughter, we all love you the same, all the years you've been away. Come to table, no one sits down to a feast alone." We walked to the house the way he'd brought Genny out, arm in arm.

I was done for with the Sinclairs.

Cullum looked back at us and waited for his da to hand me over. Robin ambled on into the house, to wash up.

His son checked with me before we went inside. "You alright, lass?"

I bobbed my head and glanced away, pressing my lips together. I knew this visit would unnerve me. "Fine."

"Yeah, you look fine to me. Are you well enough for tea?" He was amused and didn't bother to mask his pleasure.

"You think it's funny?"

He tried to sober, but failed, relented and laughed. "One thing I've always loved about you, Bel, is tha' you have steel for nerves, but tha's also the thing that vexes me most. So, what? Do you wanna run away again, or are you brave enough to face Mam's tea?" He rested his hands on his hips and let me decide.

"I'll brave your mother's tea, Cullum, though for the life o' me I don't see how they can forgive what I've done to you...us." I wiped my nose and studied my handkerchief. It would go into the dustbin.

He took a deep breath. "If we can't move past this one thing, we won't go far."

"Help me, Cullum. I don't understand." I leaned my forehead onto his shoulder.

"You're forgiven. Aye, there was a difficult bloody road to tha' conclusion, but there it is. You must accept it, or the race we ran was in vain, darlin'."

I raised my head and studied him through tear-studded lashes. "Accept it?"

"Aye, just let yourself accept that no one here wishes you harm, only good. Accept that through all the darkness there's light near. Accept that real love doesn't die, just deepens over time. Even when the one loved is absent. Will you stop lovin' Min just because you can't see her anymore?"

"Nay, I'll always treasure every moment we had together."

"Aye, love's like that, Isabel." He lifted my chin and kissed my mouth slowly. When he finished he took a long look into my eyes. "You taste just like you did the last time I kissed you before I climbed onto that plane to Germany thirteen years ago."

"You remember tha'?" I felt I'd drown in his eyes.

"Aye, I've relived it every hour of every day. It's kept me hopeful." He removed his hand from my face and stepped back, arms spread. "So, what'll it be?"

I wiped my cheeks on my sleeve and reached for him.

He wrapped me up tightly. "Oh, God! I've waited for this for thirteen long, hard years, woman."

***

Liam unlocked the door at the cottage and stepped to one side. "Mum, did you stay with Aunt Min when you were younger?"

"Aye, not here though. She and Uncle David lived in the country at his home after they married."

"And Uncle David was Gram's brother?" His face screwed up, one eye almost closed when he concentrated.

"He was a widower, when he met Min. Your dad and I were six-years-old at the time of their marriage. Min moved from her tiny house, in town, to the country and lived there for twelve years. Uncle David passed and she bought this place. She tutored until four years ago, when she retired."

"So she wasn't married until Uncle David?"

"Nay, she was what my mother called an old maid. Aunt Min chose to view herself as unclaimed treasure." I smiled, remembering my aunt's outlook on life. I couldn't profess being unclaimed, because I was once. Treasure would be a matter of opinion.

Cullum stepped in behind us. "Have you collected the post?"

"Aye, there was a card for me. Come, I'll show it to you. I reserved it for fingerprints, though it probably has none." We went to the small yellow kitchen. I handed the bagged card to Cullum. "I think it's local but that could be a ruse."

He sighed. "Alright then, pack your clothes. You're going home with me." He tossed the bag back onto my stack. "It's more convenient anyway. John called about Min's beater. It was the battery and alternator. It'll take a few days to get parts. I told him to fix it."

I stood in the kitchen and considered the place. "I'm not afraid to stay here, Cullum, really."

"Isabel, *I'm* afraid for you. If you're wi' Liam and me, we shan't have to be concerned. We'll be safer all around." He waved his hand toward the guest room and his tone sharpened. "*Now* suits me, lass." He wore a frown that wasn't to be challenged.

"Aye, alright, it's not so awful a thing. I've seen a lot of death threats come through the department, Cullum. I'm not afraid." I made tracks to the guest room.

He was on my heels. "It may be a daily occurrence for the police, but it rarely happens round here, Isabel. I've no intention of havin' you harassed on *my* watch. It'd be a sorry thing to have you killed when you've just returned to me." He surveyed the room quickly, eyes alighting on the bed. We'd made love there a few times, eleven to be exact.

I swung my suitcase up to the mattress and opened it, snatching blouses from hangers and hooks, folding neatly to tuck away. I glanced back at his sullen silence.

"What?" I placed a stack of tops in the lime green case.

He brushed his hand over his beard and growled. "Will you marry me? I didn't intend to ask like this, but I realize it may be difficult to exist in the same space without....So, what say you?" He turned the frown on me again.

I stopped folding clothes and sat on the bench at the end of the bed.

Liam popped his head in the door. "Mum, are you well?"

The word forced its way out my mouth. "Aye."

Cullum glanced back at our son. "Let us have a moment, lad. I'm tryin' to talk her into marriage just now."

Liam's face lit up. "Really, you're getting married?"

His dad waved him back into the living room. "Only if she relents. I cannot drag her back to the altar." He stripped his wool tweed jacket off and tossed it on the bed, rolling up the sleeves of his dress shirt. He knelt at my feet. "Isabel, will you do me the honor of becoming my wife, forever and always?"

A thousand thoughts raced through my head. "Cullum, you don't have to do that. We don't have to marry to share a living space. What about this…I'll call Wetherby House and see if Craig has a room available? That'll solve the problem." I held his face in my hands.

He was disappointed. His eyes narrowed. "Tell me now, will you have me back or nay, Isabel? Do I love you in vain, after all?"

I tried to stifle the tears. Sobbing followed, and I felt like the biggest fool for refusing to realize he was earnest in his plea. "Nay!" I choked down a sob and shook my head. "Cullum, I love you more than life."

His tone was harsh but what I needed to hear. "Then say aye, woman."

"Aye, I would be honored to become your wife again—forever and always." He blurred in my tear-shrouded vision.

Plucking a handkerchief from his trouser pocket, he dried my cheeks. "Well, then, let's see to it. Bring your clothes and we'll go to the registrar's office. The waitin' period is 14 days but I can get it down to 7. Do we take birth control or ship him off to his grandparents in a week?"

I shrugged…beyond words. He could decide. He chose the baggage of us.

"Right, I'll call Mam and have her make up my old room for the lad."

My tight voice squeaked. "He's due back at school in two days."

"Yeah, we discussed tha'. He wants to transfer." He stood and pulled me to my feet and into his arms. "Will you consider tha', mo chroi?"

I bobbed my head like the plastic pup on Aunt Min's dash, in the old VW Beetle.

"We'll tend that issue next, then. Is there a school nearby that we can transfer to, whatever suits his needs?"

"I'll check into it tomorrow." There was freedom in touching him. He felt wonderful.

I don't have to be afraid of him anymore.

"Let me help you, lass." Cullum folded clothes and packed my suitcase, snapping the latches closed. He hefted the bag and headed to the living room. "She said aye, son."

I followed with an armload of Min's diaries.

Our son's response could be heard a block away. "Whoo-hoo!" He jumped from the settee, the closest seat to the bedroom door, and grabbed me for a big kiss. I hugged him and wondered what he felt, besides excited.

Cullum stood at the base of the steps waiting for us. I believe he was concerned that the next seven days might be a struggle, though I had no inclination of making them hard.

I'd forgotten to tell him that Bernie annexed my time indefinitely and I'd have to resign to get away from the duty.

Chapter 6

The following morning, we sat down to breakfast, once again presented by the chef of the hour, Liam. Cullum sat beside me at the same spot as a day earlier but with the promise that we'd be married in a sennight. He *had* circumvented the fourteen day waiting period. Very soon, we'd be husband and wife again.

"I need to tell you that Bernie called yesterday and…he'd spoken to my boss in Edinburgh. Harry consented to loan my talent out for an indefinite period of time to the constable's office in Nairn." I felt guilty keeping quiet, as though somehow I was lying to him. I watched for an adverse reaction.

"Hah!" Cullum smirked. "Tha' sly fox. Allow me to guess the rest. You do the work, take the blame if it fails to produce the desired results, and he takes credit if you succeed."

"Almost word for word what he said." I nodded.

"At least he didn't lie to you, lass." He hefted his mug and sipped his tea. "Mmm, might that mean you can work here instead of Edinburgh?"

"Aye, if I don't quit first." I sipped coffee, rich, strong, acidic, full-bodied, and heaven when I'm not sleeping.

He mumbled behind his coffee mug. "You don't have to work at all if you'd rather not."

"Really?" I smiled over my mug's rim. I could choose to use the money in my trust. He didn't know that, though.

He leaned almost close enough to touch me. "You can stay home and have bairns. We have a few more years left us, you ken?" His eyes narrowed when he smiled.

Strange, I'd thought the same thing a few days ago, but somehow coming from him it sounded threatening. "Is tha' what you want?"

"It's with you, Isabel. I'm just makin' conversation." He moved my mug back for Liam to deposit my plate on the bamboo mat in front of me. "Looks fine, lad, no better way to start the day but a full Scottish breakfast." He cut into a sausage and winked at me.

53

"Dad, do you think I cook well enough to get a job at the pub?" Liam sat with his own plate and peered hopefully across the table at Cullum.

"I think it's a good idea, however…your mam has the final say. What say you, Isabel; we find a school here and let the lad work a few hours on weekends?" He didn't bother to glance my direction, as the smug look on his face might make me mad.

"I think it's likely we can find a school and he'd be able to work a few hours a week." I tapped Cullum's shin under the table.

He turned a warning look that time, the smirk still in place. "It's the way I started with Da, bussing tables and prepping vegetables with the cook. I was your same age, Liam."

Liam grinned. He was carrying out his first family tradition.

"What're you gonna do with Aunt Min's cottage?" Liam passed toast.

I took a piece and held the tray for Cullum. "I don't know yet, rent it out maybe, until you're old enough to need a first place on your own."

"What about the estate and all that?" Liam bit into one of the three types of sausage on his plate.

"I won't live there, Liam. I wish it was different on my side of our family, but it is what it is and that's never been pleasant except for Aunt Min. Someday I hope to place it all in national trust. "

"I have a question about you two. May I ask?" Liam set his utensils down and watched us.

I answered after a glimpse at Cullum. "Sure."

"Were you married when I was born?"

"No, our marriage was annulled, by a judge who was a friend of my father. We were married when you were conceived. You are very much a child of love, Liam." I dropped my voice. "Cullum was in the Royal Scot Dragoons, another family custom, and shipped out to Bosnia, on a peacekeeping mission with the United Nations. We'd married two months before he left. He didn't know about you for a long time unless Min told him."

Cullum sat back and studied me. "You were five, Liam, the first time I laid eyes on you. I kenned you were my son, there was no doubt."

Liam nodded and sat quietly for a moment pondering the implications. "I knew you belonged to me the first time I saw you, too."

Focusing all his attention on our son, Cullum leaned forwards. "When was that?"

Liam's words came slowly. "Outside my school one day. You came from the office and you walked past the window of my science class."

Cullum's gaze dropped. "Aye, how old were you then?"

"Eight, sir. I remember thinking there goes my dad. Then I prayed and asked God if I'd ever meet you." Liam looked down at his plate, still half full. "If you'd ever come for me."

"You never told me." I mumbled, feeling a bit betrayed.

"I'm sorry, Liam. I was near you hundreds of times but didn't ken how to approach you. I wasn't sure what you believed about who you are." Cullum shrugged and looked at me his eyes pleading.

I jumped into the lull. "That was my fault. I didn't tell anyone that your name was legally correct. They didn't know you would have your dad's last name and not Brad...my married name. So, when Dad went to your school to inquire about you, they didn't have a student by the name of Liam King." I traded a glance with Cullum. "It's alright, we dodged each other for years and half-believed the lies that cost us our marriage and...."

"Our very lives. But they could never steal our love." Cullum finished my sentence. "Liam, you were wanted and loved, even from a distance. Min gave me pictures that your mam sent and I shared them with my parents. We prayed for you, lad, and loved you from afar. When your mam came to Nairn I tried to see you both. The last time, one of Min's friends said somethin' outta the way about how much you looked like your dad and, fearful, your mam ran away again."

"I remember that, when Grandfather died, wasn't it, Mum?"

"Aye, the nosey old bitty." I bit into a piece of toast. "Look, our breakfast is getting cold and we have things to do today, like finding you a school. Eat up then, and we'll get on with our day."

"It's good for him to ken what happened, that it wasn't because we didn't love him and want him...or each other." Cullum gently grasped my arm, his voice softened. "Stay steady, woman. Have you any more questions, son?"

Liam's eyes were big as saucers. He'd never heard *anyone* tell me to shush.

I nodded to him. "It's okay."

He shifted his gaze back to Cullum. "Not now, sir, but I ken it isn't easy for you to talk about. If you love me half as much as I love you…."Liam held his stoic expression for half a minute before crumbling.

Cullum was out of his seat and next to our son. I slid closer as we each took part in comforting him. Our glances met, as his sobbing took center stage. Cullum's eyes were wet and mine began to seep. We were a damp mess.

***

A key scraped in the front door and opened to the man of my dreams clutching a bouquet of flowers. I met him in the living room, having just returned from a run, windblown and clammy.

"What are you doing home this time of day? I thought you were at the pub. Liam just left a while ago with Kyle and Lachlan for a football match."

"I ken, they stopped by. When I found you were free, I decided to spend the evening with you. I brought a peace offering in case you had objections." He kissed my lips.

"I have none. May I take those? They're lovely." I pressed my face into the center of a tea rose and hellebore bouquet studded with a few sprays of heather. "They smell so sweet. Thank you. I bought king scallops this afternoon. Would you like them for supper?"

I found a carafe above the sink for a vase and filled it with water.

"Absolutely." He produced a bottle of white wine from a bag. "Hope this'll compliment the meal." He stowed the bottle in the fridge.

"May I have a few minutes to shower?" I pushed my rain damp hair from my eyes.

"Aye, I think I'll change. It's cool enough for a fire. I'll build one directly."

"That'd be nice." I placed the bouquet in the center of the dining table and dashed off to the bath.

We set ourselves up for a romantic evening. What were we thinking?

I pulled on soft black knit pants and a pretty, layered top that I purchased a few days earlier. I needed to make the trip to Edinburgh, soon, for personal belongings.

Walking down the well-padded hallway, I overheard Cullum on his cell phone.

"Aye, I'm here, just trying to decipher your meaning. I'll consider…wait, no I won't. I've caught on to the game you play. I can be finished with you by phone or tender my resignation on paper if it's what you want." A moment passed in silence. "Nay, I'm busy tonight. There's your choice, Skye, it's naught to do with me." He was quiet for another moment and turned to find me standing nearby. He winked. "Yeah, I think not. Goodbye." He switched his phone off.

If Kyle or Liam needed someone, they'd probably call me anyway. Cullum had no grasp of phone protocol when you have a child away from you.

"Everything alright?" I walked slowly toward the kitchen.

"Um, probably." He ran his hands through his hair. "I'll build that fire I promised."

"I'll start the scallops." I quickened my pace, wondering what he had to do with Skye and if it was SSP business or personal. *If personal…?*

"These are fantastic. When did you learn to cook?"

"When I didn't have someone doing it for me. I learned a lot of things that way." I lifted the glass of wine and sipped. "Good choice of wine." I took another minuscule bite of scallops, layered with fresh asparagus and rocket, in a ginger-sesame sauce.

"You do a good job. Are you going to ask why I was talking to a woman on the phone earlier, or does it not matter?" He watched through narrowed eyes as he chewed.

"It matters. Might it be business?"

"Unh-unh."

I took a deep breath. "Personal, then?"

"Does it concern you what I've done or who I've been with these past years?"

I felt lighter than air, as though levitating above the dining room and watching from a distance. "Only if you think I must know, Cullum. I'd rather not. We'd been us for a lot of years, before we weren't. You don't owe me explanations."

He nodded and continued to study me. Science experiment again. "Well, the truth is, there've been a few who've wanted to eradicate your memory, but none successfully." He took another bite and moved his scrutiny to his plate. He delicately laid his fork aside and glanced up. "Isabel, I've never been unfaithful to you."

"We haven't been married for thirteen years, Cullum."

"I was. I refused to recognize the annulment." He held up his hand and twirled the wedding band. "This has never left me, nor have the vows I gave you the day you put it on my hand."

"I see." I glanced down at my plate. "Then I guess I can tell you that I've been faithful to our love, as well."

"What of your husband?"

"Bradley's homosexual. We had the marriage annulled as soon as his father died. He would've been disinherited unless we married. I thought at first he was being kind, not bothering me while pregnant. But after Liam's birth, the truth came to light. It took a while, but we became friends and he shared his sadness with me. His lover became an obsession that I was happy to let into our lives."

"He lived with you?" He pulled an incredulous look.

"No, he visited, had dinner occasionally. He was very nice and I saw it made Bradley happy. We only lived together the first few weeks anyhow. I got the job in Edinburgh and moved back to the flat you and I shared a few months before Liam was born. It wasn't large enough to accommodate a baby and au pair so I purchased the one we live in....Well." I sipped wine. "When Bradley's father visited I made an appearance in Glasgow at his home and went away after."

Cullum threw his head back and laughed. "I don't believe this. And all these years I was afraid to approach you, couldn't bear the rejection. What a fool I've been, Isabel. Please forgive me."

"Ditto. I wanted you more than anything. It shot arrows through my heart just to hear your name. Still, I couldn't face you. After all, I'd been party to the lies that destroyed us." I picked at the congealing ginger sauce on my plate with my fork.

Cullum reached across and held my hand. "You feel like dancing? Tomorrow we wed, mo chroi. We'll begin celebrating tonight." He stood and held my chair.

The music changed. I smiled. He stacked it intentionally. I laid my hand into his to begin the dance. "Bob Dylan? Did you do that on purpose?"

...offer you a warm embrace, to make you feel my love.

He smiled. "Am I so obvious?"

"Aye, you are." I laid my head on his shoulder and relished his scent, his feel, and the pulse of my heart. *Cuisle mo chroi.*

***

I stripped off my clothes in preparation for bed. Slipping a gown over my head, I turned to look in the mirror and unbraided my hair, shaking out the dark auburn wavy mass. I turned covers back and stretched out.

How can I sleep? In a few hours we'll be married again. There's so much more trepidation than the first time. Then, we were wild children with our whole lives ahead of us. Now we're careful adults, dancing as though we know what tomorrow holds.

I reached to turn out the bedside lamp when my door opened.

The man I love more than life stood there, his robe tied over his thick chest and a sheepish expression on his handsome face.

"May I help you?" I sat up with a smile.

He chuckled. "Aye, Bel, in more ways than one." He closed the door behind himself, though we were completely alone.

I tossed back the covers on the opposite side of the bed. "Join me, if you like."

He sat on the side and kept his back to me. "There's something I failed to tell you, Isabel."

"It can't wait 'til morning?"

He rolled onto the bed and kissed me. "I think not."

"By all means, talk then."

"With the vote for independence looming, there may be rough spots ahead."

"I ken tha', Cullum. Some of us have waited for this opportunity our entire voting lives, wanting to make a difference for our children and grandchildren."

"Aye, but with SSP itself…there may be a rift coming. Anyway, I don't ken how you think of the politics of the day, but it's time for radical change. There won't be many safe places for you and Liam, but with me, or on the farm with my family. The danger lies all around us. I want you to understand that it may come to a heated standoff. In fact, it's almost at that juncture now."

"Do we need to delay our marriage? Would it make it easier?"

He shook his head. "Nay, it's all relative. I just need for you to be aware that I may ship you out to the farm if it looks like it'll blow." He twirled a lock of my hair, then brushed his hand over me.

I closed my eyes and calmed. "Alright then."

"Do you trust me?" He whispered in my ear, his breath tickling my neck.

"Aye, I'll do what you say." *I think.*

"You know you're my heart?"

I opened my eyes and met him, a scant six inches from my face. "I know for certain that you're my heart, my breath…."

He covered my mouth with his and pulled me into his embrace.

When I woke alone, as it has been for thirteen years, I heard the shower running in the master bath. I rolled out and headed towards my own to prepare for our wedding day.

I donned a sage tea length silk and linen sheath with a side slit cut to just above my knee. My hair swept back and up to a twist. I slipped on a few gold accessories and a cloisonné nosegay in my chignon. It was discovered in Minerva's jewel box, among her costume jewelry, but I know gold when I see it. I slipped into a pair of brown leather pumps with a sassy, but slight heel. Cullum's only two inches taller and I'm not into competition.

Stepping out of my room, I spotted cuisle mo chroi, the pulse of my heart, his back to me, gazing out the French doors. I approached him, noting the fine cut of the dark brown suit he wore.

"How are you this mornin'?"

He turned with a grin. "It's the second best of my life."

"What's the first?" I wrapped my arms around his neck and kissed his willing mouth.

"The first time we made love, the morning after we wed. I'm guessing tomorrow will exceed expectations." He kissed me again.

"Mmm, you taste like coffee, which would be welcomed."

"I heard you moving about and poured you a cup. I would've brought it to you, but we'd be late."

I left him for the kitchen. "Thank you very much." I sipped the cooled brew and joined him to savor the sight of the mountains on Black Isle, across Moray Firth, sporting a fresh cap of snow in the brilliant sunlight. "Snowed last night."

"It's what I heard on the radio. Around Pitlochry and Blair Atholl, they had six inches. Makes it hard on the lambs. Kyle says we've been blessed not to lose many this year. They're having a tougher time of it, further south. My brother's an excellent shepherd."

"It was good to see Caleigh, but we failed to have a moment to talk. What's the shepherd's wife up to these days?"

"She's nursing now, at one of the traveling nurse organizations. Some days she'll put two hundred miles on her little car and see ten or twelve patients." He sipped his coffee. "She went back to school, when Lachlan started, finished a few years later and he was old enough to walk himself to the bus without her or Kyle."

"She was always a smart one. It's good she's gone into nursing; she has such a way with people. I wish I had her gentle touch."

"I like your touch just fine." His brow furrowed. "You're sure of this, mo chroi?"

I smoothed the crevices on his forehead with my fingertips. "Absolutely, more than the first time, I think."

He kissed me again and checked the time. "We better head for the chapel, then. We'll stop for breakfast on the way home."

"We'll see about that." I grabbed a wrap and headed for the door.

***

Vicar Angus MacBride awaited us in the front pew of the chapel. He rose as we trod the path down the aisle toward him. "How're you fairing this fine morning?"

"Well, sir." Cullum replied. He patted my hand, hooked on his bent arm.

"Ms. Fielding." The vicar offered a curt bow.

"Thank you for agreeing to marry us." I smiled.

"Mmm, I have no problem with mixed marriages as long as the children are given an education, with both sides represented in the best possible light." He pursed his thin lips. "I take it your son's been baptized?" He peered down at me through the bottom of his half-moon glasses.

"As his own choice, sir." I smiled and nodded.

Cullum patted my hand again. It hadn't been discussed.

"Well, then do you have the ring, lad?"

"Aye." Cullum reached for his jacket pocket.

"I have mine." I answered. I dug into my tiny bag and produced my first wedding band.

"Mo chroi, how'd you come to have that wi' you?" Cullum was surprised.

"I wore it on a chain beneath my clothes, until last night." I passed it to him.

He grasped the one he wore and sighed.

"You don't have to remove it. Let it be." I loved that he hadn't taken it off, even though today marked thirteen years ago our marriage was annulled.

The irony, that Cullum chose this day, wasn't lost on me. I selected Angus MacBride because he was chums with my father and signed the paperwork for the annulment, alleging coercion.

Things change in thirteen years. The power base shifted and the vicar was now marrying the two people he so callously had torn asunder when we were young and at the mercy of our elders.

"Alright, let's begin, vicar." Cullum turned to face Angus MacBride.

"Shall we pray fer the Lord's guidance? Father of all things, direct our steps this day and let the words of our mouths be fruitful, bringing glory to Your blessed Name. Amen." He opened his prayer book.

***

"Are you hungry?" Cullum led me from the chapel toward the car.

"For you." I had to be honest.

"Me too. Let's hie to the bothy, then; we'll get a bite later." He grinned and opened my door.

"Are you sure your strength will be adequate to the task, sir?" I hiked the long dress to climb into the red Mercedes.

He rounded the car, opened his door, and leaned in, grimacing. "Well maybe not. I'll dash down to the café and be back for you, in a bit."

"Get in the car, Sinclair." I growled.

He laughed and climbed inside, stretching to kiss my mouth. I'm glad he's taken up mouth kisses again.

Once home, Cullum slowly walked round the car, opened my door and offered his hand for me. I took it and climbed out to his embrace and a kiss so deep and erotic that I seriously considered going no further. But he steered me to the house and through the door. Inside he removed my wrap and his jacket and kissed me again. I thought the driveway kiss was incredible, but he surpassed himself.

He enjoyed teasing me, knowing me too well for my own good and drew out the promise of the bedroom through the whole house. The kitchen kiss was fantastic and fooled me into thinking the kitchen counter may not be so bad, though the granite's hard and cold. I was game if that's what he thought worked for him, but no....

Finally he led me to his bedroom. I hadn't seen it before, so I didn't know what to expect and from the brief glimpse I had it was masculine and tastefully done though I didn't care if it was a bare mattress in the floor, by that time. Not ordinarily a wanton hussy, but for this man I'm liquid in his glass, putty in his hands, and strings to his bow, to be played anytime.

Undressing was as leisurely as the rest of the program. Left to Cullum we might still be in the process but I'm about results and I've longed for him for thirteen years. "Enough!"

He chuckled and whispered along the line from my shoulder to my ear. "Patience, mo chroi." His tongue did wonderful things to my skin and I began to think the ecstasy was almost upon us when the phone rang. Minor bump in the road to satisfaction, it continued to ring until the caller surrendered.

My husband, I love those words, sighed and looked me over. "I love you more than life, Isabel."

"And I you, Cullum." I ran my hand down his shoulder, over the eight inch long wound with a wad of flesh missing, to his chest. "You're as wonderful as I've dreamed all these years."

He released the pins and nosegay keeping most of my hair aloft and nestled his face in the mass as he combed his fingers through to the ends. "You're beautiful, cuisle mo chroi. Are you sure of this?"

"I already said I do." I reminded him as he kissed me again.

He pulled back to peer into my eyes and nodded. I ran my fingers through his hair and caught the back of his neck.

He lifted me onto the bed and we became one.

Joining brought us to fulfillment at once. Our joint energy came to a peak and we left this squalid, grey existence for a brief flash of exquisite delight.

He paused and gruffly whispered, "Almost like the first time, eh?"

Spent, we stayed united and reveled in the warmth and intimacy that followed.

We were seventeen that summer. I was away at a posh girl's school in Switzerland, but my heart remained in Nairn. Cullum attended university in Inverness. We wrote to each other several times a week. I called as soon as I was home and out from under my father.

"Hullo, Cullum, I'm here. When can I see you?" I was wild just to look at him.

"I'll meet you at the burn in a half hour, will tha' do?" He responded with a chuckle.

"'Til then, Sinclair." I rang off and lay back on my pink bed, in a magazine perfect designer room. There was nothing of *me* in it. Mummy had a penchant for rooms looking as though no human inhabited them.

I changed clothes, from the prim suit I'd worn on the crossing, into denims and tee shirt, from my cedar chest. I had to hide them for fear Mummy would torch the lot, while I was away. I tied on my shoes and considered bailing over the balcony, to scale the drainpipe at the side of the house, and avoid meeting adults. In the end I crept down the servant's stairs and through the massive kitchen area.

Mrs. Humphries caught me. "An' where do ye think ye're off to when yer mam has plans fer the evenin', then?"

"What're the plans?" I put on my innocent face.

"Why they're takin' ye out to the club, wee one. Don't she tell ye to get all gussied up, so ye can go to the dance tonight?" She stirred something that smelled great, in a wooden bowl.

"She said naught to me, ma'am. She mentioned that she and Daddy might have dinner away." I lied. I needed to see Cullum and could avoid the stuffy club if I left and didn't turn up again in time.

Mrs. Humphries appeared thoughtful for a moment. "Well, then perhaps she's changed her mind already. I canna imagine bringin' me lass home and leavin' her, but then I ain't the high and mighty now, am I?" She continued to stir, while I pouted.

"I'm going for a walk, ma'am. Be back in an hour or so." I left for the burn, loping across the extensive lawn, an English affectation, into the woods beyond.

Pausing for a breath of sweet rotting underbrush, moss, and the crisp clean fragrance of the cold stream, I sat and waited for my friend. Fifteen minutes later Cullum wandered through the trees to our meeting spot. I studied his approach, enjoying the voyeurism, for a moment, before he glanced up and caught me.

His jet black hair was longer than a few months earlier, caught back in a ponytail, his pale grey eyes as startling as ever. His lanky frame filled out, his shoulders broadened. I imagined he'd taken up weight lifting. He had to be buff to play rugby.

He stopped and grinned. "Hullo, Bel." His voice was deeper.

Suddenly shy, I stood and threw up a hand. "Hey."

His quick strides ate up the distance. He grabbed me, lifting me off the ground, and spun around. "You're skinny. Don't they feed you in that place?"

"Ah, occasionally." My hands rested on his chest and, in a flash, I became aware that we were no longer children. When our eyes met I could tell the realization had just struck him too.

He pushed me away a bit and his face blushed pink. "Um, how's school?" He tried to draw on our history of friendship, over the past eleven years, to put us both at ease.

"Fine." I sat on a protruding rock, picked up a stick and broke it into tiny pieces.

"What else do you do there? Tell me everythin', Bel, I'm keen to know what your life's like away from home."

I turned to study him. "It's inconsequential to the best things in the world, Cullum. I'd trade it all to be able to spend the day with you, like we used to be."

"How's that, lass?" He smiled, but there was something else in his eyes.

"Friends, you know." I felt uncomfortable. A new and exciting event was about to take place, and I had no understanding of the consequences.

He sat near me on the thick moss carpet as we listened to the song of a nearby lark. I closed my eyes for a moment and imagined being an ordinary girl.

"Do you have a girlfriend?" I dreaded the answer, jealousy twisting my insides.

"You're my girlfriend. You're a girl and my friend, right?" He teased me mercilessly, at times.

I moved to the verdant carpet beside him. "That wasn't what I meant. We're mates, you ken. I meant romantic."

He fell silent, as he does on occasion when he's pondering something profound. He watched the cold, clear water gurgle across the rocks. "I'll never love anyone but you, Bel." He smiled, but I knew he was serious.

Relief washed over me and I sighed. "Tha's good, Cullum, because I'll never love anyone but you." I leaned towards him and he kissed my lips, as he'd done a thousand times.

This time was different.

A dance began. A waltz more than a rhumba, as we fell into each other's presence, perfectly suited to compatibility. Spoons nesting together could not fit tighter than our bodies. We loved for the first time…but not the last.

The affair continued until Cullum left Inverness UHI, with a degree in business, to enlist in the Royal Scots Dragoons and I stayed on at University of Edinburgh to finish an advanced degree in science.

Edinburgh Castle garrisoned the Dragoons and we had a tiny flat in a rough neighborhood. We married and threw caution to the wind. Conceived a month before Cullum shipped out to the Balkans, Liam came to be.

***

Aunt Min's diary:

I received a letter from my darling ones today. Isabel and Cullum have married! What a wonderful way to begin my dull week. I shan't break the news to Naomi and Arthur. Isabel requested I keep it quiet, for now. Cullum called his parents and requested the same silence. He has only a few days left with his wife, before deploying to Germany and processing out to Kosovo, as part of a UN peacekeeping force. My heart and prayers are with him, my dear lovely boy and my sweet, sweet girl, my heart, Isabel.

They'll make beautiful babies and I shall indulge my grand maternal yearning by spoiling each of them rotten!

I closed the diary for a moment and fought the sense of nostalgia for those sweet days of bliss when Cullum and I were so entangled, in body and spirit. How did Min know what we felt unless she'd experienced the same at some time? I never thought of her having a lover, but then, what did I know about her past— before my memory? Not much. I dug through the journals and found one dated thirty-five years earlier, two years before I was born. Min would have been twenty-eight, an elementary educator, and according to her photos, striking in appearance.

She wrote:

I do wish I'd forgone joining summer camp this year. The new parish priest, Father Ralph is teaching the lads and I the lasses. He's a handsome man with a winsome smile and too much interest in the fairer sex. He's a bit of a flirt with all the ladies except me, which chaps me more than it should. I hate to feel silly about any man, especially a priest!

Today, when passing, he nodded briefly and turned to watch me walk all the way to my cottage. I closed the door and felt flushed at his attention, yet he hesitates to laugh, even smile, in my presence. The infernal man is vexing. Tomorrow I'll ignore him completely. I shan't allow him to ruin my summer.

Another of the coaches is an Englishman, Arthur Fielding, who's quite handsome, with the loveliest eyes and such a rigid, almost military bearing about him. I think I may have formed a crush. It'd be my first. Sometimes I think men fatuous, obsessed with cars, their careers, and girls in scanty clothes.

Oh, to meet my forever love! He'd be handsome, serious I think, love reading, and taking long walks in the rain. He'd never need reminding to take the dustbin to the curb or trim the roses. He'd watch me approach from the bus, of an evening, with burning passion simmering in his eyes.

My, my, I read like a torrid novel! I'm sure he'll come along someday, hopefully before I'm past childbearing age. I do so want children, loads of them, six or eight or ten. Well, in the future, perhaps.

Tomorrow I'll be sure to cut a wide swathe around the priest. Perhaps I'll enjoy a few moments of Mr. Fielding instructing the lads on rowing techniques, in one of those sleeveless shirts he favors.

Aunt Min had a crush on my father and from the sounds of it; the priest had a crush on Aunt Min. For some reason it made me smile.

I opened to the following entry as my husband returned to our bed.

"You're smiling, that's a good sign." He carried a tray loaded with our late brunch.

"I'm with the man of my dreams; why wouldn't I be smiling?" I watched as he sat the tray on the side of the bed, unloading mugs of tea to his side table.

"Move over here, mo chroi."

Scooting a few feet across the bed I propped with his pillow behind me, against the headboard. He sat the tray across my lap.

"When did you do this? You haven't been away ten minutes." Luscious strawberries, cantaloupe, and honeydew melons cut into bites glistened in the light. Brown flaky croissants made my mouth water.

He grinned. "A chef lives beside us. I called him yesterday. He just delivered it to the kitchen door."

Smiling, my heart lingered on 'us' and I sighed. "Thank you."

"What were you up to while I was gone?" He dipped a strawberry in clotted cream and held it to my mouth.

Biting into the tart fruit tingled my nose. "Mmm, good." I wiped with a white napkin. "Reading some of Aunt Min's older diaries has led me to discover she had a crush on my father when they taught at the same summer camp. Isn't that wild? She also wrote about your friend, Father Ralph. Apparently he was a flirt and made over all the gals, but Min."

Cullum chuckled. "I can see that in him when he was younger. I remember when I went to summer camp and Min still taught lasses and Father Ralph, the lads. Your da wasn't there then."

"No, he wouldn't be. He was busy making millions, by that time, and tending my high maintenance mother. If she is my mother."

"What does that mean?"

"Min wrote about me like I belonged to her. I don't ken, maybe an adoring aunt, but there are places she refers to me like she gave life to me, then passed me on to Naomi. I know Arthur Fielding's my father."

"How can you be sure? You don't favor him."

"Nay, but I have a Fielding birthmark, identical to one he, his father, and grandfather bore in the same spot. Min always said I had Daddy's eyes." I bit into a buttered whole grain croissant.

"The mark right here?" He traced his hand down my thigh and slipped between my legs. "Looks like Scotland with England conspicuously absent?" He grinned.

"Aye, but I favor Min. I've never wondered about that, a lot of children resemble an aunt or uncle more than a parent." I shrugged. "It doesn't matter...to me." I leaned against the headboard. "But...it might matter quite a lot to Naomi."

He sipped his tea. "How's that?"

"Inheritance. Min relinquished her rights as first born. But I have controlling interest in the estate, with Naomi, a second at twenty-five percent."

"Naomi wouldn't adopt you then?" He buttered another croissant and swirled on a tiny spoon of local honey laced with a drop or two of Balvenie single malt Scotch.

"I'll have to check county records and see. Then again, my father kenned she doesn't have the brains to tend anything beyond her physique. Still, I'm going to look further into this question." I popped a bite of melon into my mouth. "This is such a treat, husband, thank you."

He leaned over the tray and kissed me. "We have to keep up our strength, wife."

"Did you check the phone call you missed?"

"Aye, not important."

Peeking from under my lashes, I caught a look cross his face, agitation at the caller or my question? I reached out and ran my hand up his shaggy arm to his shoulder and stopped at the wound, exploring the roughness, just above my name, tattooed over his right pectoral muscle.

He met my eyes and tried to smile. "Left a bit of a hole. They grafted skin from my thigh."

"Can you tell me what happened or is it too soon?" My voice softened and my fingers raked through the mat of hair on his chest.

He inhaled and looked away. "Not a lot to tell. I was between secure areas, carrying a missive to Military Intelligence. A sniper caught me and pulled the trigger. Knocked me off my feet. Next thing I knew three brawny lads carried me away. I felt relief for a moment, before I realized we'd been fighting 'em for three weeks. Then I passed out. I woke in their medical camp, but after a few days, gangrene set in. They traded me for one of their own. Field docs did the best they could to clean me up and sent me out, by chopper, to hospital in Germany. That's it." Lips set in a firm line, he looked away.

"Aunt Min called and told me the Dragoons had you back. I was relieved, but distraught at the same time. All I could think of was getting to where you were. Then my father called and threatened your life should I stray. I asked Aunt Min to tell you that I loved you...."

He touched his fingers to my mouth. "Shh, she did, lass. It wasn't the same as having you and our child together. It's past. What do you think about having another?"

"I tendered my resignation to the department yesterday. I owe them two weeks, took a week vacation, so I've one week to work. I can do it here with Bernie. Right now I'm supervising the investigation, under the table of course."

"So you're sayin' what? Aye or nay, lass?"

"Aye, let's complete our family, Cullum." I kept a hand on his arm and studied his reaction.

He smiled, though sadly and nodded. "Well, finish eating and we'll get back to making up for thirteen years apart."

Smiling, I sipped tea and watched him over the mug. "I'm all yours, anytime."

He took the tray away and I made a dash for the loo.

***

Click, click, boom. I heard the echo of the shot; saw my beloved, handsome lad lying in the dirt, blood seeping into foreign soil. I woke with a gasp. Cullum jerked awake beside me.

He mumbled into my hair. "Wha's wrong, Bel?" He wrapped his arm over me and pulled in closer.

"Bad dream." I felt his hand and arm, his shoulder and his hair in the dark. It was really my lover. *This* wasn't a dream. "I love you, Cullum."

"And I you, cuisle mo chroi." His breath felt hot and moist on my chilled skin.

He stirred against me. I turned into his embrace and we welcomed dawn making love. It's what he wanted to experience again, like the first time we married.

Thirteen years lost, but now—bliss.

***

"Hullo, lad. Are you having a merry holiday with your grandparents?"

Liam laughed at the other end of the line. "Mum, I love the farm! Lachlan is so much fun and he kens all kinds of farm things I could never imagine." He gushed, as he recounted yesterday's events. "We had new puppies last night. I helped Uncle Kyle and Grandpa deliver them. Then I lay down in the hay beside Kelly while the pups had their first meal. That's the bitch's name, and it's okay to say tha' because it isn't cursing."

I laughed aloud and wished Cullum would finish his shower to hear Liam's enthusiasm. "I know."

"Did you and Dad get married yet?"

"We did yesterday. You could've come with us but I didn't want to ruin your first week at school."

"It's great! I like my teacher. He says he looked over my transcripts and I'm very clever."

"We knew that." I glanced back to the hallway.

"Aye, we did but I like to hear it because Gram says you're clever and Dad's clever so it's only natural that I'd be clever, too." I heard Genny's voice in the background. "Are you comin' out today? Gram's calling me. It's breakfast time."

"Aye, we'll see you later. Go eat, I love you."

"Love you more." The line went dead.

After I showered, I padded down the hallway, but stopped short, when Cullum's voice resounded on the phone.

"Look, give her a month and she'll self-destruct. That's her history, and she'll be outta the way. If not, I'll take her in hand and move her on. Nay, darlin' it's alright. I ken what I'm doing. I'll handle everything."

I continued on to the living room, then the kitchen, turned on the kettle, gathered tea cups, and a pot. I measured out loose English Breakfast tea leaves, dumped them into the pot, and wondered who my husband was calling darlin' and who she was, who would self-destruct. There was plenty of self-destruction in *my* history.

I heard his steps coming my way and tried not to look suspicious. When you work for the police, it becomes second nature that you question everything.

"Hey, love, how's our lad?" He opened the refrigerator without looking at me, grabbed out a bottle of juice, and knocked it back.

"Fine, delivered pups last night and he's having a blast with Lachlan, Kyle, and his grandparents." I smiled.

He turned to watch the surf of Moray Firth from the west window. "Good, I want 'im to enjoy his family."

Either his mind was only half on our conversation or he was evasive. It's hard to tell when he won't look at me.

Pouring hot water over the tea leaves, I tried another tactic. "I'm going out to see him in a while. Wanna come?"

"Mmm." He was not in the same universe.

"Then I thought I might buy a piece of land and build a nightclub, maybe put in a pool instead of a dance floor." I glanced at his broad back.

"Mmm."

"There's a traveling dance act we might employ for opening night. They use elephants, dressed in pink tutus. They're very talented underwater ballerinas."

"Mmm, good." He nodded.

I gave up and left him to ponder the surf, sorting out his problem with the woman he would handle.

***

"I need to make a quick stop at the pub." Cullum flipped his keys in the air and caught them without looking. He can juggle too. He wore denims and a tee shirt so I knew he wasn't spending time at the pub or anywhere else but the farm. He always wore a suit to work.

"Alright." I slung my handbag over my shoulder and followed him out as he held the door. He looped his arm through mine and opened the door to the Mercedes.

"I need to run down to Edinburgh soon." I vied for his attention for a moment.

"Sure, we can do tha'. When?" He circled and climbed inside.

"I'm running out of clothes; need to put the flat up for sale, or let, and it would be nice to have my car." I watched to see if he tuned in to my voice.

He cranked the car and pulled out of the driveway. "When, love? I can take off and run down with you whenever you want or we can fly down and drive back. We have three more days before we both have to get back to work, do you wanna go tomorrow?"

"Wow, you're paying attention." I smiled.

He glanced at me. "Wha'? Ah, I'm sorry, mo chroi. We have a personnel problem I may have to tend. I hate firing people."

"It's alright, I understand." I sat quietly, figuring on a trip to the flat. "I can go without you if you're tied up."

He stopped at a traffic light. "Nay, you'll not be going anywhere without me. We'll leave tomorrow mornin'. Will you see to it?"

"Aye, if you're sure."

"I am." He pulled into the pub and left me in the car while he dashed inside. In less than five minutes he was out again.

We drove towards the farm.

***

We boarded a flight from Inverness to Edinburgh. A taxi carried us the five miles to my home in the Old Town district.

It seemed a lifetime past that I left for a quick hop up to Nairn for Min's funeral. I'll feel the hollowness inside the remainder of my days. Aunt Min was my lifeline to home, the buffer zone I'd always run to, when my circumstances became unbearably lonely.

I unlocked the door to my flat and stepped inside, Cullum on my heels. He looked around, surveying my former domain and helped me with my jacket, removing his and hung both on a hall tree. I immediately crossed the room and opened the drapes to let light inside and glanced down at the street level concrete steps.

"It's lovely, lass. Did you decide to sell or let?" He glanced over at me, sunglasses on top of his head, like a hairband, and smiled.

"Selling, with as many furnishings as possible. What with Min's cottage full and living with you...."

He met me on the other side and wrapped his arms behind me, keeping space between us. "Aye, you don't need the place. On the other hand, if you let it, fully furnished, perhaps it would bring a decent income. Show me the layout?"

"There's not so much to see. The kitchen opens to the dining room." I walked to the left of the entrance, and through a closed passageway, past the place I'd prepared meals for more than a dozen years. "The dining room's a nice size, but I use one end as a home office." I indicated an armoire at one side.

"Bedrooms are opposite." I plodded across the living room, beyond the tapestry sofa and matching chair to open Liam's bedroom door. "Liam's," I turned to the guest room. "Mrs. Peterson sleeps here when she stays over."

Opening the door to my bedroom felt strange. No man had ever put a foot inside, if you don't count my son and the movers. "This is mine." I flipped on lights and stepped inside. I crossed my arms and studied his reaction to the rich cerulean blue and gold pumpkin room and accessories.

He smiled. "I wanna make love to you in here." He began to unbutton his dress shirt. "Come along now, be co-operative, love." He teased, as though I'd ever been otherwise.

Embarrassed, I smiled and blushed. "I was just thinking, other than Liam, no male person's ever entered my private space."

"I let you into mine. Now it's your turn." He stripped off his shirt, hanging it neatly over the back of my vanity chair. I admired the smooth muscles of his back and chest, when he spun back my direction.

He began work on my shirt, pulling it over my head and stopping, as he does, to ponder my breasts. I inherited that feature from Min as well. She was busty.

He took another moment to unhook my bra and removed it by way of running his hands over every millimeter of newly exposed flesh. My clothes landed over his shirt. He unzipped my skirt, feeding it past my hips with the flat of his hands, all the way down my thighs. He followed it to the floor where he knelt and reached for my panties.

I stood still, braced against the mattress, not trusting my balance, but certain he would catch me if I passed out.

It was the most erotic encounter we'd had yet.

He pressed me back onto my bed and joined me, smiling.

A little while later, I lay on Cullum's arm and enjoyed the skin smell of him, beyond the clean soap of his morning shower. I looked over his thick chest at the picture on the side table. It was of our wedding day, shortly after we pledged our eternal love.

He lifted the frame and studied the subjects. "I didn't have a copy of this. Never thought I'd need one, as that day's engraved on my brain." He lay the photo face down on the table and glanced down at me. "I still can't believe this has actually happened. Keep thinking I'll wake up and it's all been a dream."

I smiled and ran my fingertips up to his chin. "I never dared hoped that we'd...I thought a thousand times we'd meet, maybe talk, perhaps share a kiss."

"I ken. Me too." He kissed my hair.

"I never believed you'd want me back." I wrapped my leg round his and squeezed.

"Darlin', I never left you."

Cullum's phone rang a third time. "I'll just be a moment, love." He left me to pack a box alone but rejoined me in a flash. His eyes brimmed with laughter. "Hold on, son, you're mum's right here."

Cullum handed me his phone. "Hullo, Liam."

"Mum, the most amazing thing just happened!"

"I hope I don't have to guess."

"I suppose I can tell you, since I told Dad."

I tossed a glance towards Cullum, hands on his hips, grinning. "It's only fair."

"I just now, this minute, am riding a horse in Scotland." Satisfaction abounded in my...our son.

"That's incredible! Who's with you, Uncle Kyle?"

"Lachlan. I tell you, Mum, he kens animals. I wish I had his magic. He can approach any horse, even a mostly wild one. I watched him do it yester...whoa! Mum, may I call you back?"

"Concentrate on the ride, Liam. We'll talk about particulars later." I handed Cullum's phone back to him.

He burst out laughing and grabbed me in a hug. "Bel, I wanna dozen just like him."

I joined his amusement. "A dozen? Wait until you stay up all night with a sick one. Then we'll see how many more you want."

"You mean he didn't come like he is, loo trained, and all? Well, I might have to rethink my order. At least a few more. Gaud, he's a great lad." He pulled back and looked me over. "I wanna be part of your pregnancy, feel our child move. I want to be there to catch him when he's born and the first to lay 'im to your breast. All the things I missed with Liam...." His eyes teared. He inhaled. "Everything I missed with Liam, I want to experience with our next child. Promise me you'll always stay with me, you'll never leave me again."

I held his face in my hands. "I promise." I kissed his mouth.

We finished packing the last box. The estate agent was on his way over to view the flat and take pictures. Movers had most of their truck packed and we had half a day to get home before returning to work.

Cullum managed the pub and brewery by phone. He was right. He hired good people.

"After next week I'll be a lady of leisure…." I slid a box out toward the entry door.

"I'll get tha', mo chroi." He snatched the container filled with Liam's summer clothes that still fit. "Don't move heavy items. You may be pregnant even if you're not, don't hurt yourself. I'm here. So, lady of leisure, wha's up your sleeve?" He sat the box into the hallway with a dozen others for the movers to load.

"I don't know yet. I wanna get Min's cottage into shape and may let it to tourists, self-catered. Then, we'll see. Before we have babies we'll need to figure out living arrangements, what with bedrooms and such. With three, we'll have enough for now." I stretched forward, touching my toes to loosen my lower back.

"If we need more I'll build you a bigger house." He grinned, imagining, I supposed, the prospect of a home full of scampering children.

"I like the one you have. Maybe add another bedroom. Shall I keep Min's cottage for our getaway love nest?"

"Tha' sounds sexy." He wrapped me up for a squeeze and pinched my bum, followed by a long wet kiss.

One of the movers tapped at the door and stuck his head inside. "Is there more? We have a wee bit o' room yet."

I gave a quick look around and landed on the rocker I'd used with Liam. "For the rocker, perhaps?"

"Aye, that'll be all, Mrs. Sinclair." He grasped the antique platform base rocker Min brought to me when my…our son was born. Even after he was older, we rocked whenever Liam was ill or felt sad. Unconsciously, I swiped my hand across my belly, not realizing my husband watched.

He stepped behind me, placing his large mitt over my abdomen. "I bought that chair for you and our child. Min helped me find it and brought it down. The night Liam was born, Kyle sat with me on her settee and waited for word from you. I wept like an old woman when you called and said we had a son, would she tell me." His voice broke. "She held the phone away from her ear and I heard your voice…broken, crying."

"I don't remember asking her to tell you. I was alone in the hospital until she came down the next day; then my father arrived late in the afternoon."

"Where was whose it?" He asked blandly.

"Away—with his better half. He came by to see me when he returned, brought flowers, and played the part for his father. As soon as I could leave hospital, I returned here. I couldn't even pretend to bring Liam up in a divided house with such sad people, as we were." I turned in his arms. "I thought I grew up with angry parents, but the more I read Min's diaries, the greater my grasp of their dysfunction. If Min gave me birth, with my father's cooperation or participation, which it appears, is what happened, Naomi was out of the loop. She didn't want a child, my father did."

His eyes narrowed. "Could she have murdered Min?"

I grinned. "Oh, you've never seen her in a full tilt rage. She's a force of calculated terror, for sure, and not just her mouth. She kicks, screams, and throws large objects. Once she—I hadn't thought of that before. I should've remembered."

"Wha', love? You must tell me."

"Once she hit Min with an onyx paperweight from Daddy's desk. Clipped her on the chin with it; knocked her out cold. It fractured Min's chin and jaw. She was in a brace and drank through a straw for months. The impact left her with a spur and a bit of a crooked smile for a long time. Several surgeries and a dental apparatus was all it took to straighten her face. I overheard my father on the phone with her, apologizing. He said something I didn't understand at the time. 'Min, I married the wrong woman. You'd have been so much better for our daughter and for me.'"

"It sounds as though Aunt Min *was* your birth mother." He frowned. "That makes more sense of the gibberish Naomi shouted at me about blood ties, when I returned from Germany. I went out to the estate to confront your parents. Naomi didn't realize what she was giving away. I thought she was witless, but she never forgot for a moment tha' you were not her child."

Nodding I continued to pile a case against her, as though for court. "While pregnant with Liam I developed stretch marks on my hips, breasts, and belly. Naomi always paraded around the pool in a string bikini, nary a stretch mark in sight. I thought she'd had them nipped and tucked, as she's fond of the knife and laser."

"I love those marks on you, mo chroí." He kissed my neck.

"Mmm....In one of Min's summer camp entries she wrote about buying a conservative one piece bathing suit for her fuller figure. It was the summer after I was born—in Spain."

"You never told me you were born abroad." He kissed my forehead. "We need concrete proof." He released me.

"I'll go through Min's belongings, after I become a lady of leisure, to see what surfaces."

"I'll help all I can." He crossed the room and stood in the bay window, overlooking the plaza. "I should've told you this before. Naomi came by the pub a few months ago and offered me a bribe."

A chill swept past.

"We were hit by a hacker who took over our bank accounts and bled us dry in a day. Damian found out, probably from Bernie, and told her. She offered to cover our loss. She asked me to contact you and invite you to come home. You ken? Get to know Liam, see you, perhaps we could work through our issues. She even went so far as to apologize for her behavior in the past."

"I see." I busied myself straightening the ottoman in front of the sofa where my son and I cuddled to watch movies.

He stuffed his hands in his trouser pockets. "I didn't take her up on her proposition, Bel, but she told me somethin' I didn't know. She let it slip that my feelings would be reciprocated. I had no clue you'd even talk to me prior to that conversation. It gave me courage to approach you." He turned, his back to the sunlight streaming through the window. Particles danced through the air, around him, like tiny sprites.

"She wouldn't know tha', Cullum. Aunt Min must've told her. I always asked for an update when I called or visited, wishing I'd hear something to give me the courage to call you. According to her diaries she experienced a great deal of remorse over helping my parents destroy us and keep us apart."

"I'll not lie to you, love; *I* accused her of meddling, more than once." He sighed and brushed his hand over his beard. "May I shave this off?" He scowled.

I stepped to his side and ran my fingertips over the graying hair on his face. "I like it but...I miss the dimple here, on your cheek, when you smile and then the cleft in your chin has always fascinated me. Anyway, why ask?"

"It was my penance after I healed. I made a pact with God tha' I'd only shave off the beard if He brought you back to me." His eyes dropped to study the edge of the wool rug on the floor.

"Talk to *Him*, then." My smile reassured him.

He kissed my mouth, without touching me with his hands. "I'd have done anything to get you back. But I couldn't make a deal with the devil. You ken?"

"I do." I laid my hand along his jaw. "Just wish we'd crossed this bridge sooner. Min would be alive. Liam would've had his dad," I whispered in his ear, "and I my lover."

***

Dozing in the passenger's seat of my brown Toyota Prius, I focused on the surroundings when we stopped at a layby.

Cullum glanced over. "Lovely, I need to move around a bit. Will you walk with me?"

"Sure." I unbuckled my seatbelt and opened the door to climb out. Looking around, I recognized that we were on A9. "Where have we passed?"

"Just north of Aviemore." He reached for my hand and tucked it into his arm. "There's a trail beyond that stile." He pointed into the sunlight.

Shading my eyes, I glimpsed a pasture full of sheep. New lambs scampered amongst the wild flowers and thick grass, their faces smiling as they baaed. Two lambs, twins by the look of them, wrestled for the prime spot under a ewe. She patiently stood by, while they sorted themselves out, and became attached to her udder.

My husband's hands gripped my waist, from behind, as he peered over my shoulder. "What's this? Ah, the playful babes. Looking forward to another child, mo chroi?"

My cheeks flamed. "I am. I've not allowed myself to even dream of children. You're the only man I've ever loved...ever wanted. Liam asked once, when he was about six, why he had no brothers or sisters like all his friends." I led out to the path.

"What did you tell him?"

"That we didn't have his dad to be their dad."

We walked on in silence for ten minutes, the light breeze refreshing.

"I would have been, had I been able." He shot a sidelong glance towards me.

"Now, I know that's true. Bradley suggested I contact you and try to make amends. He even implied we should just pick up where we left off, that no one would be the wiser, should we live together as man and wife." I turned to face him. "Accommodating my father when he visited, of course."

"I would have considered it, mo chroi. Trouble is, I'd never have been able to send you off to play at bein' the other man's wife—even if he'd lose everything." He parked his hand on my back. "You belong to *me*. I'm rather exclusive about that, Bel."

I smiled. "I like you that way, lover."

We'd gone about a mile before turning back for the car.

"We'll stop for petrol and a cuppa in Grantown-on-Spey before we turn onto A939 home." He held my hand.

"That'll do. Cullum, how many times have you made this trek in the past thirteen years?" There was no avoiding the question, nowhere to run.

The rumble of a diesel truck died on the breeze.

Cullum quietened for a moment. "I came down to Edinburgh fifteen times last year. I followed you to work, to lunch, home after picking up our son from school. I was nearby when you went to the grocer, the doctor once, the dentist, and a store that specializes in those cute little things you favor that cover your fine bottom."

"Thank you." I clasped his arm and leaned into his shoulder. "Thank you very much."

"You're welcome." He nodded. "Another time I waited to see you leave your office with a…co-worker, perhaps…a man."

"What'd he look like?" I pulled in closer to him.

"Abou' my height, weight, reddish hair. You laughed at something he said, and my blood ran cold." He glanced past me.

"That was Harry, my boss. He's married, with five children and a beautiful wife. There's been no one in my life to make your

83

blood run cold. The closest I've been to any male, since and until you, was our son, unless I sat beside a man on a plane. Those seats are really tight in coach and I have a big bum and…."

"I love your bum. Come, let's hie to the bothy. The movers will arrive soon and we need to decide what to do with all your clothes. I've never seen so many garments stuffed into one wardrobe my whole life." He stepped up the pace and we climbed across the stile to the layby and back into my car.

"I can leave them at Aunt Min's cottage until I figure it all out. We don't have to wade through it today. What do you say to a run this evening? Celebrate our last night as adults, tomorrow we're parents again. Our lad's comin' home." I squeezed his shoulder.

"Well said, lovely. A run it will be."

Chapter 7

Liam helped me clear the table after tea. He carried the china service to the sink on a tray and unloaded.

I watched him and felt a pang for the child he'd been, and the young man he was becoming. "Do you recall the conversations we had, in the past, about why you're an only child?"

"Aye, Mum. I ken it's because Dad wasn't there to be the dad of brothers and sisters." He carefully placed the cups on the rug in the sink.

"Right, well that's changed. Now Dad's here, to be your dad, and a brother or sister's dad as well." I inhaled, unsure how'd he feel about a sibling.

"Are you sayin' you're having a baby?" Liam met my eyes frankly.

"I don't know yet, but your dad and I want more children. He missed out on so much with you, he wants to know all that you and I went through first hand. I want you to have brothers and sisters."

Liam dropped his gaze and studied the dishes in the sink for a moment. "I'm not enough?"

"I didn't say that. Do you love me less since you have your dad?"

He looked up, brow furrowed. "Nay, Mum."

"Then how can I love you less because we have another child, or more than another, what if we have two or three? Will there be less love, concern, and time for you?" Warm water ran into the sink.

"I guess not." He looked uncertain while he added washing up liquid.

"You're still who you are, but then you'd also be a brother, not just a son and a grandson. That's a lot of responsibility. You'll have to help teach a child to walk, talk, and stay out of trouble. You'll need to help feed and watch over him to be sure he's safe. All the things I taught you and you're learning from Dad have to be passed to a brother or sister. Are you up for it?" I dropped a soft cotton rag into the sudsy water.

His shoulders straightened and he nodded. "Aye, Mum. I won't let you down."

"You'd not disappoint me, Liam. A new life is a huge charge. I knew nothing about tending a bairn when you were born." I reached across and ran my wet finger down his straight nose. "Thank goodness Aunt Min was there to show me what to do." I ruffled his wavy hair with a smile.

His face screwed up, one eye almost closed. "Do I have to change nappies?"

"It'll *probably* come to tha'." I nodded and handed him a clean cup.

"Will Dad change nappies, too?" He looked hopeful as he rinsed dishes.

"I'm *sure* it'll come to tha'."

He grinned. "I can do it, then, Mum. You may count on me."

"Good, it's bedtime." I dried my hands on a towel.

"Can't I stay up 'til Dad gets home?" Liam rinsed the last glass.

"He might be late. Better you get your shower and do your nighttime routine. We have an early mornin'." I headed to the office through the living room.

The door opened to the love of my life. He smiled. "Where's our lad?"

Liam shot out of the kitchen. "Dad! Mum said you'd be late."

"I must return for a bit, yet, but I wanted to say goodnight." Cullum gripped Liam's shoulder and led him to his bedroom. "Now, finish your chores and I'll tuck you in." He left our son in his room and returned to me. "How's he doing his first night home, mo chroí?" He brushed back a lock of my hair that slipped the braid.

Watching the two people I loved most interact, left me with a stupid grin. "Good, we had a chat about brothers and sisters."

Cullum grimaced and whispered. "What'd he say?"

My voice dropped. "Wondered why he wasn't enough."

"Did you tell him…that he's always our firstborn and…." He covered his mouth and cleared his throat.

I wrapped my arm around his. "I told him that loving someone else could never diminish our love for him. It won't, will it?"

He shook his head, choking out words. "Death wouldn't change it, Bel."

Chapter 8

Click-click-boom! My charming man fell to the ground in slow motion, grabbing his shoulder. Tears sprang to my eyes and I couldn't breathe. I gasped, struggling for oxygen.

"Bel, wake up, darlin'!" Strong hands shook me aware.

"What?" I took in a bushel of air.

"You're dreaming again, love. Wha's happenin'?" My husband propped on one elbow, hovering. His hand caught my hair and smoothed it away from my face. "Talk to me, mo chroi. Tell me wha' the monsters look like. If I don't know, I can't slay 'em."

"Cullum?" I wrapped my arms around him and wept.

"Shh, shh, shh, my love, it's alright. Whatever it is, we'll sort it, just tell me." He rolled to his back, me above him and wrapped me in a tight embrace. "Is it Liam?"

"Nay, you…shot in the shoulder, falling to the ground."

"Ah, maybe I shouldn't have told you all tha'. It's over, Bel. All over. Shh…." He smoothed my hair back and kissed me. Fear became longing for something more. I turned my lips to his and found contentment.

***

I dressed for a run and stretched my weariness away.

Liam opened his bedroom door, appearing dressed, ready for school. "Is Dad up?"

"Nay, he didn't get home 'til really late." I poured coffee and prepared toast.

"He's drivin' me to school."

"Might I do?" I glanced back with a smile.

He can't help but respond, smiling. "Aye, you'll do fine, Mum."

Dishing up porridge and plating toast, I checked his progress with juice and water at the table. "Alright then, we'll have a bite and go to school."

We sat, held hands, and blessed our breakfast.

When I looked up, Cullum stood in the doorway stretching and yawning. "Somethin' smells good."

"Here, take mine. I assume you're up for school duty." I left my place and prepared another bowl of porridge, and a mug of coffee.

"Aye, said I'd take our fine lad to school this morning." He ruffled Liam's hair then poured a glass of juice and drank it down, refilling before sipping his coffee. He sat at my bowl and I swapped it out for one twice as full. His hand grasped and tightened on my thigh. "You runnin' this mornin'?"

A burn crept up my neck at the physical familiarity in front of Liam. He needed to see our affection in actions and words to understand. But it was all new to me too. "Aye."

"Wait for me, I'll go with you."

"Okay, but how far do you *normally* run?" I took my smaller bowl of porridge and sat beside Liam. I wanted to be able to see my husband, blood-shot eyes, and all.

"Generally six miles. You?" He scooped up porridge and watched me, while rubbing my socked foot with his.

"I can do three in a pinch." I couldn't help smiling, when he winked.

"I don't want you pinched. We'll run two together and I'll continue on while you shower." He scraped the bottom of his bowl, pulled a bread plate of toast and the clotted cream forwards.

"You have a deal. I'll wait for you, or shall I ride with you?" I checked with Liam, but he was watching his father.

"Can your mum go with us?"

Liam nodded, his mouth full, swallowed, and mumbled. "Sure."

I rubbed his back. "Slow down, the toast won't run away, lad."

He stuffed a quarter piece of bread in his mouth.

Cullum realized he set the pace and slowed down himself. "I apologize. I was hungry."

"Me, too." Liam mimed.

I reconsidered my escort. "Tell you what. You two go to school. I'll have the kitchen cleaned up when Dad returns and we'll go for a run. Will it work?"

Liam smiled. "Sure, Mum."

I piled dishes into the washer and dried my hands.

My men left. I rubbed my hand across my abdomen and wondered if we'd brought another life into being. I looked forward to knowing in a few weeks. Then I remembered my mother's—Naomi's fertility treatments. Curiosity peaked, I went to find Aunt Min's diary that corresponded with the times she accompanied her sister for the procedures. I could only guess at the schedule. Pulling a journal dated the year before my conception, I opened to the beginning.

Arthur left me this evening a bit earlier than usual. He felt he needed to put in an appearance at home, as it would be his first before midnight, this week. It is good to have his love, but know we cheat and sin against God and my sister, no matter the circumstances. Arthur feels justified, but I do not.

He brought up an idea that I'm considering. He asked me to give him an heir as Naomi continues to fail to conceive. This is the third year she's undergone fertility treatment, so she says.

Arthur has never accompanied her, but I've gone several times. She appeared to be in pain, which the doctors warned might happen. However, while in the loo at their home I found a current package of birth control pills and several missing. She's never been brilliant, but I'd think she'd try harder to hide them if she was being duplicitous.

The library had numerous volumes about infertility treatments. I checked two and came home, pouring over the tomes until the wee hours. Her symptoms seem very near the double treatment, fertility injections, and added birth control measures. I hate being suspicious of her but she is a lying little minx. Daddy doted upon her, then passed her off for Arthur to dote upon. Neither realize that her type of allure is temporary. At some point, the pretty wears thin and one is left with the reality of her evil nature. Then there were the lies she used to ensnare Arthur.

I'm fast approaching the age, beyond which, it is no longer safe to have a child. I do so want to experience life growing inside. For that life to be an extension of the man I love, to provide him with an heir, would have the upmost gratification. Perhaps he'll even see what companionship, love, yes...even sacrifice, means to a relationship.

I shall seek God's answer in prayer and pray He agrees with me.

"Oh, Min, you precious, foolish woman." I closed the journal and dried the tears on my face. "You had no idea he'd never leave her. He gave her his word. You didn't see the ruthless side of him that took whatever he wanted, leaving you bereft, desolate...and me abandoned."

"Wha's this, mo chroi?" Cullum entered the guest room quietly.

Startled, I jumped, heart racing. "I didn't hear you come in. You scared the life outta me."

He sat beside me on the bed. "Liam was quick to bail once we arrived at school. He'll ride the bus tomorrow." My husband stroked my back and pulled me into his safe embrace. "Now, tell me, why the tears?"

"I read Aunt Min's diary from the time she was considering having a child, to give my father an heir. While at the mansion, she discovered birth control pills, prescribed to Naomi." I snuggled into his unshaven neck. His roughness felt like sandpaper.

"Ah, and history repeats itself. She abandons you to Naomi for your father. You abandon me to another kind of hell, for your father." He rubbed my arm. "He was a demanding man, Arthur Fielding. Unfortunately he left those who loved him dead and wounded in his wake, as he dragged along that little tart he married."

"Yes, we complied out of misguided loyalty and fear. At least I knew he was no saint, but an underhanded liar and thief of all I held dear. When he threatened your life, I realized he was afraid he couldn't control me. I came so close to mutiny...had I only be certain that you'd have me back."

"I was a hot mess, mo chroi." He released me. "It was two years before I could be trusted alone. I didn't drive for the first eight years." He studied the carpeted floor. "It may have been better *for me,* had you been here, then again, it would've been hell for you. And to bring a child into the terror...no, the more I think on it, the more I realize God protected you and Liam from the chaos of my return."

Leaning into his thick arm, I wrapped my hands around his bicep. "It wouldn't have been fun, but you may not have been the mess you were, had I been here. I'll spend the rest of my life tryin' to make it up to you." I kissed his shoulder.

He smiled and nuzzled my hair. "Well, you're welcome to try." He patted my knee. "I'll pull on clothes and we'll run."

"I'll wait in here. Maybe read a bit more." I watched the man of my dreams leave the guestroom and glanced back at the stack of journals. "Aunt Min, how can I think of you any other way, after all these years? Yet...Naomi is so easy to divorce in my heart and mind. I feel like a pawn in an unending match. All that's left to do battle is me and the dark queen."

***

Leaving Cullum to finish his distance, I headed straight to the shower in the guestroom. Closing the door softly, out of habit, I stripped. Warm water streamed through my hair and banished the damp chill of the shoreline run.

Lab results should be in at Bernie's office, then I'll head over to Aunt Min's, and go through her papers. Where would she hide my birth certificate? I'd bet money she kept at least a copy squirreled away.

I've had a passport all my life and Daddy's office always handled those things. The attorneys handle it now, so the original may be on file with them.

Pick up Liam from school, unless Cullum's doing that, too.

A door closed somewhere in the house. I stepped out onto the bamboo bathmat and snagged my towel. Wrapped securely I checked the clock in the bedroom. *Too soon for my lover to have returned.*

My running clothes were damp, from the rain that caught us the first few minutes we were out. The guestroom door was still closed.

I quickly donned a bra and slid into a denim skirt. Pulling a knit shirt over my head, I crossed the well-padded floor to the entry.

The door opened silently, on well-maintained hinges.

I glanced up and down the hallway.

No one was there.

A deep breath later, I crept toward the living room, keeping to the south wall.

A grey hooded figure was tossing my handbag; one item at a time examined and laid out the dining table. The body structure was female or small male, 5'4 or thereabouts.

I kept moving in his/her general direction, avoiding reflective surfaces. I was almost within arm's reach when she turned.

Skye Paisley.

Startled, she backed away.

"What're you doing here?" Moving towards her slowly, I prepared myself to make the confrontation physical, if necessary.

"I was looking for Cullum." She glanced behind her.

There's an outside door in the kitchen.

"He's not in my handbag." I took another step closer.

"I just wondered who was living here with him." She glanced back again.

"He told you that his wife and son live with him. I heard him on the phone with you." I took two more steps.

"Well, I had to be sure. He's broken off with me before." She backed away, her hand out to catch the door frame to the kitchen.

"I see. Well, you can consider it final this time." *How did she get in?*

Her chin tilted up, eyes fiery, teeth clenched. Her voice lowered as she growled. "I only take orders from him."

The kitchen door opened and my husband entered.

Skye made a dash to pass Cullum in the doorway, but he caught her arm.

"Yeah, thought that was your car in the street. What're *you* doing in our home?"

She laid her hands on his chest, as though she'd done it a hundred other times.

Cullum grimaced and peeled them away, stepping back.

Her voice became a whimper. "I just dropped paperwork for you, from David."

He barked. "How'd you get into our home?"

"The door was open. Thought I'd leave the packet on the table and *she* came out and accused me of going through her handbag."

"Bel, wha's going on?"

Mute, I turned, scooping up my handbag and belongings, and walked back to the guestroom. *Let him sort her out.*

I combed out my hair and slipped into clogs, leaving by the front door while he was still in the kitchen with her. No time or energy left for drama. I still had Bernie to deal with today.

Cullum escorted his challenge out through the kitchen door as I relocked the front.

***

The steps up to the station left me almost breathless. I'd walked from Cullum's house at a quick pace, putting distance between us. My car keys were in the kitchen, but Min's house key was in my handbag.

When I finished with Bernie, I'd walk to Min's and search out the information I needed.

Jimmy gave me a nod and a smile, then jabbed his thumb towards the back. I passed him and tapped on Bernie's door.

He bellowed. "Come in, Isabel."

Opening the door, I stepped inside, curious. "How'd you know it was me?"

"Cullum called after you, a few moments ago. Told 'im I'd tell you."

I perched on the chair in front of his desk. "What do you have for me, Bernie?"

"Lab results came in. You were correct. That was Min's blood on the rug and hearth. Suppose Cullum was right about the statue bein' moved." He shrugged. "How was I to ken? I ain't a bloody decorator." He tossed a file across the desk.

"Even though you thought it was an accident, you should've had the big-shots in to investigate. Better safe than tryin' to cover your rump later." I picked up the file folder and rose. "I'll be at Min's a while, if you need me."

He sang out, "I have your number." Constable Leighton shot a sly grin my way.

"Don't give it out, Bernie. It's personal information." I wondered how deep he was into Scotland's Socialist Party, and if Skye had her fangs into him too.

"I'll guard it wi' my life." He laid his hand over his heart.

I headed to the door. "See that you do."

There's a cozy little café down by the harbor. It's the opposite direction of Min's, but I needed tea and solace.

Coming up the lane was one of Aunt Min's dearest friends, Liddy Anderson. "How are you, Miss Liddy?" She is a delightful old gal.

Her poodle wagged all over, a pink bow in her hair. I bent to rub her frizzy ears.

Miss Liddy gushed. "Oh, Isabel, I didn't get to speak with you at Minerva's funeral. Dear one, I so hope you find the culprit behind her murder. Your aunt was very proud of your work at the police department in Edinburgh." She laid her wrinkled hand on my arm.

"Thank you, Miss Liddy. I didn't realize anyone knew we were investigating Min's death."

"Bernie's wife told us, last night at Bunco, that you were on loan to help him. It wasn't a secret, now was it?" Her faded blue eyes were merry, her wrinkled brow creased with a frown.

"Nay, no secret. I'll do my best. I must be off. I need a cuppa this morning." We parted.

She looked back and called to me. "I saw your lad a few days past. Looks just like his da, he does."

Smiling, I waved, gritting my teeth. "Aye, he does that."

The door to the café swept open and was held in place by an elderly gentleman I should have known, but couldn't recall his name. "Thank you, kindly."

He tipped his hat, smiled, and winked before closing the door. I scanned the blackboard menu and found a table.

One of the ladies behind the counter looked up. "Tea, with milk, please."

She nodded. "Aye, it'll be right there, Isabel."

The bad thing about being away, so much and so long, was that some folks remembered me. But I struggled with names and sometimes faces. Later it wouldn't prove a problem.

I opened the folder and perused the lab results. The broken button was carved rhinoceros horn. *What?* I pondered that revelation for a moment, before reading further. The hair was not Minerva's. Tests revealed it salon-dyed and the follicles indicated regular high-end shampoo and treatment.

I wondered when Naomi last visited her sister. Obviously, after Aunt Min last hoovered the rug. I stared out the front window at the colorful harbored sail boats.

A couple entered the tiny space, their Springer Spaniel on a short lead. They took the table beside me. The dog looked up; his large golden brown eyes searched mine before I reached to brush my hand over his silken fur.

Daddy brought a Springer puppy home when I was seven and a half. He was very pleased with himself. Aunt Min and Uncle David had married and moved to Melross Manor, a few miles away.

I named my new friend Charlie and he slept with me, ate with me, and wound up in the cellar with me, after one of Naomi's tirades. She tossed him down the stairs. He yelped in pain as his roly-poly body slapped the stone stairs. I'd preceded him and caught myself on the landing. I was able to stop his fall, grasping his warm, whining softness close.

Mrs. MacDougle brought lunch down later. I shared my sandwich with Charlie. He nibbled a bit of bread but had no appetite. Inside I knew he'd die, if not this time, perhaps next. Naomi took delight in destruction. I talked the housekeeper into letting me out through the wine vault and sneaked my precious cargo away from the mansion.

I walked to Aunt Min and Uncle David's home carrying Charlie in my arms. Upon arrival I handed him over to Uncle David.

"Mummy's tryin' to kill him. Could you protect him from her, please." I broke down; my stalwart spirit finally succumbing to Naomi's hatred.

Uncle David hugged me close as he cradled my puppy. "Leave him to me, lass. He'll never want for a thing." He probed Charlie's body gently. "I think maybe he's just sore, but I'll run him over to Cullum's da for a look, okay?"

It was the only time I heard him raise his voice with Min. He demanded I not be returned to the mansion. She screeched that the constable would be called and she could be arrested for kidnapping. He paced and swore he'd have revenge on Naomi. Min cried and begged him to not create a stir, as it would surely cause us more pain once Daddy discovered the truth.

Aunt Min drove me home after tending my scraped knee and skinned elbow. She protested when I insisted she drop me at the wood. I left her crying as she watched me scale down the embankment and over a fence. I looked back and waved. Sneaking in through the wine vault, I spent the next day and a half mourning the loss of my faithful companion, in chilly silence, but for an occasional creak in the floor above and Mrs. MacDougle's brief visits.

Two weeks after my eighth birthday, I was sent away to school for the first time. Fortunately Gordonstoun was nearby. Aunt Min and Uncle David, with Charlie, and sometimes Cullum, in tow, could catch the train and come see me at least once a week. Daddy stopped in before he left or returned from business trips, secure in the knowledge that Naomi held no power over either of us any longer.

Boxes and furniture were stacked throughout Aunt Min's cottage. Lady of leisure couldn't come soon enough. I longed to get the lot sorted and look at a clean, livable space.

If Cullum couldn't manage without Skye, this may be my new home.

I know that sounds crass, but I've always felt I had to land on my feet. Whenever I didn't I nearly died—just better to be prepared.

I picked my way through a narrow path to Min's bedroom. Starting at the top drawer of her bureau, I gently moved aside personal articles of clothing. They'd all have to be packed away and sent to the needy…but not today. I couldn't bear the pain.

The third drawer revealed an interesting feature, a false bottom. Discovery depended on the fervor of the examiner, and I was nothing if not dedicated. I removed all her jumpers and the sachets scenting them. Stacking them carefully on her bed, I fingered an azure blue cashmere turtleneck I'd given her for Christmas last year. I lifted it to my face and inhaled her fragrance, lavender...all I had left of the real woman who mothered me throughout my life.

The false bottom lifted away, revealing a few papers stacked to one side of the drawer and an old pistol case. I picked up the case and opened it on the bed to find a Glock 17. Uncle David retired from the Black Watch, an elite unit of Scotsmen in service to England's queen. The weapon may have been standard issue, in 1983, before he left the regiment.

I checked the loaded clip. The weapon was clean and well-oiled, with a bullet in the chamber. There was spare ammunition in the case.

Min had a formidable weapon at hand, had she *felt* threatened the night she was murdered. I knew she was capable, as Uncle David made sure she was trained in self-defense.

I perched on the side of the bed and pondered her visitor. It had to have been someone she knew, and while she may not have trusted him or her, she didn't consider the person frightening.

A key scratched in the door. I'd had enough intrusions for one day. Hefting the Glock resurrected reminders of qualifying for my job. I'm an expert shot and value the feel of a powerful weapon, though I don't own one.

I picked my way through my belongings in the front room, and waited for the door to open.

Cullum walked in. "Ah, I wondered where that pistol had got to. This row isn't a shooting offense. Why'd you walk outta the house, Isabel?" His manner was dry. He was angry.

"You were occupied and obviously needed privacy. I wanted to get to work. *And* I've had all the drama I can bear just now, Cullum." I laid the weapon on a nearby box.

"Why didn't you call me?"

"*My* phone didn't ring. I assumed you were busy with your intruder." I turned back to the bedroom, feeling justified in my own resentment.

He sighed and followed. "It's not what that vixen makes it look like. Isabel, turn and face me!"

"Not just now, Cullum. I'm busy." I glanced back and steeled myself, winding through boxes.

He was at me in two steps, grasped my shoulders, and twisted me back. "Not too busy to hear me out. I've nothing for her. She makes it look as though she's with every man in town, but not me. She never has been. She never will be. Do you hear me?"

I met his eyes. "I hear you."

He sighed again. "Do you believe me?"

"I haven't decided. It may take a little time to work through all our…bumps, Cullum. Honestly, I didn't expect you'd be faithful to our marriage vows. You're a handsome man and I'm sure there've been more tempting offers than Skye Paisley yanking your chain."

"I told you the truth, wife. I've not been intimate with another woman. You're the only one I ever wanted, and ever had. Ken?" He stepped a wee bit closer, still holding my arms.

"Alright, I believe you because I want to. I've never doubted anything you've told me. You've never lied to me. But *shut her down*, whatever that takes. I won't have people talking and Liam being the object of pity or supposition. Do *you* ken?" I stepped back as far as he'd advanced. The smell of his soap and the smidge of aftershave he used made me weak in the knees.

He smiled. "Aye, Mrs. Sinclair, I understand." He studied me a moment. "Bel, we didn't have to be married. I could've had relationship with Liam, without you. But I'll love you 'til the day I draw my last breath. I have no choice in the matter. I couldn't bear to see you and you not bein' my wife and my life forever. You were made for me, lass, and I for you." He pulled me into his arms and held me, kissing my hair until he found my neck. He buried his face in the curve.

I tried to resist for almost fifteen seconds, before caving in to wrap my arms around him. Closing my eyes, I remembered another time we'd argued...and made up. Making up is great but I'd like to skip right to that and avoid the argument. I hate confrontation, but can't back down when pushed.

***

On a sunny Friday afternoon in May, Cullum met Liam at school and they headed to work at the pub. I was to meet them for a bite later on.

I hadn't decided when I'd make my appearance at the Fielding estate, but I knew I didn't want Naomi wise to what we'd discovered.

Before I made accusations against my former mother, I called Leah Mabry-Mitchell.

Aunt Minerva's neighbor, all of eighty-five, was as sharp as a bird. She owned a textile business for fifty years and worked it every day until her son, Saul, forced her to retire.

She began a new hobby. Tying fishing lures had not only been a godsend for wise use of her time, but was also turning out to be a profitable venture. Saul advertised his mother's handiwork online and in fishing mags, to the delight of the people who'd become her fans and customers.

Leah has a great eye and she knows a thing or two about expensive buttons, having bought them for her textile business. Even fifty years ago she was very shrewd about the origin of materials. Maybe she could enlighten me on the source and purpose of the shard we found on Minerva's rug.

We met in her front garden, where she rested from cutting flowers, her old yellow Lab lying beside her feet. They both dozed in the warm sun. Butterflies and bumblebees skirted their presence for the fragrant Hellebores and Hawthorn blossoms. Lovely, profuse pale pink blooms covered a nearby rose bush, heads sagging towards the ground. A dozen buds, in a heavy vase, soaked in a water and sugar mixture at the base of the plant. The bouquet would soon adorn the breakfast table, if I remembered this dear woman well.

The squeak of the garden gate hinges and tinkle of the bell attached to the weighted chain caused her to stir. Hazel, the old Lab looked up and yawned, cataracts mostly obscuring her vision.

Leah slowly rose to her feet and stood erect after a moment's pause. "Ah, Isabel!" She tried to shuffle through the pea gravel mulch of her tiny bit of paradise, in my direction.

We met in one step. "Leah, how are you?" Hugging briefly, she resettled herself on the bench.

"Oh, darlin', lonely without our precious Min. Hazel and I were chatting 'bout her a few moments ago, weren't we, old girl?" Leah bent forward to scratch Hazel's chin. "What a fine companion you are." She glanced back at me, perched beside her. "We'd just returned from a walk, dear. A brief nap does wonders for the mind, doctors now tell us. Hell, I've know that all my life."

I failed to mention, when disagreeable, Leah curses like the son of a sea cook. When pleasant, she seeks to shock her audience with her verbal aptitude.

Smiling, I patted Hazel's arthritic back end. "Probably keeps you both going."

"Aye, true that. To what do I owe the pleasure of this visit?" Leah's faded green eyes brightened with curiosity.

"I found a button that might interest you. It's broken, but thought you may shed some light on its use." I produced the evidence bag.

"Let's go inside, dear. I could use a spot o' tea. Grab the vase of roses there and bring them with us. Place them on the breakfast table; we'll enjoy their fragrance. Use caution, the thorns on that bush are a bastad on tender skin."

I obliged her and collected the urn, following her inside, through another rose covered arbor.

"Saul will drop in. I told him you were coming. I knew you wouldn't mind. Did you know his son? Evan was very keen on you when you were younger." She glanced back over her shoulder, a knowing smile in place.

"Nay, I only knew him to say hullo."

"Well, I never encouraged his infatuation. After all, Cullum always hung about. Min supposed by now the two of you'd have a brood and be covered with nappies and teats. She'd never dreamed you'd grow up to be a criminalist."

"Really, Leah, I'm just a scientist." I was beginning to feel annoyed. I *wanted* to be shoulder high in nappies and bottles. It just wasn't in the stars, or my father's political and social ambitions.

She parked her narrow bum on an antique office chair and turned on a brilliant desk light, swiveling her mounted magnifying glass to her face, and held out her hand. "Give me the button, lass."

I unsheathed the broken piece and laid it in her cupped hand. "Lab says it's made of rhinoceros horn."

She snorted. "Bah! I haven't see rhinoceros horn in decades." She held the object with a long pair of tweezers and gave a careful look. "Hmm...well, I'm wrong. It *is* rhino." She leaned back, stared up at the white ceiling, her tongue worrying the corner of her mouth. "I wonder...." She peered through the glass again. "Have you checked Min's apparel?"

"Aye, nothing even comes close." I longed to peek over her shoulder, but would receive a sharp reprimand, unless invited.

"There are designers who use antique buttons, when they can get them. The last time I saw one as fine as this, was about 1958. The specimen definitely dates to the forties." She glanced back at the shard and handed it to me. "Have you spoken to Naomi?" Switching off the light, she swung the magnifier to the side.

"I saw her a few weeks ago, at the solicitor's office." I tucked the evidence away.

"She was over to see Minerva *twice* on the night she died." Her eyes gleamed with facts I didn't know.

"Really? There's nothing in Bernie's report."

"*Pootosh,* he's a clown. I told him. He just refuses to believe, as so many *men* do, that a beautiful woman cannot be guilty of murder." She checked her watch. "Damn! Saul should've been here by now." She left her rolling chair in a leap and hurried to the window, peeping through the sheer curtain, then demanding, "Come here." She waved her twiggy arm at me.

I took the few steps to her side.

"Look where that jackass priest's parking!" She scowled at the old man's vehicle, a timeworn rusting Citroen.

"Aye, I see him. I thought you were Catholic."

Father Ralph struggled to pull into a small space at Min's curb. His thick shoulders bunched turning the wheel in a tight circle.

She sent a sour expression my way. "It doesn't mean I like 'im. I don't like the Pope either, if you must know. He's spooky, that one. Better dressed in a black frock and pointed hat of a wizard than white of a holy man. They say he's steppin' down and a good thing tha'."

We watched together as Father Ralph left the car, mopping his face and brow with a handkerchief, as he furtively glanced around.

"He won't see us in here. I survey Min's house all the time. This is a perfect lookout; the windows are tinted one way." She stretched to watch the elderly man huff as he waddled up to the door and applied the knocker. "Are you going to dash over and entertain the old devil?" She switched on a speculative smile.

"Nay, I need to go to the pub. My men await my arrival for a bit of tea." I gathered my evidence, then thought better of rushing out. Father Ralph might catch me. "Was there anything else you told Bernie that he neglected to write down?"

Her eyes rolled to the ceiling again. "Probably quite a few items. The fool was more interested in my roses than who's been frequenting Min's door."

"Who else has been there, Leah?" I was into playing her game. She knew far more about Min than I'd ever discover.

"That friend of your mother's, the solicitor...?" Her wrinkled, knotty fingers snapped. "What *is* that lad's name?"

"Damian?" I really didn't want to put words in her mouth.

"Tall, wide shoulders?" She made motions with her hands. "Nice arse?" She checked the window for Saul.

"Sounds like him." I saw Father Ralph relented and strolled back to his car.

"Then, aye, him. He went with Naomi once, a few weeks ago, and came by again, alone. He looked as sneaky about it as that priest, who's tryin' to back outta the parkin' space without hitting your car." She held herself erect and smiled. "That means somethin' to you. I see those wheels turning', lass!" Her knotty finger wagged at me. "That lad was in school with Evan, my *grandson* and your mam's shagging him."

There was no way to keep from laughing. Few people hit a nail squarely on the head with the first whack. This little old lady hid an excellent mind beneath a headful of thinning white hair and a ragged fisherman's hat.

I tried to recapture my sense of propriety. "Leah, sometimes your honesty's too...real."

"Balls! I don't have so many minutes of breath that I can screw around tryin' to make dummies understand what I'm sayin'." She scowled.

"*It was a compliment, old thing!*" I headed to the door and turned back. She shuffled my way, on my heels. "Give Saul my regards, and Evan. I'll be comin' and going over there. Call me if anyone else goes in or out, please." I handed over a business card with my phone number circled.

She studied the card a moment and lowered her voice. "Isabel, please tell me you'll not return to Edinburgh. Your husband's heart would break." Her thin lips set in a straight line; her chin tremored.

"No, we went down a week ago and let the flat. It's why mover's brought a truck full of boxes into Min's—to store. I'll sort them out once this wretched mess is done, and figure out what to do with the cottage. I don't think I can bear to sell."

She patted my arm. "I'll be your snitch, lass. If Naomi, her squeeze, or anyone else darkens the door again, I'll call you straight away."

I leaned down to drop a kiss on her leathery flesh. "Thanks so much, Leah."

Leaving through the fragrant rose arbor and the weighted gate, I glanced back to wave at the window where she perched, when not tying fishing lures.

***

Pulling into the parking lot at Jacobite's Folly, I spotted Skye's little red MGB. I prayed not to have to butt heads with her or my husband over her. I opened the door and relished the sound and smell of the pub. I've always loved the scent of single malt Scotch. The scent of fine ale is just as effective. I was born to be a publican's wife.

The camaraderie of the community melds for drinks in the evening. Folks out walking their dogs stop in for a pint while their faithful companions sit beside them and enjoy passersby offering treats and rubs. There are few disputes as proprietors tend to keep strict order. I scanned the light afternoon crowd and found my son and beloved behind the bar.

Cullum worked with Liam, slicing citrus from Spain or Greece. Enjoying the interaction between the two, I was disappointed when my husband looked up and caught me, lost in my thoughts. He smiled and motioned me to the bar. Liam peeked up and grinned. I approached slowly, to lengthen the moment and slid onto an oak barstool.

Cullum met me with a kiss and leaned to my ear. "The reason she's here is to meet with Ferrell. He's dismissing her." He kissed my mouth again, sure Liam watched.

"How'd you manage that?"

"Just told him he could lose the baggage or find somewhere else to meet and by the way, I'm resigning." He grasped my hands and locked eyes with me.

"You're leaving SSP?" I'd never even dreamed he'd make such a change.

"Have more on my plate these days and I'm not interested in pushing it back." He shrugged. "I've waited too many years for you, Bel. I'm still a member, just not tied down to office."

If I doubted him before, it passed. The look in his eyes at Min's, changed my mind for a moment. Stern determination emanated from my husband. He would fight for me, even if it was me he had to take on in the battle.

Excellent.

Chapter 9

I should have hired someone to spy on Naomi, but a stranger in town is suspect, if not a tourist, and they aren't familiar with the hiding places around the estate. On a fine morning in June, I set out after getting Liam off to school and leaving Cullum a note. I took a few tools with me and a very good camera with several lenses.

Parked at a layby two miles past the drive to the estate, I slipped on my rucksack and jogged back to the wood. I ducked branches and vines, finding the burn cluttered with wild brambles and undergrowth. It had been more than thirteen years since I visited the place where Cullum and I met for our lovers' trysts.

Picking my way carefully through the host of snags and rocks, I finally arrived at the edge of the estate's lawn. I set up camp and pulled out my camera, focusing on the house, most specifically Naomi's bedroom.

Once settled, I poured a cup of coffee from my thermos. I waited to see what stirred in the early morning mist, settled over the low places of lawn and pristine flower gardens. A pair of roe does eased out of the wood accompanied by their fawns. I sat, without moving, to study their progress. The fawns ate freely from a flower garden, near the trees, while the does kept watch.

Movement in front of the mansion caught my attention. I raised the camera to find James, the butler, walking out the drive for the morning paper, having been deposited by the delivery company in a special drop box at the gate. I wouldn't think there'd be a lot of interest in a newspaper.

I don't recall Naomi ever reading more than a menu at a restaurant. Her secretary took care of thank you notes and invitations. Anything that required signature was signed or stamped by whomever currently held that office, in Naomi's monogram.

As the telephoto lens was already attached, I scanned the bedroom windows on the second floor. The curtain to her room moved aside, the door opened, and a young man stepped out to the balcony. He wore denims but no shirt, revealing several tattoos on his muscular upper torso and biceps. I snapped off a few picks He stretched, as he gazed blankly across the lawn. For a moment he stared directly at me, but I felt confident he couldn't see into the blind.

I lowered the camera and speculated on the lad's identity. He appeared to be in his late teens. Seems Naomi's taste in flesh leaned towards the adolescent these days. What about Damian's role, only her solicitor and friend, or something more?

I leaned back against a tree and sipped my coffee, concentrating on the stirrings of the mansion from outside. My escape from the house used to be the downspout at the side, from my bedroom balcony. That was twelve pounds and fifteen years ago.

Teen angel was no longer alone on the balcony. Naomi joined him, clad in a short negligee and a smile. She hung her well-toned arms around his neck and pulled him back into her bedroom.

When Max appeared to trim spent flower heads, I watched a moment longer, then packed my thermos and left the area. I trudged back through thick undergrowth and up to the road. Once clear of the hazards, I strapped on my rucksack and jogged the mile to my car.

***

"Sir William Carmichael, please." I held the phone in my left hand while spooning porridge with my right.

"May I ask who's calling?" his secretary, Annmarie, asked rather coolly.

"Isabel Fielding-Sinclair." I scooped up the Irish oats with a raisin and tiny shard of walnut.

"At once, Ms. Fielding, did you say Sinclair?" Annmarie's mind must be spinning. She was party to the plot thirteen years ago.

"Aye, it's what I said, Annmarie." I ate another bite and waited for Sir William to answer.

The line clicked when he picked up. "Is this a joke, Isabel?"

"Nay, I've not been in any kind of mood for joking, these days. My aunt, I should say my mother, died and we believe she was murdered."

"What's this nonsense?" He was a ration short of patience today.

"If you're awfully busy just now, perhaps you'd call me back?" I grinned at his exasperation. He'd been furious when my father left him the chore of executing the trust and remaining as the Chief Financial Officer of AIM Enterprises.

"No, no, dear, I apologize. I was in the middle of reading a letter Naomi sent. It seems she requires an increase in her allowance. She says she's appealed to you and was refused. Is that true?" He must be mopping his face with the fine hankie he snatches from his suit pocket when I'm in the room. I tend to unnerve the man.

"She has *not* spoken to me, but she *is* the reason I'm calling."

"What do you need, Isabel?"

"To rid myself and the Fielding Trust of the constant drain on income that Naomi has been allowed. That stops today." I sipped a glass of juice.

"I see. What's caused this rift in your relationship with your mother?"

"She's not my mother, as you well know. Check my birth certificate, if your memory needs refreshing. Minerva gave birth to me. Now, let's arrange a meeting, perhaps in your office? Sometime later this week will do nicely." Orange juice tasted exceptional that morning.

"I'll telephone Naomi and see if she can get away."

"By all means, see if she can fit us into her schedule."

"Annmarie will telephone you, when we set a date and time."

"Sooner is better for me." I ended the call and scooped the last of my porridge.

Cullum was awake. I heard him in the living room headed for the kitchen.

I called out to him. "The newspaper is in here, already."

He smiled as he entered the kitchen, bleary-eyed, dressed in boxer shorts and a ragged pullover. "Good mornin', mo chroi." He bent for a kiss and plucked something out of my hair. "Tell me where you've been this early, to collect twigs in your hair?"

"I'll pour your coffee and fill you in. Come sit. Do you want porridge?"

"Aye, thank you." He opened the refrigerator and poured juice, then sat to peruse the Edinburgh Evening News from the previous day. He studied the front page while I prepared his breakfast. "Are you working for Bernie today?" He glanced towards me, as I served his porridge.

"I've been on the job already this mornin'. Why?" I sat opposite him and slid round the curve to be close enough to touch him.

"Wanna take a drive and show you a piece of land. So, wha's this job you've been on so early?" He folded the paper and attacked his porridge.

"I visited our secret place by the burn." I massaged his muscular thigh.

"You've been to the estate?" He lowered his spoon to glare at me.

"I went in the back way, erected a blind in the woods, and watched with a telephoto lens as the inhabitants awoke. Naomi has a new lover, not much older than our lad."

He crossed his arms. "Bel, stay away from that place." He glanced out the kitchen window and winced. "Darlin' it's poison. If you get caught trespassing...."

"Cullum, I own it. I wasn't lying when I said she could be put out if I take a notion. When I spied her newest toy, who *may* be seventeen, I decided she's has to go. You called her a tart the other day, when we were discussing my father. How is it that you ken she's loose?"

He looked away and sighed. "When she came to make me the offer of cash to lure you home, she...." He waved his hand and grimaced. "Um, what? Made a pass?" He scowled at me again.

I chuckled and leaned back against a cushion. "Sounds like a rugby match. Husband, all you need to qualify is equipment. You were supposed to fall over yourself gettin' to her, drooling like a teething babe. What did you do?"

He blushed. "It made me mad, at first. Then, I don't know why, but I felt sorry for her. She's been catered to her whole life and she's still searching for the love that she's missed. Then I thought about wha' she'd done to you and was angry all over again."

I patted his arm and ran my hand over the wavy hair that covers the hard flesh beneath. "Thank you. She'd have shed her clothes for you in a heartbeat. She doesn't seem to have a moral barometer, you know?"

"I've always kenned that about her. It's in the eyes; the way a shrew looks at a man…like he's a piece of meat." He attacked the porridge again.

"Women are treated like that by men all the time. Welcome to our world."

He cut a sidelong glance towards me. "Have I ever looked at you that way, Bel?"

Shaking my head, I smiled. "Nay, you always make me feel like…I'm the most special girl in the world. Dancing with you at the pub, I feel like a queen in your arms. There's nowhere else I'd rather be, Cullum."

"There's nowhere else you're *going* to be, mo chroi." He leaned towards me and met my lips. "Are you free for an hour or so?"

"You still want to take tha' ride?" My hand landed on his thick thigh again.

"Something's come up. I think we'll stay in for now."

***

"Were you serious about exercising ownership of the estate?" My lover poured another cup of tea, sitting across from me at the kitchen banquette.

"I made an appointment with the attorney who handled my father's affairs. Sir William Carmichael is also the executor of the estate. His office is phoning for a meeting with Naomi. She's recently contacted him, asking for more allowance."

"How much does she receive?" He bit into his chicken salad, avocado, and tomato sandwich and chewed.

"More than I make at my job in a year. Considering she has no bills, that's way too much. Anyway, we'll discuss her moving out of the mansion." I smiled as I bit into my own prawn mayo on ciabatta.

"Wha'? I ken tha' look on you, lass." He took another gigantic bite.

"I'm considering giving her a flat in Edinburgh. Would you mind awfully if I gave her our old place?"

"A one bedroom flat in a shoddy neighborhood?" He considered my request and popped the remainder of his sandwich in his mouth. "Mmm, no don't, please."

"Why not? Do you think we should keep it? It's currently let." I nibbled my prawn mayo.

"It was ours, darlin'. The first place we had together. I don't even want to think of her living there. Let her have the one you just left?" He tipped his teacup and wiped his mouth on a napkin.

"I can do that, though I think it far too nice for her. She'll probably kill herself rather than leave the luxury of the mansion." I stared into my teacup, as though the few floating leaves had answers. "I don't want that, but...." I glanced out the window. "I need to settle a few things between us, Cullum."

"That'd be appreciated."

"I inherited all of Daddy's money." I met his eyes. "I've never touched my trust fund. I own the controlling shares in AIM, and five," I held up one hand, fingers spread, "five houses. The mansion's the principal, but the others are very large. There's a villa in Spain, where I was born, another on the Mediterranean, in Greece, a fourth in Tel Aviv, where Daddy purchased a lot of technology. The fifth is a flat in Lima, Peru. AIM doesn't have connections there. I have no idea why my father acquired the property, unless he hoped to skip out on his obligations and flee the country."

Cullum sat back and crossed his arms. "What're you going to do with all tha', Bel?"

"Sell everythin' but the estate. That belongs to the people of Scotland. Since owning the controlling vote of AIM, I've raised wages, opened in-house care centers so Mums and Dads can be close to their children. We've partnered with a bank AIM holds shares in, for home and auto loans for employees. I've done my best to be sure all of our people are treated superbly on my watch."

"How many people work for the company?" He frowned with concentration. The math genius I married might have been impressed.

"Worldwide, almost 120,000 people depend on AIM for their living." I felt proud of my accomplishments with Daddy's company.

"What does the future hold for you there?" His frown deepened.

"What I wanted is finished. I carry the deciding vote at board meetings and keep an eye on the profit column. Otherwise, Sir William's in control. He lets me know when my presence is required. You're looking at me oddly. Does this change somethin' between us, Cullum?"

I'm not sure why I didn't consider telling him all this before we remarried. I tried to inhale, steeling myself, but my breath faltered.

He stood and stretched, heading to the kitchen window that looks out at the Moray Firth. "How could it not, Isabel?" He quietly pondered my declaration.

I sat, mutely considering why my financial situation was a bad thing in his mind. "You knew who were marrying, Sinclair—both times." I studied the change in wind direction, blowing spray onto the nearest windows. "It's not as though I live off the funds. It goes into the trust. But, my dream is to turn over the estate to the National Historic Trust and provide the money to finance upkeep on the place. Though I participate in the business, it isn't my living."

He turned to face me, skeptical. "And you're going to abide in a place *I* provide you the rest of our lives?"

"Of course. Is that the difficulty?"

"Are you sure you can do tha', lass?"

"Cullum, when we were growing up, all I wanted to be was a plain everyday girl. Since university, I've been an ordinary woman, who lived off her own earnings. Nothing's changed about me." Tears sprang to my eyes.

He nodded and stood there looking at me like…the science experiment gone wrong.

"Do you doubt me? I'll show you my bank records. Daddy left me a monthly stipend that goes directly to an orphanage in Russia. I don't even *see* actual cash, earned by means other than my own."

He returned to the booth and sat. His expression was far from encouraging. "I'll consider it, but you ken how I feel about extreme wealth?"

"I'm not rich, Cullum. The trust confines the wealth."

"Aye, lass you are. You just don't dabble in the proceeds…right now. What'll you do, if we need somethin' big? What if Liam needs medical care not available in Scotland? Will you be tempted to tap into Arthur's funds?"

"That's not fair, Cullum. I'll go to the moon and back but I won't let our child suffer. Look, I paid for my car out of my salary, took out a loan like anyone else. My flat, the same." I held up one hand. "That's not entirely true. My paternal grandmother left me a piece of land in England. I sold it, and paid off the debt with the proceeds."

"Have you explored unloading the corporation?" He leaned on the table.

"Nay. When Daddy died there was a move afoot to sell, but I voted against the offer, which was pence on the pound. It fell through. There have been a few more offers. I wanted to finish the improvements before letting it go."

"How did Carmichael position the proposals?" His eyes narrowed.

"He encouraged me to sell on all occasions. I supposed, because he didn't want the job of executing the trust. If we sold out, he'd be out of a job, but literally rolling in cash. He owns a large block of company stock."

"Where was Naomi in all this?"

"She never said anythin' to me. We don't talk. Once, Sir William mentioned she was helpful referring a buyer and the offer was very generous. Tha's all." A puzzle piece, that had been missing, clicked into place, but I couldn't connect it correctly at that moment. The picture was far from complete.

Deb Kemper

Cullum's phone chimed. He held up one hand to me. "Hullo, Mam. Aye, we're having a bite o' lunch just now. Aye, we're home, come along then." He rang off. "My parents are on their way over. They went to the safe deposit and retrieved their inheritance from Aunt Min. A few dozen shares of stock in AIM awaited them." He crossed his arms.

***

Genny and Robin sat round Cullum's dining table, a rough 17th century piece he built from the original bar in the pub. We'd served drinks and passed the time catching up, until Robin pulled out a heavy envelope.

My father-in-law slid it across the table to me. "What can you tell us abou' this, Isabel?"

I looked inside. A letter, from Daddy to Aunt Min, lay atop the paper stock certificates.

My dearest Min, I've loved the time we've had together, but alas all good things in my life must end. It seems only the tortuous last eternally. I'm happy for David, that he found the most special woman in the world. I'm happy for you, that you finally have a true love to belong only to you. But my sadness is deep for myself, and of course, Isabel. I'm sure your new husband will occupy as much of your time as possible, denying us the pleasure of your company as often as we've come to expect.

Enclosed, you will find my gift to you both. If you decide to sell, by all means do, as what's enclosed will leave you a wealthy woman. Dance, celebrate, and enjoy life. No one deserves the chance more than you do, my love. I only wish it was me holding your hand.

Always yours in heart,
Arthur Fielding

My hands shook as I folded the letter. "Oh, my. Well, what do you know about their relationship?"

Genny answered quietly. "I ken that Minerva called this blood money. I want to understand why, darlin'."

I gazed at Cullum's wonderful parents across the table. "Aunt Min and my father were lovers. I'm a result of their effort to give

115

the Fieldings an heir." My voice broke near the end and I pressed my lips together to stifle a sob.

"Naomi...?" Genny began to question even as she left her seat to comfort me.

"No, she didn't give me life or make it pleasant. That was her elder sister, who birthed me out of love for my father, then handed me over to Naomi, no strings attached."

Robin cocked his head to one side, with a frown. "How long have you kent tha', lass?"

"Only two weeks. I've been pouring through Min's journals." I glanced at Cullum and leaned my head into Genny's chest. "I found my birth certificate hidden in a false bottom drawer, at the cottage."

Robin propped his chin in his hand and studied me. "How're you standin' this? Tha' has to be like havin' a land mine blow up on you, girl." He glanced at Cullum. "Son, you should've told us."

I sniffled. "It becomes even more gruesome. It's all part of investigating her murder, digging into her past. The more I discover, the more anxious I feel about having Liam in range, and Cullum susceptible to the consequences." I wiped my wet face. "If we uncover the real plot, it may put all of us in dire straits."

Genny patted my back. "We can take our lad to the farm with us. He'll be safe there. He and Lachlan will ride the bus together. Robin can drive them down the lane and meet them in the afternoon."

"Tha's a good idea, Mam. I hate to ask you to take on the responsibility of a child, though."

Robin chuckled. "You hush that kind of talk, son. We've waited for twelve years to know tha' boy. It's a pleasure. Not as though we have to change nappies."

Cullum glanced at me and grinned. "Hopefully, we'll be doing nappies by lambing season next year." He watched his parents with delight.

Genny hugged me closer. "When?"

I closed my eyes and took a deep breath. "I resigned my job in Edinburgh and reluctantly took on this murder inquiry. I'm planning to leave the police, and a babe on the way is a good excuse."

"Aye, it may look better if we let the plot run its course, knowing what we do." Cullum agreed.

Robin pondered the news, his head bobbing. "Tha' sounds like wisdom."

"We were going to wait to tell you, make sure Bel's pregnant, but," Cullum shook his head and scrubbed his fist over his chin, "I'm too excited."

Genny squeezed me. "She's healthy and strong; she'll be fine. But that does increase my concern."

"We'll be careful. I promise." Cullum patted his mother's hand, propped on my shoulder.

After Robin and Genny left us, we sat quietly, watching the tide come in and reveling in a breeze from the open French doors.

"You can pack Liam when he gets home from school and take him to the farm."

"Aye, are you going to the pub?" I rubbed my hand over his back.

"I need to go for a bit to cover the bar, until Duncan arrives. We have a couple of hours. How about a run? I feel like I need to stretch out and work through some of the angst."

I grinned. "Aye, let's dress warmly. I smell rain on the wind."

We met in the dining room, changed for our run. Cullum watched Moray Firth rush into the North Sea. I slipped my arms around his waist and pressed my face on his back.

"You smell good."

He turned and gathered me into his arms. "Bel, about earlier, before Da and Mam came, we need to resolve the money issues so we're standing together, or it'll blow us apart."

"I know. When I meet with Naomi and Sir William, I can ask if there are offers for the company. I'll sell it, Cullum. Nothing's more important than being a family. I won't risk losing you to the socialist agenda or Daddy's amassed fortune."

He frowned. "I ken. Do you know what the AIM acronym represents, Bel?"

"Artificial Intelligence Modifications."

"When did your dad change the name of the company?"

"Change it? I don't know."

"Come, let's check the internet."

I followed him to a small front room he used for an office. He sat at the desktop and input his password: my full name.

AIM Enterprises was formed a week after my birth. Prior, it was known only as Fielding Enterprises.

Cullum whirled in the armless office chair and bit his lower lip as he studied me. "Did Arthur have anythin' to do with Liam?"

"Aye, he came to Edinburgh once a month, stayed at his club, and visited a few days. We went to the park or zoo, a rugby, or soccer match, sometimes to dinner and a movie. Why?" I sat on the low sofa against the wall.

"Did Naomi...?"

I shook my head. "She met him at Daddy's funeral for the first time."

"Arthur, Isabel, Minerva...AIM Enterprises. Naomi must be wild to rid her world of Minerva influence. She birthed you, loved you, and your da. He loved the both of you, in return." He stared out the window, eyes narrowed. "Naomi set us up, thinking we'd be so naïve, we'd fall for the trap."

The realization hit us both at the same time.

Crossing my arms, I frowned at my lover. "This whole thing's been to push me....."

"Aye, lass, what else? I kenned it was bigger than what we believed. Naomi's directing the players somehow. I'd bet next month's profit Damian has his hands in the mix as well."

"You'd object to the wealth and press me to sell, so we could live without Daddy's billions casting an ominous cloud over our lives." I rose and went for a glass of water, suddenly nauseated. When I returned, he stared out the window again.

"You can't let on tha' we've figured it out. We'll have to play the game in public, at least." He caught me before I sat, grasping my thigh. He gazed into my eyes with a smile. "I've finished being a hostage, Bel."

"Aye, I feel the same. What of Liam?"

"He's with me or you or at the farm. He'll be fine. But, no new friends or sleepovers. Let's keep a low profile. Makes us less of a target." He stood and kissed my lips. "Let's run, then we'll fetch our son from school."

Only an hour later…

Click, click, boom. I turned to the shore from my trek to our home, to see my lovely man tumbling onto the sand. He didn't get up. I dashed to his side and skidded to a stop, dropping to my knees. A fountain of blood spurted from a wound in his upper thigh.

He snatched my arm and growled. "Get down, Bel."

I pulled away to strip my shirt over my head and followed with my sports bra. "In a minute. I must stop the bleedin' or at least slow it or you'll die." Wrapping my bra around his thigh as a tourniquet worked. Sleet pelted my bare back and shoulders.

"Get your shirt on, woman." He actually chuckled.

"No one's around to see anythin'. Where are all the normal walkers?" I glanced up and down the beach, to no avail. The constant rain kept even the hardiest inside, on this chilled afternoon. But not us.

I tugged my phone from its waterproof pocket inside my pants, and pressed nine-nine-nine, with my thumb. With my foot turned sidewise, I pushed sand beneath Cullum's left side to elevate his thigh. One ring and the call dropped. I checked for coverage. The screen went blank. Then my phone died.

"Can you hold this tightly?" I placed Cullum's hand on the tourniquet. "I have to run for help."

"Just stand and wave your arms, lass. There're a half dozen sets of binoculars trained on you at the moment." He kept a firm grasp on my bra.

I slipped my cold wet shirt back on and stood to wave. Two men were already on their way to our position from different directions. I yelled with all my strength, to make my voice heard over the gale force wind, rain, sleet, and surf. "Over here!"

"They ken where we are, Bel." Cullum tried to sit up; but surrendered when the pain in his thigh won out over his desire to be presentable.

One tall chap, wearing runner's pants and a hooded sweatshirt, leapt over the dunes and reached us first, sliding in the deep tan sand. "Cullum?"

"Aye, right here, no' going anywhere." He tucked his arm behind his head and blew out through pursed lips.

"Ma'am, Randy Ross." He offered me his hand and I shook it, dazed.

"Help me elevate his thigh." Together we pushed the rough sand beneath my husband's left side.

"Mel's on his way to get you an ambulance. Land line would have been handy today. Our cell phones died a minute ago."

Cullum's voice croaked. "As did Bel's. I considered that. They used a scrambler to block service." He took a deep breath and shivered.

"I don't want to move you, but we have to get you warmed. Randy, run up to our home and fetch as many quilts and rugs as you can find, forgoing the quilt in the blue room." I handed him my keys.

He left at a sprint when backup arrived, breathing heavily. "Kent Hudson, Isabel. Kevin's following the shooter. We all spied 'im when he raised his tripod, but he was quick about the hit and took off like wind before any of us made his position. He kens Nairn."

"Anyone see him or was he cloaked in a dark hoodie?" I rubbed Cullum's arms to warm him with one hand while holding the tourniquet.

"How'd you know tha'?" He smiled with admiration. "We spotted his vehicle. Black motorcycle."

"Usual suspects. How many black bikes might there be in the area?"

"No more than a hundred or so. We'll find him," Kent assured me.

Randy Ross leapt over the dunes and slid down to us with three quilts and a blanket. He wrapped Cullum well. "The ambulance should be here shortly. Hang on, boss." He tossed a grin my way. "You alright, Isabel?" He stripped off his jacket and handed it to me.

"Aye, fine. It's just not every day my husband's shot, you know." I checked my cell phone. It was back on line and had coverage. I dialed Bernie's number and pulled on Randy's still warm hoodie.

"Hullo?" The constable sounded surprised that his phone rang.

"It's Isabel, Bernie. Cullum's been shot. We're on the beach beyond his house. Get someone ASAP, please." I left Kent holding tension on the tourniquet and backtracked Cullum's steps as we spoke, spotting the bullet's entry into a dune two feet away. The trail of blood was a good indicator. I dug, with my nails, to free the still warm shell.

"I'll call an ambulance."

"It's done. We need a forensic technician; phone the proper authorities. No dodging it this time." I ended the call.

The bullet that passed through Cullum's meaty thigh was stopped by a massive tangle of sea oat roots. It was a high powered rifle shell. I considered the opportunities for its disappearance and decided to keep it a secret for now. It was tucked away in Randy's jacket pocket, my fingertips only slightly scorched.

I returned to my husband's side. Releasing the tourniquet, I held as much pressure as possible on the artery, before retightening the hold on my bra. "How you doin', my love?"

He watched my face, his own white with pain. His words slurred. "I'm with you, Bel. How could I be anythin' but fine?" His eyes closed.

Chapter 10

The ambulance's siren sounded near, a police car followed close behind. In moments, the place crawled with men in uniforms and I was hustled to the side. I waited, still wearing Randy's jacket, while the paramedics diagnosed and treated my husband, biting back the dread that lurked, waiting to consume me.

As soon as they had Cullum on a gurney, we were ready to leave. Local police were in process of securing the area.

Randy had also been kind enough to return to the house and fetch my handbag, Cullum's phone, and dry clothes for us both. He failed to retrieve a bra for me, though.

Robin and Genny's phone rang six times before Cullum's breathless mother answered. "Hullo?"

"Genny, it's Isabel. Is Robin handy?"

"Right here, darlin'." She called out for him. The echo of her voice sounded like she caught the phone in one of the barns.

Robin's voice was tense. "Hullo, Isabel. Are you alright?"

"Aye, fine. Cullum's been shot—in the thigh. We're about to leave in the ambulance. An artery's been torn, causing a lot of blood loss." I followed the paramedics to the ambulance at a trot. "We're headed for Raigmore Hospital in Inverness."

"I'll be on my way in a tick," Robin muttered.

"Robin, take care of Genny and take your time driving there. I need you to fetch our lad, please."

"I'll do tha', lass. We'll be along within the hour. Cullum's phone has our numbers."

"It's in my handbag. Liam will be upset. He's like Cullum. Don't be alarmed if you can't comfort him. He'll be fine until you get there." I climbed into the back of the ambulance, catching a glimpse of my husband's pallor. "I must ring off. We're driving away now, and they'll switch on the sirens. Cullum's doing well."

"Take care, daughter." Robin disconnected.

I wasn't sure if I'd lied to him, but the medical response team seemed to have everything in hand. I looked on as they attached Cullum to a heart monitor and an IV. His sand-covered left side was elevated with an air-filled wedge. The oxygen they'd administered helped him come round.

I sat back and prayed for our health and well-being.

***

Raigmore Hospital's waiting room for surgeries was not crowded. For all its glory throughout history, Inverness is not a city city, with a population of only a few over fifty thousand.

My son balanced on my right, snug against my thigh, holding both my hands. "Are you worried, Mum? Is Dad going to die?"

"I think not. He has too much to live for, Liam. He just found you. I'm sure he's not about to give up on life. We need to talk."

He lifted his bloodshot grey eyes to mine and nodded solemnly. "Yes, ma'am."

"There are unpleasant things happenin' that makes your safety uncertain. I'm going to take you out of school and you'll go home with Gram and Grandpa until this is over. Okay?" I stroked his black wavy hair. Our son looks so much more like Cullum than me, yet he came from my body. It isn't fair.

"Okay then, my teachers could email lessons." He nodded, looking for some stable ground to stand.

"Aye, tha's a good idea, like when you had your appendix out. I'll stay here with your da, until we can come back to Nairn. The surgery shouldn't take long. He'll be here until the wound heals enough to go home, perhaps no more than a few days."

Liam nodded, brushing tears off his freckled cheeks.

"There's something else I need for you to know. We can't trust many people. Don't think, because you know someone belongs to our family, that they're trustworthy. You're going to Gram's because they *can* be depended upon to have our best interest at heart. No one left in my family is honorable; that died with your grandfather." He was a scheming manipulator but would have protected Liam with his own life.

My son's bottom lip quivered and he nodded again, even as he firmed his chin, to keep from crying.

"You're a brave lad. You'll be fine." I kissed the top of his head and pulled him into my arms. *What have I brought you into?*

This is becoming a hornet's nest and it's not nearly over. "There's no place on earth safer than where you'll be, Liam. I promise." *I'm glad the other one is securely tucked away, for now. Perhaps we can be done with this vile mess before he's born.*

"Sinclair family?" A middle aged woman held a file in her hand while we queued in front of her. She looked at me. "Mrs. Sinclair?"

"Aye, there's two of us." I indicated Genny as well. "But I expect you want me, as I signed Cullum into hospital."

A smile brightened her pasty, powdered complexion. She read from the file. "Your husband's out of surgery, recovering. The surgeon will be out shortly."

"Thank you." We sat again and waited.

Genny squeezed my knee. "Are you alright, Isabel?"

I tried to smile, but tears clouded my vision and throat, so I nodded instead. "Just...relief setting in." I choked on words so I leaned back, closed my eyes, and thanked God for Cullum's life.

"Isabel Sinclair?" A man with dark, weathered skin and bright blue eyes spoke to the waiting room in general.

I stood and nodded. "I'm Isabel."

His accent denoted south London. "Jack Flannery." He extended his hand, which I took. "You may come wi' me, if you like."

"I will." I glanced back at Genny, Robin, and Liam and felt undeserving, of the special treatment. They all three smiled. Liam laid his head against Genny, who snugged him in her arms, and kissed his forehead.

We strode the corridor, our steps matched. "The bullet nicked the femoral artery. You saved your husband's life with the sports bra. How'd you know to use that as a tourniquet?" He grinned, as though delighted with the idea.

"I work for the police department in Edinburgh. We all have to qualify in lifesaving techniques, disaster recovery, and the firing range."

"Outstanding! If you'd not been there he'd have bled out in a few minutes." He patted my shoulder as we walked. "Are you a copper?"

"Nay, a forensic scientist." I blushed and tried to inhale.

"I'll take you in to see him, but he's still sleeping off the anesthesia. I used a venous patch. The artery was nicked. It might have been much worse; an adjustment of a hair to the left and the artery would've severed."

"Aye, I considered tha'. I'm glad he's hearty and heals quickly." We turned into another passage.

Mr. Flannery swiped the card hanging from his lanyard and a door opened to us. We went through and to the third doorway on the right. The hallway side of the rooms was glass viewed from a round nursing center. He led the way and we halted short of the bed as a nurse finished taking vital signs.

Cullum slept. I crept to his side and bent to kiss him. He stirred.

"Bel?" His eyes were closed.

"Aye, I'm right here." I found his hand.

"Are you really?" His brow bunched.

"Aye, really. Do you remember what happened?"

"Nay, just thought...you came home to me?" He fought to open his eyes.

"Aye, we're married. Your son's in the waiting room with your parents."

Mumbling, he struggled to remain conscious. "I thought I was dreamin'." He sighed, closing his eyes.

"No dream, this, my love. We went for a run this mornin'. I headed back to the house. You waited for me to make the door, before you continued. A shot was fired, hitting you in the thigh." I brushed his ebony hair, embellished with a bit of silver, off his forehead, and bent low over him. "Now sleep, my handsome man, and we'll talk again in a while."

He mumbled. "Love you, Bel."

Turning back to Mr. Flannery, I tried to keep my composure. I really wanted a quiet corner to cry this episode out. "I'll stay with him, but will you send back at least one of his parents. They need to see that he's alright."

Smiling, he nodded. "I can do tha'. Take care. We'll talk again soon." He started for the door. "Oh, he'll be here at least three days. We have to keep his leg elevated and immobile."

"Thank you." I turned away, sat in a nearby chair, and held my lover's hand.

Moments later, the door opened to Genny. I rose and directed her to Cullum's side.

"He's sleeping off the anesthesia. It's a blessing, because when he wakes, he'll be in pain. His leg's immobilized and that's gonna be irritating as well." I smiled as I gazed on my husband—still breathing.

"The surgeon told us you saved his life, Isabel. That you made a tourniquet with your bra to stop the bleeding." Genny's large grey eyes searched my face.

"Aye, it was necessary." I looked away.

"You *saved* him, darlin'," She persisted.

"I love him, Genny. He's my life…my breath…my heart." My eyes gave way to the tears I'd fought all afternoon. "I'd have died with him." *As I nearly did, when told he was missing in action and feared dead.*

"I know… I know." She enfolded me in her arms and we wept together.

Genny sat with Cullum, while I scurried down the hallway to speak with Liam and Robin. I spotted a police inspector talking with Robin when I entered the room.

He swung toward me when Robin gestured my way. He was more than six feet tall and thin as a rail. His coarse black hair was short his almost ebony skin, smooth.

"This is our daughter, Isabel." Robin held my arm, gently pulling me nearer.

Extending my hand, I nodded. "Isabel Sinclair, sir."

"Inspector John Cooley." His dark complexion brightened with a splendid smile. "I've heard much praise from your supervisor in Edinburgh."

"Harry's a good policeman." I took my hand back and patted Robin's, still gripping my arm. "I have somethin' for you." I dug into the pocket of my borrowed sweatshirt for the bullet and held it up. "I'm not sure who to trust right now and didn't want to leave it to chance that the lads securing the area were on the right side."

He studied the prize in his broad palm. "Well, I'll call down and tell them to stop lookin' for it, then." He glanced up at Robin. "Sir, may I have a word in private with your daughter?"

Robin checked with me, then nodded. "Aye, I'll wait for you."

I stole a look back at Liam, curled onto a settee, asleep. "There's a business facility around the corner."

I led the way and checked to find the room unoccupied. We took our seats facing each other.

He smiled again, trying to put me at ease. "What can you tell me about this incident, Isabel?"

"We were out for a run along the shore, our usual time. Cullum runs farther than I. We stopped, as we do, while I headed to our home. I had the key in hand when I heard the report, turned, saw him fall. A fountain of blood erupted from his thigh and I hurried to him to try and stop the bleeding. I was busy getting the flow lessened and didn't look around for anyone. When I couldn't locate phone coverage, Cullum said to stand and wave my arms, there were half dozen men watching us through binoculars. I thought he was...I don't know...teasing, maybe. I stood and waved my arms as two healthy lads loped out to our position. There were more, but they took up separate posts. I don't believe I met them all, as one followed the shooter, and another ran for a landline to call an ambulance. No one had phone coverage. Cullum said something about a scrambler used to cut our service. He expected it to happen." I shrugged.

"This wasn't a surprise to him?" He frowned, his brow wrinkling deep gullies.

"No. He told me a few weeks ago, no, more than six weeks now, to prepare for there to be serious consequences resulting from a rift in SSP. I'm not sure they're involved, so don't take that to mean he suspects them. I've been busy trying to discover who murdered our Aunt Min. We know more than I've shared with Bernard Leighton. I'm not sure of him. I've been winging that investigation on my own. Only Cullum knows what's been uncovered."

"You say that as though he's assisting you. Is that the case; are you investigating together?" He leaned forward, entwining his long fingers.

"He's my sounding board. We think that events more than three decades ago were the catalyst behind Aunt Min's death. The culprits were untouchable then and are dead or untouchable now. There's a well-woven network of treachery, Inspector Cooley. I intend to get at the truth."

His voice was gentle. "At what cost, Isabel?"

My head dropped, for a moment, as I considered the worn red patterned carpet. "That's my quandary." I met his eyes. "I can't endanger my husband and our son again."

He detached a business card from a silver case and held it out. "Check my credentials and let me know if you'll consider a partnership."

Accepting the card, I held his eyes. "I'll do that. I've submitted notice, I want to leave the force...."

"Not just yet. Give us a chance to settle this matter. I may need you in place. I promise I'll protect your contribution to our investigation and any information you provide. If you decide you can trust me, I'll take the other matter off your hands."

I nodded. "I'll consider it, then."

The door flew open. Genny huffed, breathless, her face pale. "There you are! Isabel, please hurry to Cullum. He's frantic, love."

I jumped up and headed for the door. "What happened?"

"He needs to *see* you. He won't believe you're alright." Genny followed me for a few steps before I broke into a run.

I rounded the corner and sprinted through the doors, closing behind a doctor, to reach my objective.

A nurse hovered, trying to reason with Cullum. "Mr. Sinclair, you *must* lay back and calm yourself. I'm sure your wife stepped out for only a moment." She pushed down on his wide shoulders.

"Cullum!" Striding toward the struggling duo, I approached opposite the nurse.

He grasped my hand and fell back on the pillow. "Bel!" He gulped air and closed his eyes.

"What's happenin'?" I looked to the nurse for an explanation. Truth couldn't be as frightening as the thoughts running through my head.

His heart rate slowed a bit. The ping of the monitor slackened as he inhaled and exhaled. He opened his eyes. "I thought you were hurt. I had to see you. Tha's all, mo chroi."

The nurse took a step back and began to type information into his chart. Her hands shook. She clutched them close and tried again. She glanced back at Cullum and appeared doubtful.

"I'm unharmed and right here. I went down to speak with Liam, but he was asleep." I rubbed his fine arm, around tubes and monitor patches. "Everyone's well, but you."

He nodded, inhaling deeply. I checked the screen for his blood pressure.

"I apologize." He looked at the nurse. "Please forgive me. I lost—my nerve for a moment."

She smiled. "Happens all the time." She left us, harried.

I bent to kiss my lover's cheek. He turned his head and caught my lips.

"What happened?" he breathed.

"Do you recall our run this morning?"

"I don't ken. My brain's foggy." His eyes searched the room. "I bent to tie my shoe…what then?"

"Your mind will clear as the anesthesia wanes from your system." I stroked his arm again. "I turned back from the door to see you falling, blood spurting from your leg."

"I was terrified they'd hurt you and Mam wasn't telling me the whole truth. She kept sayin' you'd be back soon." He inhaled and widened his pale grey eyes.

"And I was. Stop fighting and rest, my love. You'll heal faster and we can go home." I nuzzled his neck, pressed close to his rough, clammy skin, and whispered. "You must be here at least three days, perhaps more. Then you can move to hospital in Nairn for therapy, then home." I remained against his neck or cheek until the chiming monitor slowed to normal.

That trick works with his son as well.

***

"Why did you think Genny was lying to you?" I leaned back into the lounge chair beside Cullum's bed.

129

He sighed and closed his eyes. "Mam came and stayed with me, in Germany, at hospital after I was returned to my battalion. I needed you. She said you were away and they couldn't reach you. She said they'd keep trying."

"Oh."

"She stayed for a few weeks, then returned home when Kyle came. He remained until I was released. We flew home together. He told me the truth, as much as he kenned. We didn't know you'd tried to kill yourself when the messenger told you they presumed I was dead. All he knew was that you'd left with another man. He couldn't find out where you were, until Aunt Min let it out that you were in America with your husband."

"I see. We were only there a fortnight. No one called me." I stared at the ceiling tiles, a few tinted brown with old water marks. "Reading her journal, I've discovered that Aunt Min wasn't tryin' to protect her relationship with Naomi. It was Daddy she couldn't live without. He'd threatened to withdraw his affections...."

"Oh, hell!" Cullum rubbed both hands over his face. "To think we suffered all tha' for what? So Aunt Min could have her token kiss now and again, a pat on the head from her lover?"

"It wasn't the way she viewed it, Cullum. At least she saw the error of her ways before she died." I grasped his arm and brushed my fingers down to his hand. Entwining mine with his, I squeezed. "Let it go. Those years are lost to us."

"I ken tha', Bel. It still makes me mad as a hornet when I realize the cruel game your father played, with Minerva accompaniment. We were mere puppets to them, no feelings, no love at all. They never even took Liam into account, that he needed his da." He turned a fierce grimace toward me.

"I know, my heart, but it's gone. We're here now and we need to determine who pulled the trigger of that sniper's rifle or, more importantly, who paid them." I released his hand and sat back in the chair. "I met Inspector Cooley while I was out checking on our son. He gave me his card." I passed over the business card. "I dug the bullet out of the sand and kept it for him. He's on our side in this, I think. I'll call Harry and ask for advice. The inspector said if I help him, he'll take Minerva's case off our hands."

He scrutinized me a moment. "That would be good. Unless I'm mistaken, we've got a bairn on the way."

"How'd you know?" I smiled at beloved.

"I ken you, woman. It comes in handy to have years of experience understanding you. When were you going to tell me?" His frown made my heart ache.

"I was planning on supper tonight. Unless my nose deceives me, I think it's time for your tea."

***

I walked back into the room, hair wet from a shower. Genny kindly went by our home, on the way, and brought me fresh clothes, including a bra. The dry clothes Randy retrieved, while we waited for the ambulance, were my pajamas and no bra.

Liam came to me for a hug. He laid his face against mine. "Mum, will he recover?"

"Aye, he will. He's a strong man with lots to live for, Liam. He'll be here three days before he moves to Nairn for therapy." I pushed him back. "Stop fretting. I called the school. Your instructors will email your work."

"Good. But I'll really miss my classes."

"You'll be back soon. I promise."

Robin bent over Cullum and brushed his hair back like he would have most of his childhood. "I'm pleased you're alright, son."

"Thanks, Da, take care of our lad and use caution." Cullum grasped his father's hand.

"I will. Talked to that inspector fellow. He's a sharp one. No Bernie Leighton." Robin nodded and turned to Liam. "Let's go, lad, let your parents get a rest."

Liam left me for another pass at Cullum. He laid his face beside his da's and nuzzled his neck, turning to whisper something into Cullum's ear as tears sprang to his eyes. Liam stood and hugged me again. "Bye, Mum. Will I come back tomorrow?"

"That's with your grandparents." I glanced up at Robin, who bobbed his head. "Most probably." I kissed his cheek and

131

squeezed him again, before he pushed through the heavy door and left us alone.

Turning back to Cullum, I caught him wiping his eyes with a corner of the sheet.

His voice was husky. "Our son…you've done a fine job, Bel." He sniffed.

"He has good genes. Thank you for tha' and for having me back, giving him a home."

"It was almost stolen today *again*, all we hold dear." He sniffed.

I fetched a tissue and handed it to him. "Aye, now tell me about the lads with binoculars stationed along the shore." I sat and leaned back into the chair.

"Well," he began. "I told you I expected resistance to the division in SSP. I figured the one pushing hardest would do her worst. Seems she has."

"Is this about Skye?"

"Nay, she's but a wily puppet. It's more complicated. I don't ken *her* identity. I think David Ferrell knows, but she stays in shadows. She's poured a mountain of cash into the organization the past few years. Purchasing favor, currying popular opinion toward her own agenda."

"Sounds intriguing. What's the catch? Are the seasoned members taking her interference as a threat?" A woman in charge wouldn't do for the lads, I supposed.

"It *is* a threat. She's made that clear enough. I figured promoting the split might bring her out of hiding. I don't care for shadowboxing and she's had us at each other's throats for months on end." My love tried to shift in the hospital bed, with an agitated glance my direction.

"What's her agenda?" I hopped up to help him readjust his pillow.

"That's the devil of it. She hasn't proclaimed an agenda. David assures me she's on the right side of SSP. I think he's daft." He growled as he settled back. "Bloody hell, my leg hurts!"

"I can ask for pain medication." I reached for the buzzer to alert the nurse.

"No! Maybe in a while. Sit, tell me about America. When you were there, where'd you go?" He blew out heavily, staring at the ceiling.

"A small town north of Atlanta, Georgia. I stayed at a bed and breakfast, in a place called Mallory. It was named for a Scottish family who helped establish the area."

"What's it like?" Pain was wearing him down.

"Mountains shrouded in blue mist, lovely, rocky burns, beautiful rivers. I went to a local church one Sunday and met a lady, Caroline Brogan. She has a ranch where they retrain race horses when they've lived beyond their usefulness at the track. I drove up to her ranch, Mallory Ridge. Her family was the one that moved into those mountains first. They hailed from down around Dundee." I mused on that visit a moment.

"Where was what's-his-name? You were on your honeymoon, weren't you?" He glared at me.

"He stayed in Atlanta with friends. I was gotten outta the way because you were coming home."

"Aye, tha's when Kyle and I flew home. It's why he couldn't find you. So, tell me more."

"I became well-acquainted with Caroline. I always felt she knew more about me than I told. She'd look at me sometimes, like she had a sense of my heart, you ken?" I glanced back at my lover.

"Aye, go on."

"Liam and I have been back four times. He loves the place. He learned to ride there. Caroline's husband died in an auto crash and she remarried. Remember the British actor, Will Mason?"

"Aye?" He frowned and tried to breathe normally.

"She married him. Turns out, they'd met 30 years earlier, on a nearby army base. He was smitten, he swears, and looked for her for years. They finally met in an airport terminal."

"You're kidding."

"No, they married and have a daughter, Adelaide. She's adorable. I so want a daughter, Cullum." I peeked up at my husband.

His voice was barely a whisper. "I'll do my best, love."

"Adelaide has a touch of autism. She's an artist, like her grandfather, Thomas Mallory. She paints lovely sunsets almost every day, on a professional easel, set up at the end of the veranda."

"Sounds idyllic." He murmured.

"Nothing like as wildly beautiful as Scotland, especially Nairn. But I do see why so many of our people settled there. Liam and I had just returned, a week gone, when you called about Aunt Min." I stood and kissed his forehead. "Seems a lifetime ago. It's only been two months."

He opened his eyes. "Alright, I'll take medication. Where are you sleeping?"

"The chair reclines." I jabbed my thumb toward the vinyl covered seat.

"Get a room." He grimaced with pain.

"No, I don't wanna be far from you." I kissed him and rang the nurse.

"Your meeting with Naomi and Carmichael is tomorrow, love."

"I've called to reschedule. Under the circumstances…well, I'll tend it after you're safely home."

"You're sure?"

"You take priority, husband." I smiled and squeezed his hand while the nurse injected medication into his IV.

Ten days later the rehab center in Nairn released Cullum to home care. He had to stay off his feet most of the day…and night. No bartending for a while. Robin stepped in while Cullum recuperated and hired a new bartender to cover his turns at Jacobite's Folly. Kyle's wife, Caleigh, tended Cullum once a day and a physical therapist came by every morning to work him over.

Still, my man had to go to work. I drove him, with Liam in tow. He hobbled to the office and propped in his chair for a few hours for two weeks.

Liam learned to prep veggies in the kitchen and bus tables. His dad pouted because he wasn't the one teaching him. He'd have a man drag his chair to the kitchen so he could, at least, observe.

Quiz nights, on Tuesdays and Thursdays, Cullum sat behind the bar on a stool, for two weeks, reading questions and keeping score. He was well enough, at the end of a month, to pull a five hour shift with one break. It would be another month or so before he could run, so we bought gear for home. He worked out twice a day for thirty minutes and was still unbearable.

While his health improved, I continued to read Minerva's diaries. The more I discovered, the less enamored I became about my aunt/mother. She was lulu for my father, even after she and David married. It took several years for him to truly win her heart. I was happy to find he succeeded, as I could hardly bear the words she wrote comparing him to her beloved Arthur.

My phone rang. "Isabel Sinclair."

"Mrs. Sinclair, this is John Cooley."

"Inspector, it's good to hear from you. I hope this is a progress report."

"I wish I had good news. We've not been able to track the shooter; however, we have a lead on a rifle that may have been the weapon used. The day prior to the shooting, a rifle matching the description went missing from a home in Nairn."

"I suppose it's too much to ask who reported the rifle stolen."

"You *are* still on the force, are you not?"

"Aye, still plodding through the muck of my treasured aunt's life."

"Well, as a fellow peace officer, I may inform you that a local solicitor, Damian Ferguson, was the one to report the theft."

I tried not to smile. "That's more than interesting, Inspector. He happens to involved with the muddle surrounding *my* family."

"On the down side, the shooter vanished like a puff of smoke. We interviewed Cullum's chap who followed the motorcycle. He lost the biker on A96, near Elgin. Black motorbikes are a dime a dozen so we may have hit a dead end. We were able to get a paint sample from a crash he caused, scraping the side of a car before the driver drove off the carriageway to avoid him. It was a Suzuki. That's all we know for certain."

"You might want to check Damian's bank account. See if he made payment to anyone for their questionable service. If not, Naomi Rose-Fielding may prove interesting in the same regard." I

135

walked towards the kitchen for water. My stomach flipped for the third time that morning.

"Isn't she your mother?"

"In a sense. She held that role for a number of years. It's a sordid story. Stop in whenever you're here and I'll be happy to share it... and what I've found so far."

"Do you believe this is all tied together, honestly, Isabel?"

"I do. The more that occurs, the deeper my suspicion runs"

"Then I'll investigate that trail. May I come by tomorrow?"

"How about dinner? Cullum usually leaves for the pub late afternoon."

"Sounds delightful. I'll see the two of you then."

***

While all this life revolved around us, we finally met with Naomi and Sir William at his office. It was anything but pleasant.

"I don't want you going alone. I'll accompany you." Cullum prepared his clothes the night before. Brown slacks, a tweed jacket, with suede elbow patches and a gold silk shirt awaited him on the valet beside his closet.

"You needn't brave the lair of the she-cat. I have to leave so early, are you sure you're up to the trip? You've only been out a few weeks."

He growled at me. "Aye, the leg works well enough to get me inside and out to the car again. If I have to fight, we'll be in dire straits, but otherwise I'm in good shape."

I had to leave the room, laughing, about to cry, because every response from him was like that encounter. My man does not like to be less than at the top of his game.

On return, I finished dressing for bed. We had a new routine, since my body began to change. I had to undress deliberately and dress at an even more unhurried pace. He studied my shape, the poochy, softness of my abdomen. He wasn't content with visual inspection, as he's always been hands-on.

"Come here." He wiggled his finger at me.

I strode to his side, feeling like a runway model with her dress on backwards. "What?"

He propped in bed to watch my approach. "I wanna feel you grow, Bel." His broad hand spanned my belly, then my hips. "I like the feel of your silk robe across the back of my hand when I touch you. How's the nausea?"

"Not too bad. It slows me down in the mornin'."

He pulled me down to sit beside him and cupped one breast. "I'm slowing you down, too, eh?" He watched my reaction as he caressed sensitive areas, made more so by hormonal responses.

I bit my bottom lip and gazed into his eyes. "I'm good with it. I didn't have the opportunity to care for you when you came home from Bosnia. I have the pleasure of doing so now."

"You can hire help, if you want." He ran his hand over my loosed hair to my shoulder, down my back to my widening waist and parked on my wee bit of a belly.

"I don't want. Liam and I will tend you. Are you finished?" We went through this routine twice daily.

"Nay, come to bed like you are, in the robe. It's almost as soft as your skin." He reached to switch off the lamp on his side table.

I had the pleasure of tending more than his ailments.

Chapter 11

Cullum tossed the cane he used for balance into the back seat.

"Wouldn't that be handy if we have to fight our way out?" I shouldered my handbag and tugged the corners of my flyaway jacket to disguise my small weight gain. Naomi needn't know we were having another child.

She'd always chided me for my full figure, failing to be as rail thin as she, with the exception of implants in her breasts and tush.

He took my arm in his and gritted his teeth. "Don't ever let 'em see fear or weakness in you, Bel. They're like tigers prowling for their prey. We're not playing their game any longer."

He stood straight and tall, walking without so much as a hitch, which I knew must cause pain.

We entered the Art Deco brass trimmed lift in the marble lined foyer.

The lift man asked, "Which floor?"

"Three," growled my lover.

We rode in silence until the antique vehicle creaked to a stop.

"Three," the lift man announced formally.

My love rumbled, "Ta," and led me out to the doorway of my father's friend and solicitor, the executor of his estate.

We paused at the portal. "You know what the best news would be? At least for us?"

He turned a charming smile my way. "Tha' if we remarried all your rights, as heir, are revoked?"

"You know me too well." I waited for him to open the door.

We entered a plush waiting area. A nearby settee was clad in dark green velvet. Deep red leather wing-backed chairs with nail head trim sat juxtaposed two by two around ebony tables with brass lamps topped by Tiffany shades. Thick pile carpet absorbed every sound in the room.

A shapely blonde, propped behind a mahogany desk topped only with a slim phone, spoke coolly. "May I help you?" Her expression could not have been more vacant.

"I'm Isabel Fielding-Sinclair to see Sir William." I smiled warmly, still attached to my husband's arm.

She regarded Mr. Sinclair, who grinned. "Please sit. I'll call through." She raised the phone to her perfect lips and mumbled something to the person at the other end.

We seated ourselves and held hands across the narrow table. I whispered to Cullum. "Are you alright?"

"Aye, fine, lass." He winked and kept a lock on my gaze.

A door to the inner sanctum opened and Annmarie, Sir William's personal assistant appeared before our chairs in a sober navy suit. "Isabel, how lovely to see you." She graced us with a hint of a smile. She extended her hand to Cullum. "I don't believe we've met."

He stood and took her hand. "Nay, I'd remember that." He released her hand as she dropped her eyes.

"Well, follow me, please." She turned to the inner sanctum.

I stole a glance at the blonde receptionist. She stared blankly into space above our heads.

We followed Annmarie into Sir William's private office and found Naomi already perched on a chair beside his desk, like an expectant schoolgirl.

He rose from the tall leather chair beyond her and bowed. "Isabel, how wonderful to see you." He leaned to my cheek for a kiss. He turned to Cullum and extended his hand. "And you must feel a lucky man to finally land my charge."

Cullum clutched the older man's heavily veined offering. "She was my wife *before* she was your charge."

"Ah, yes, well, we're here to iron out the wrinkles. I apologize for my part in the disaster. Annulling your marriage was the worst decision my dear friend, Arthur Fielding, ever made. He was a fine man, but overly emotional when it came to Isabel." He released Cullum and waved towards chairs pressed together to suit us.

We sat and faced Naomi and Sir William.

Naomi spoke with great confidence to Sir William but had not offered us even a glance. "I'd like to conclude *my* business before you get into the deeper matters of AIM Enterprises, William." She smiled in a coy way she used on all her victims.

He returned her look with mock severity. "Naomi, you haven't even greeted the newlyweds."

She arched one shapely brow and considered us. She spoke to Cullum. "Congratulations, Cullum. You finally got what you wanted." She didn't bother with me but turned back to the executor, her coiffed head cocked to one side. "Will that do, William?"

He passed a glance my way. "Naomi, you must at least be civil if you intend to ask for an increase in allowance. Isabel dictates. I merely execute her commands."

I ended the discussion, addressing Naomi directly. "The answer is no, if that makes the day pass easier. You needn't grovel or humiliate yourself. Your allowance is more than I make at my job in a year and you have no expenses but your own whims. The people who work for the company won't prop you up any longer. I want to revoke your allowance entirely." That got her attention; she whirled and glared with her steely eyes. "But Cullum's convinced me that perhaps it's best to freeze your assets until you learn to live within your means. You have one year to do so and we'll reevaluate your situation."

I turned my eyes to Sir William. "She needs to leave our presence." I looked away.

"Well, Naomi, there's your answer." He rose stiffly and offered her his hand while she dabbed at her eyes with a lacy hankie. "I'll see you out, my dear." He took her fragile hand and tucked it into his arm and exited left to his private living space. We all knew what that meant.

A few weeks after meeting with Sir William, our lives settled into a strained sort of normalcy. Cullum's hours at the pub extended. I worked on sorting out Min's life, past and most current. Liam stayed tucked safely away at the farm.

I was not so naïve to think that the dark queen's arm couldn't reach our son there. There was just a better chance to see the culprit approaching from a distance.

Then one evening, I parked in the drive and climbed out, tugging a bag with fresh salmon, a baguette, and salad greens along with me. Ignoring my surroundings, dangerous considering all the turmoil of the past four and a half months, I was startled when someone called my name from very near the back of my car.

Glancing up, I found the man I married in name only for almost a dozen years. "Bradley?"

He smiled. "Hello, Isabel." He stuffed his hands in the pockets of his Savile Row trousers and smiled. He's a handsome man, blond, tanned, with very green eyes.

I thought they may be enhanced contacts though I'd never ventured close enough to tell. "Bradley, what are you doing here?" I tried a pleasant look but it wasn't natural and certainly not what I felt.

"Oh, I'm sorry. I must have frightened you." He reached for my bag, hanging loosely at my side. "Let me carry this." He scooped up my groceries and motioned toward the door. "May we go inside?"

I recovered. "Aye, we may." I slammed the door of my Prius and preceded my guest into the home I shared with my husband.

I turned and took the bag from him as he closed the door behind us. "I need to put this away. My…Cullum will be home any moment."

"I know. I just left the pub."

Halfway across the living room, I stopped and glanced back. "You were at the pub?"

"Yes, he doesn't know I was there, but I wanted to speak with you both and waited until he showed signs of coming home. He should be behind me, no more than a few minutes." His hands stuffed into his pockets again.

"What do you want to talk about?" I frowned.

"Let's wait until he arrives. There'll be questions and I want to be clear with you both. My intentions are…Isabel, it's nothing bad." His hands left his pockets and he held them up defensively. "There are a few things to discuss concerning business. That's all." He remained standing.

I left him to hurry to the kitchen and cram the bag into the icebox. I washed my hands and peeked into the living room while I dried them on a towel. "Would you like a glass of wine?"

"Sounds delightful," he grinned.

Smiling back, I turned away and gathered glasses and a bottle of white wine from the wine cooler. I put it all on a tray and carried the lot to the living room.

Bradley looked at the table before the couch and moved a book to clear a spot for me to park the tray. "Shall I?" He hefted the screw.

"Sure, that'll be fine, then." I perched on a nearby chair, while he opened the bottle, until I heard Cullum at the door.

Hastening to the foyer, I waited for him to enter.

"Bel?" He hung up his jacket, frowned, and met me for a kiss.

"Be nice." It was all I had time to say, as Bradley walked in behind me.

"Wha's this?" Cullum glared as he studied our guest.

Inhaling deeply, I introduced them. "My heart, this is Bradley."

Beloved paled. His mouth set into a thin line.

"Bradley, Cullum." I swept my hand between them.

Bradley felt the tension, but reached beyond it to offer my husband his hand with a smile. "Cullum, I'm sorry to intrude like this, but I must speak to you and Isabel at once."

Cullum looked at me and took the proffered hand. "Did you call first?"

"No, I wanted to see you together, so I waited at your pub until you prepared to leave. Had I phoned, well, I was afraid Isabel would refuse me. I've only been here," He checked his watch, "three minutes." He paused for consent.

"All right, then." Cullum motioned to the living room. "Go— sit." He was cautious with his movements. He glanced at me and I took his hand, squeezing tightly.

The three of us chose our seats, Bradley in the chair I'd left, Cullum and I together on the sofa, our thighs pressed together.

I leaned forward and poured the wine. Bradley picked up a glass, sipped and nodded approval. Cullum accepted his glass and propped his arm behind me. I turned for a glimpse of his furrowed brow.

Bradley began. "I've heard scuttlebutt in business circles, Isabel. They say you're looking for a buyer for AIM Enterprises. Is it true?"

"Aye, though the only ones discussing it are sitting before you. I was about to approach Sir William, but then my husband was shot. We've been preoccupied with recovery and...I haven't broached the subject with the board yet."

"There's a flurry of gossip, which you know is a really bad sign that drives down the price of your shares."

"Aye, no doubt. But, they can't sell without me and I doubt there are many buyers out there who want less than forty-nine percent of the company. I hold fifty-one percent and Cullum's parents ten." I crossed my legs and sipped the wine.

"Ah, well, it's a moot point unless you're *willing* to sell."

Cullum's deep voice sounded threatening. "What's this to do with you?"

"Cullum, I owe a great deal to Isabel, to Liam, and to you. Had she not held fast to our agreement, but divorced me when *her* father died, I'd have still lost everything. Because she kept her word and saw me through that ordeal, I feel compelled to offer to buy her out."

"What? You want to...Bradley, how?"

"I've done very well. It would stretch me to my limit, but if you agree, I have a partner for the investment and we'll purchase at the going rate of one week ago."

Cullum growled. "Who's the partner?"

Bradley glanced at me. "Ron and I separated two years ago. I've met someone new. He's solid. We've been on for about a year now. He's fairly well off and proposed to come in with me for a small portion, enough I can offer you the better rate for your fifty-one percent. He's a solicitor."

Cullum's volume decreased ominously. "*Who's* the partner?"

Bradley appeared cornered as he swung his gaze to me for help. "Isabel?"

"Is it Damian Ferguson?" I have a suspicious mind.

He started and leaned back in the chair, crossing his long, elegant legs, and frowned. "How'd you know?"

I glanced back at Cullum who ran his hand through his thick black hair and shook his head at me.

"He keeps popping up, wherever we go." I smiled, for the first time, mildly amused by the turn of events.

Cullum laid the dining room table and Bradley poured more wine around. I shredded ginger and garlic into a sauté pan with two tablespoons of excellent Spanish olive oil. Stirring with a bamboo spatula, I replayed our conversation.

I had a solution to the dilemma that would keep Damian out of the mix.

I scooped seasonings out of the hot oil and slid fresh salmon filets in to sear each side for about two minutes. Cullum filled bowls with greens and headed to the table while Bradley tore the baguette. I poured olive oil into two bowls for dipping bread and laid one between Cullum's seat and mine, and the other beside Bradley. Removing heated plates from the Aga, I slid filets onto each one, then quickly added the seasonings back to the oil and a quick dash of white wine to finish. Once the sauce warmed, I poured it over the fish and plated steamed asparagus spears.

I turned to present our plates to my husband, who kissed my lips and whispered, "I love you, Bel."

"And I you, mo chroi." I carried Bradley's plate to the table and caught him checking his phone. "Dinner's ready."

He joined us with a smile, but it was obvious he was confused and a bit hurt.

I reached across the table for his hand. He laid his fingertips in mine and we bowed our heads to bless the food. After, when he removed his hand, it was a quick, uncomfortable moment.

Cullum attacked the salmon and salad. He eats heartily.

Bradley tasted a sample. "This is very good, Isabel."

"Thank you."

"Tell me how Liam fairs. Is he away at school?" Bradley dabbed his mouth with the napkin after every bite.

Cullum answered. "Nay, at his grand's farm." He glanced up and chewed. When he swallowed, he sat back. "He comes to visit, but we're afraid the same people who killed our aunt, had me shot, and are tryin' to ruin AIM Enterprises will strike out against our son. The sooner the company's sold, the better, in my mind. Maybe then, our son can come home for more than a night."

"I may have a solution, at least for Bradley's offer. What do you say to whatever you have without a partner as the sale price of the company?" I popped a bite into my mouth, the first time that day I wasn't nauseated.

Bradley frowned and shook his head. "You mean selling me the whole fifty-one percent for what I can raise alone?"

"That's what she said." Cullum laid his hand on my thigh.

"Why would you do that? You can ride this out, wait until the rumors die out, and receive top market value."

"It isn't about the money. I'm more interested in the rights of the people who work for the company. I implemented changes that caused the bottom line to shrink at first. But the changes are beginning to pay off with tenure. We don't turn over our work force. We refused to lay off laborers because the economy takes a dive. We tighten our belts at the top, instead of walking out with huge bonuses, at the expense of our work force retirement plan, things like that. If you'll keep those changes in place, Bradley, we'll sell for whatever you can raise...comfortably. Don't get yourself into a jam trying to give me somethin' I don't care about."

He laid his fork on his plate, dabbed his sculpted mouth and cleared his throat. "You don't really care about the profit?"

"Not a tick. Do we have a deal? Can you promise me that you'll keep the covenant I made with the people who work for AIM Enterprises?" I took another bite and savored the pepper and garlic burn.

He turned to Cullum. "And how do you feel? Will you be satisfied to walk away from millions of dollars?"

Cullum smiled. "I'll be thrilled when it's gone. However, you must be sure to keep Bel's word to the people who work for the company and not sell them out. Otherwise, it'll contractually revert back to her control. That'll be part of the agreement, made easier, to inject the clause, because you were...married." He sat back in his chair and we both considered Bradley.

"You know I have questions about Damian. Like, what do you know that I obviously don't?" His green eyes widened with irritation, and a touch of fear.

"Do we have a deal on the sale of the company?" I placed my napkin beside my plate, having eaten every bite.

"Yes, absolutely. We'll get something in writing tonight. Then will you tell me?"

"I'll give you that information free of charge." My husband leaned forward. "Run like your life depends on it, because it does. When he gets his hands on those shares, you're a dead man. Has he wormed his way into being named trustee of your estate?"

Bradley turned grey. "How'd you know?"

"You need to change that provision before bedtime tonight. The other, we can shake on and sleep tight." Cullum exchanged glances with me. "You good with that, mo chroi?"

I smiled and nodded. "Very good."

"Bradley." It was the first time Cullum spoke his name. "You don't want to take the notion to face down Damian Ferguson. It'll get you killed, savvy?" He checked his watch. "It's abou' time for Liam to be in bed." He looked at me. "You comin' with me?"

"Aye, let's do a quick clean up and we'll go to the farm."

"You can stay here tonight, in Liam's room, if you need a place." Cullum addressed Bradley again.

I turned at the kitchen entry.

"Thank you, but I remembered Isabel's friend, Craig Forsyth at Wetherby House, and booked a room. She's always said how fine his full Scottish breakfast is, so I decided to try it, as this will likely be my last visit."

Cullum turned to me. "Bel, shall I have my attorney draw up paperwork for the sale?"

I smiled at him. "That sounds grand. Have it ready by two tomorrow afternoon?"

"Aye, it shall be." Cullum offered his hand to Bradley. They shook and walked to the door. My husband's voice drifted to my hearing though I couldn't make out his words. The front door closed and we were alone again. He met me in the living room. "So, mo chroi, are you satisfied with the outcome?" He propped his hands on my hips.

Rubbing my hands up his arms I locked them behind his head. "Very much, thank you. I appreciate that you were kind and not overly put out that Bradley was here."

He chuckled. "Not really. I wanted to kill 'im the first ten minutes, but realized it might behoove me to listen. I'm glad I did.

What're you gonna do with all the money?" He pulled me into his body.

"I have a plan. Let's go see our son."

We left for the farm.

The drive out to the country was silent. I watched sheepdogs rounding the herds for night watch.

The sun hung near the horizon, refusing to give up on daylight. The moon was full and appeared as a shadow in the sky. The land was verdant, wild, and lovely. It was good to be back in the Highlands. Edinburgh has its charms, but no place on earth is as beautiful as this part of Scotland. But then, I could be prejudiced.

We pulled into the mile long drive up to the house when my phone rang.

"Hullo, Liam."

He sniffed. "Mum, you're late!" A sob followed.

"We're on our way up the drive, darlin'. What's wrong?"

"Can I come home?"

I didn't hesitate. "Yes. Pack your bag and we'll be together for a few days. Okay?" I glanced at Cullum, who hung on every word. "We're parkin'. I'll be right inside." I rang off.

"Wha's wrong?" He looked concerned.

"The lad needs some Mum time."

He grinned. "I can understand that. Let's fetch 'im, then." We climbed out.

Genny waited at the door. "I cannot fathom wha's wrong with 'im, but, I think he needs to go home for a few days."

"Aye, he does. I've never been away from him for more than three days at a time. I'll help him pack." I left Cullum and his parents for his old bedroom, upstairs, third on the right. I peeked inside and caught Liam wiping his face on his sleeve.

He turned when I stepped inside.

"Mum!" He wrapped his arms round me and we held onto each other for a few minutes.

I heard his da's heavy step on the stairs. He pushed away from me. "I'm sorry to be such a baby."

I dried his tears with my hankie. "It's alright. I've missed you somethin' fierce. If you hadn't needed to come home tonight, I was going to ask you to come anyway."

Cullum pushed the door open and reached for our lad. "Let's take you home, lad. Mum can stay with you. The two of you'll have to stay inside until I get a bodyguard at the house."

Liam turned his face up to Cullum's. "Is it *so* bad, Da?"

"Just wanna be careful. I ken you can take care of your mum, but I'd rather play it safe." He hugged Liam again and kissed his forehead. "Grab your bag and I'll get your laptop."

Liam obeyed, still wiping his eyes. "Will Gran be awfully disappointed, Da?"

"Nay, she understands. Besides, you'll be back. We aren't going far. If she misses you too much, she can come to you." He caught my glance and shook his head.

"Right, then, let's head home." I wrapped my arm around Liam's shoulder and we led the way.

Arriving, Liam headed for his room to prepare for bed.

Cullum squeezed my hand. "Quite a night, eh?"

"Aye, we need time to process our visitor and get Liam settled too. I'm sorry he melted down. He's more like you than me."

"Then I should be the one apologizin'." He grinned.

"I know you have to get back to the pub." I kissed his mouth.

"Mmm, let me tuck him in and I'll go. I don't feel good about leavin' you here on your own." He glanced around.

"I have Uncle David's Glock."

"I didn't know you brought the weapon home." His brows rose.

"There've been too many intruders. It seems locked doors can't keep us safe. Besides, I'm still officially on the force, if not in reality. Liam and I will be fine." I winked and smiled.

"The lad's quietened. I'll say prayers with 'im and get back to work, but I'll be home soon. I'm callin' Kent to see if he and his brother can keep watch, in shifts, until I hire someone proper." He left me in the living room for our son's bedroom.

I went to the kitchen for water and a glass of milk to calm my racing heart. Beloved was serious about the bodyguard.

Robin and Genny must have told him something that alarmed him enough to hire protection. I sipped water and milk alternately, pondering the threats and decided to check all the window locks. Intruders hadn't tried the windows yet, but there's always a first time.

Cullum found me before he left. "Mo chroi, are you well?"

"Aye, no problem. Go to work. We'll be alright, my love." I inhaled deeply and felt the weariness of the day in my bones.

He kissed me. "Go to bed. I'll only be a couple of hours. Don't wait up."

I nodded and walked him to the door.

When I heard him drive away, I went through the house checking the remainder of window latches.

Liam was still awake when I entered his room quietly. "Mum?"

"Aye, darlin'?" I pulled his curtains open and reached for the lock. A shadow or someone in dark clothes and a hood caught my eye. I locked the windows and snatched the curtains closed. "Aren't you sleepy, lad?" I sat on his bed. He lay on his side and I rubbed his back.

"Are you mad because I needed to come home?"

"No, not at all. I wanted to call and ask you to come home, but Dad said to leave it 'til we got to the farm. We ran late because we had an unexpected visitor and he stayed for supper. We came out as soon as we could." I brushed his black wavy hair away from his eyes. A few strokes generally knock him out.

"Mum, when is my brother or sister going to be born?" He rolled to his back.

"In about five months, give or take a week."

"I've been thinkin' about our talk."

"What've you concluded?"

He sighed. "I think it's a cool idea to have more kids. Lachlan said his mum and dad have been tryin' for a few years. What does that mean, tryin'?"

"Oh, my. Well. Did you ask your dad?" I was flummoxed. This was not a bedtime conversation.

"Nay, I wasn't sure what to say. With you, it's never mattered what I don't say right. Does it mean they really want a baby and they're, you know, being…really personal about it?"

"That's an excellent way to explain what they're doing. They're being *extremely* personal about trying to become pregnant. That happens only in the privacy of their time together." *Whew! Think that's clear.*

"Oh, right, sex and all that." He was blushing. I couldn't see him, but I know my lad and that's why he chose that time to ask. He was too embarrassed, even with me, to wait until his rosy freckled cheeks reddened in day's light.

"Aye, all that." I kissed his forehead. "I love you, Liam."

"I love you more." He rolled to his side.

I left him and headed for the dark kitchen to see if we still had a loiterer out back or if someone cut through, after a late stroll on the beach. I doused lights in the living room as I went and waited by the window, facing west, for my eyes to adjust to the lack of light. When I felt confident I could look outside, without being spotted, I opened the shade a few inches and flattened myself on the floor.

The view was great, though a cloudy night and no street lights kept my vision limited.

A darkly hooded figure stood about thirty feet away studying our home, most particularly Liam's window.

What to do? Call Cullum? Nay, I just said we'd be fine. I can protect us. Is there more than this one bloke or two or three? I'll have to keep watch until he leaves and another takes his place. At least, I can be assured of where this one is located.

I lay on the stone floor for more than an hour before the watcher's mobile needed attention. He held it to his ear, listened, and turned as he pocketed the phone. He loped away from our home and cut between houses up the lane.

I pushed myself up and dashed for the loo, intending to return to my post. Once back in the hallway, I heard the front door opening. Cullum stepped into the foyer.

I rounded the corner and whispered. "Hello, handsome."

He spun. "Mo chroi, what're you doing up so late?" He met me in a few steps.

"Did you have one of the lads come to keep watch already?"

"Nay, I talked to Kent. He'll begin tomorrow evenin'. Why? Did you see someone outside? Could've been a late walker or jogger." He reached for me.

"Don't think so, lover. I watched him at Liam's bedroom for more than an hour. Spotted him when latching windows." I relaxed in his grasp.

"What did he look like?"

"Usual suspect. Anyway, the house is tight, unless there're more keys floating round. How often do you lend your car?" I leaned back to peruse his handsome face in the near dark.

"When items need fetching from the grocer or market, one of the kids from the pub, drive it occasionally. Why?"

"I wonder how Skye opened the door the day she sneaked inside?"

He pondered the question a moment. "She worked for the brewery awhile." He blew air out hard. "I can't recall a time she used my car." He shook his head, a lank of ebony hair slipping to his forehead.

"Maybe someone else copied the key and gave it to her?"

He sighed. "Perhaps. I'll have the locks changed tomorrow, mo chroi. We'll throw the bolts on the doors." He turned back and locked the deadbolt on the front door.

"Kitchen door's done already. Do you wanna snack or anythin'?"

He reached for me. "Mmm, that I do, lass."

"I can fix that craving."

"I ken, let's go to bed, then. I had an idea to wake you slowly with kisses."

"I can pretend to be asleep."

Cullum was about, stirring, every hour. He checked the house perimeter and returned to bed, always with the Glock in hand. When he lay down the last time before dawn, at 4:30, he sighed and reached across the space of a half foot for me.

I responded. "Stay in bed, lover. I'll get up next time."

"Nay, it's my job to protect you, mo chroi, and our son." He rolled over and kissed me.

We welcomed dawn his favorite way. Afterwards, I hied to the loo and then the kitchen for a ginger tea to sip until nausea passed.

I've heard old women say that bane, which comes with the blessing of life, indicates a healthy child. Then ours should be hearty.

I'd experienced the same with Liam and he was a fine, braw boy. I smiled at the memory of the stirring of life, the first time I felt him move. In another month, it became a game between us. He'd hear my voice and wake, kicking, like his dad playin' rugby. I always imagined him, so like Cullum.

I never dreamed we'd be here, now, with another child on the way, struggling against an unknown assailant who coveted our lives. *Pray, God, lead us in the right direction, to uncover the plot and expose the dark queen...if she's the one behind the treachery.*

Liam woke and met me in the kitchen. "Fine mornin', Mum." He opened the icebox and found the juice. "Do you wanna glass?"

"Nay, I'm good. I have tea. Come sit with me. How'd you sleep?"

"Good...better. I didn't wanna tell you last night...but I saw a man at the farm. He was far away, with binoculars, but I could tell he was watching me and Lachlan."

"What were the two of you about?" I leaned on the table.

"We rode horses in the upper pasture. Uncle Kyle said it could've been a hiker, tryin' to find his way. He said sometimes they get lost and come down to the farm for directions. It scared me. I don't know why." He sipped juice.

"It's better you're home." I patted his arm.

Cullum propped in the doorway. "Aye, it is. You'll both *stay* home 'til this is over. We'll go to the farm together from now on." He approached the table. "I ken you boys like being on your own out there, but just now, it isn't safe."

Liam scooted over for his dad to sit. "Why, Dad? Why does someone want to harm us? Have we done somethin' wrong?"

"Nay, son, but they have and they ken we know what they're about." He met my eyes.

"We can't live like this forever." I massaged his thick calf with both my socked feet.

He smiled. "I've considered tha', mo chroi. It might be time to create our own catalyst."

"Aye, you may be right."

"I ken I'm right, Bel. All I need is for the two of you to stay outta reach for a little while. I talked to Inspector Cooley yesterday. We're hatching a plan."

"*You've* spoken with the police. Cullum, that's my job."

"Not anymore. I'll not have either of you harmed. If I have to handle this myself, I will. As soon as whose it calls, we'll see which way the wind blows with regard to AIM Enterprises." He sighed. "What's for breakfast? If you don't feel like cooking, the lad and I can run out and fetch somethin'."

"Porridge, I made it last night while you showered. I'll turn the Aga on." I slid out of the booth and headed for the stove. Pouring coffee for him into a large mug, I glanced out the west window as a black clad figure dashed past, very near the house. It startled me. "Ah!" I stepped back.

Cullum bolted across the kitchen, to me, beside the Aga. He stopped in front of me, facing the window. "Wha', Bel?"

"Just a runner passing, I think." I held one hand to my racing heart.

He turned, grabbed my shoulders, and whispered, "Shh, lass. It'll be fine." He hugged me. "You don't need to be livin' on edge like this. It's no good for our child, darlin'." He glanced back at Liam. "Either of them."

I nodded and calmed myself, putting the kettle on for tea. He hovered, a hand at my waist. "I'm fine, really."

"Nay, you aren't. This has to stop."

I smiled. "I agree, but we aren't finishing this by fighting each other or shadows. How do we get *her* out in the light?"

"I think when the company's sold to Bradley, it'll be over. The sooner, the better." He bobbed his head once. "Hopefully, we'll hear back today."

"Hopefully." I patted his chest and turned to stir the porridge.

It didn't happen.

Chapter 12

We supposed we knew what we faced, at the time. Truthfully, I figured the whole affair far more complicated than we imagined.

After a day together, Liam paced, longing to be outside, with his friends, anywhere but stuck inside four walls.

He was our first concern. Missing school and new friends was a challenge for him. We fretted over what to do; he needed a consistent learning environment. We decided to chance it, over shipping him off to boarding school. Cullum would drop him off, walk into school with him and pick him up, going inside to fetch him from the principal's office.

"Are you excited to see your friends today?" I placed his bowl of semolina on the table.

"Aye, Mum." He glanced up. "Are you going to be alright by yourself?" He scooped cereal.

"Won't be, love. Kent will be about, or his brother. They won't be inside with me, but accompany me everywhere I go. Today, it's Inverness." I smiled, gritting my teeth the whole time. I hate being someone else's burden, besides I had to feed the lads.

"I'll miss you but I'm glad to go back to school." He finished his breakfast.

"You don't leave with anyone but Dad. He won't send someone from the pub or brewery for you, okay?" I raked my hand through his thick black hair.

"Aye, Mum, I ken. I'll wait for Dad; even if the principal says it's alright to go with someone because Dad called, I stay put." He hoisted his rucksack and grinned. "Really, I'll be fine."

Cullum filled the kitchen portal. "Ready, lad?"

"Aye." Liam stretched for a kiss. "Don't worry."

"It's what Mums do." I watched the lad Cullum and I made together follow him to the car and wondered if education was worth the risk of Liam's safety. Then again, he needed normalcy. We all did, and had to stop living like caged animals or the bad guys had already won.

"Mornin', Isabel." Kent popped in when my lads went out. "I'll be out here if you need anything."

"Good, and thank you for keeping an eye on me, Kent."

"My pleasure. Holler if you're lonely." He ducked out the front and took up vigil in the cushioned glider on the front porch.

Windows and doors were locked tight. Nothing short of an armored truck or tank could penetrate Fort Sinclair. I'd go mad if I didn't try Bradley's cell phone. It was better to give it a go while Cullum was away.

Scrolling through the phone numbers, I realized I wasn't sure if it had changed. I tried the number on my phone. It rang seven times before voice mail activated.

"You have reached the voice mailbox of Bradley King. I'm unable to take your call at this time. Please leave a message at the tone and have a fantastic day." A high pitched whine followed.

I wrestled with leaving a message as soon as I heard the recording. He had a habit of looking at missed calls. Maybe he'd see I rang, but left no message...if he was still alive. I disconnected.

New fear crept through me. I knew that Bradley was no longer breathing. He'd met with Damian and had it out. *They* killed him, whoever *they* were.

The door opened to my husband. He must've noticed the look on my face. "Wha'? Bel, wha's wrong?" He took the steps quickly. "Are you ill, lass?"

I shook my head. "Nay." I sat on the edge of the sofa. "I called Bradley's phone. It rolled to voice mail."

"Is that significant? Mine rolls to voice mail all the time."

"No, it doesn't. Bradley's not alive. I just know it, Cullum." I looked at the man I love and tried to not act too concerned. Just giving him the information left me feeling guilty, but I shared *some* life with Bradley, too.

He dropped onto the sofa. "I feared he'd not be able to keep his mouth shut and go to Damian to vent his displeasure. I'm right then, eh?" He rubbed his hand across my back. "I have to get to the pub, love. Who can we call to check on him?"

"I'll try his office; see when the last time was they heard from him." I leaned into the strength that kept me going. "How'd Liam do?"

"He had an entourage all the way into the building. There's an older girl who fancies him. I don't ken that he's ready for that." He brushed his hand over his face. "I need to shower and get to the pub. We have inventory to complete."

"Why can't I help you? We did inventory monthly in the laboratory. How would it differ from measuring liquor and such?"

He chuckled. "It's tempting, but not today. You try and track the errant whose it and let me know what you find." He rose and stretched. "It occurs to me we could just chuck it all and take off for some foreign land, if I let you use your fortune." He turned for a glance at me. "Won't happen. I'll be damned if I'll be stalked like an animal, in my own hometown."

Chapter 13

Cullum called. "Mo chroi, any word?"

"The office hasn't seen him in three days and his mother hasn't spoken to him in two. That's alarming. They talk at *least* once each day. She's calling authorities." I paced the living room, feeling like a cat in a cage.

"Well, there's nothin' else for it, then. I'm on my way to fetch the lad. I'll take 'im to the pub with me."

"Kent and I've returned from Inverness and are about to head over to Aunt Min's cottage. Call when you're ready for supper."

"I'll take you out, if you like."

"We'll see. I'm chomping at the bit to get outta here but…will I be able to come back once I leave? I'm in a quandary, yet…climbing walls. I'll chance the wicked world for a spell." I sighed. I was bored. Dangerous stuff, that. Human tendency leans towards choosing chaos over boredom.

He chuckled, the low sexy sound that stirs me. "Shall I fetch you as well?"

"Nay, I have work to finish, just need initiative." I smiled. "Tell the lad I love him. I'll see you in a few hours."

"I love you, mo chroi. Be careful."

After ringing off, I held the phone in my hand for a moment longer. A voice is a tenuous connection to the ones we love. Much better to have a hug before parting, better yet, a kiss.

I went to the bedroom to change before leaving for Min's. I hadn't been regular with visits to the cottage since Cullum was shot. I needed to sort myself and her out and put closure to, at least, one adjustment in our lives.

Pulling on loose knit pants and a sweater, I headed to the front door, where my escort waited. Kent's a good sort of chap, easily amused and he'd eat everything I fix for a meal.

"Off to Min's, then." He slapped his library book closed and we headed for my car.

I unlocked the door to Min's cottage. Kent preceded me inside and bade me enter. I stepped in and took a look around.

"Everythin' in order?" Kent propped his hands on his hips and surveyed my other domain.

"Looks so. Something's a bit off, though." My nose wrinkled. *Perhaps an odor?*

"Wha'? Don't close the door until we know it's safe." He caught the heavy oak before it swung shut.

I took the steps to the main floor and checked between stacked boxes of my former life. "Nothin'. I'll check the kitchen."

"Nay! Stand here until I return." His long legs carried him to the rear of the cottage, while I waited at the top of the steps.

I heard a choking noise before Kent rounded the portal, stopping to lean against it for a moment. "Call Bernie, Isabel. There's a dead body in here."

I stepped back outside and phoned Bernie.

"Isabel, how kind of you to check in wi' me…oh, wait you're workin' for tha' inspector now, aren't you, lass?"

"Bernie, there's a dead body in Minerva's kitchen and yes, I'm phoning Inspector Cooley. Send a few lads over to secure the perimeter, please." I disconnected and phoned John Cooley.

"Isabel?" His deep voice sounded puzzled. We hadn't spoken in more than two weeks.

"Aye, 'tis me. John, I'm at my aunt's cottage. There's a dead body in the kitchen."

"I'm on my way. Whose body is it? Can you identify the person?"

"I've not looked. I'm with a friend who checked to be sure the cottage was safe prior to my entry. *I will* take a peek, if you like." I was dying of curiosity.

There are worse ways to go, of course.

"Please, if you can stomach the encounter, do."

I headed towards Kent. "I will. Hold the line." I took a deep breath of less than perfect air and rounded the corner to find my missing former husband in a heap. I hied to the living room. "Much as I feared; it's Bradley King, John." I hurried out the front door, Kent on my heels. "He was at our home two nights ago and we haven't heard back from him. He was to sign a contract to

158

purchase the company I own, yesterday. No one has had contact with him, meaning his mother and his secretary. Tha's completely out of character for him." I inhaled the wonderfully clean, fragrant salty air of outdoors.

"You know him well, then?"

"Aye, we were married once, part of the saga I've shared with you. He came into town to make an offer for AIM Enterprises. I'll fill you in when you arrive. Bernie's troops are here. They can secure the area. I'll wait for you."

"You know the routine."

"Aye, sir." I closed my phone and inhaled again.

I'd smelled more blood and death since my return to Nairn than in my whole lifetime. In the lab we received samples, smeared on glass. It was enough. My eyes filled with tears. I wiped my cheeks to keep from betraying emotion to the three officers Bernie sent.

Kent laid his solid hand on my shoulder. "I phoned Cullum. He's on his way."

"Thank you." I sniffed and wiped my cheeks again.

Leah Mabry-Mitchell slowed her step on the walkway, Hazel at her side. Her brows rose, her mouth compressed and she nodded towards her cottage when I met her eyes. I bobbed my head and turned to Kent.

"Tha's Min's neighbor and a dear friend. I need to speak with her."

"I'll stand vigil, then. Stay in sight. Cullum will have my hide for a rug, if aught happens to you." He kept his eyes moving, perusing all the action in the area.

"I'll keep to the garden." I let my shaky legs carry me to the lovely flower-filled patch next door. It reminded me that I must make time for pulling weeds from Min's...how could thoughts, of everyday life, block the horror of Bradley's lifeless body?

Leah glanced up, from under the ragged fisherman's hat she wore, with bright, alert eyes. "I see there's another spot of trouble at Minerva's, eh?" Smugness teased the corner of her mouth.

"Aye, a man's body found in the kitchen." She didn't have to know everything.

"I watched them bring him here last night. I thought at the time, he looked like he may've been unconscious. He didn't walk

159

in under his own steam, tha's for sure." She leaned back and closed her eyes.

"Who brought him here, Leah?"

"I canna tell you tha', lass. Two figures wearing dark clothes and those hooded things the youngsters favor these days." She kept her eyes closed, a ruse to make me think she'd nod off any second.

"What were their sizes? Man and woman, two men, ducking through the doorway?"

Her eyes popped open. "My, you're in a hurry, dear. Do calm yourself. I believe it was two men, though I couldn't see beyond their costumes. I base tha' theory on their gaits, the way they carried themselves. It may've very well been one man and a woman with sexual identity issues."

I couldn't help smiling. "Sexual identity issues?"

"I watch telly…sometimes." She snorted. "It was no one I recognized, not familiar manners, you ken? They had a key to enter, though. I marvel at all the keys floating about that fit Minerva's door. Don't you?"

"Aye, and our home as well. Our locks were changed yesterday. The smith was to change these this afternoon, but now it's a crime scene. Too late…for him, at least."

"Was it someone you know, dear? Someone precious to you?" Leah leaned towards me.

"Aye, I knew him. He was a…friend."

"One Cullum approved?"

"One Cullum met, only two nights ago."

"I see." She sat back. "You haven't asked about the car they drove."

"What of it?"

"It was an estate wagon, darlin', dark colored. The interior light had been doused."

"Alright then, an estate wagon." Max drove the estate wagon, on the property I own. What gardener, or other male servant, could be induced to dispose of an inconvenient body? Perhaps most, given the longevity of their careers. One simply did not hire a servant with a string of short-lived references. They couldn't be trusted.

"Why didn't you phone me?" I frowned at her. This qualified as important.

"I tried to find your card and couldn't. I called the pub, but Cullum had gone, they said. Then this afternoon, before Hazel's late mornin' walk, there it was on my desk, plain as day. I was going to call you, as soon as we returned." She shot a sidelong glance my way. "You were already there."

Cullum's red Mercedes parked in front of Leah's cottage. He opened the door and spotted me on the garden bench. He jogged the path towards me. Our lad bailed, when traffic cleared, and followed his da.

I rose to meet him, at the gate. "I'm sorry to interrupt the pub's inventory."

He shook his head. "Not more important than you, mo chroi." He opened the gate and passed through, embracing me, crossed arms and all. He whispered in my ear. "Is it?"

"Aye." I nodded against him.

Liam stood behind, waiting his turn. I reached past Cullum to take his hand.

I turned back to Leah. Her eyes had closed, mouth slackened. Hazel snoozed at her feet.

"Let's go home, Bel." He steered me towards the Mercedes.

"I need to wait for Inspector Cooley."

"He kens where we are. It may be awhile 'til he gets here. You need to get a cuppa into you and put your feet up." He held my arm in a firm grip.

Liam opened the door for me and slipped into the back. Kent threw his hand up and smiled. He could direct the inspector to our home. It was time to finish telling him the hateful saga of our lives.

***

I prepared supper. It was easier than not. The order of everyday life that must go on offers comfort, in the grounding of habits. That was what I knew for sure, as my life has often been a grieving process. I grieved daily for more than three years, after

161

Bradley and I married. Every morning, on waking Liam, even six months ago, I felt bereft of hope.

When the stir fry finished, I ladled our meal into large pasta bowls over whole grain rice. Liam laid the banquette table with flatware and napkins. He poured water while his dad poured wine.

I sat silently and bowed my head relishing the warmth of the hands I held on each side. My connections to life. When I lifted my eyes to my husband's, he met them with a slight smile.

"Thank you for supper, Bel. I could've ordered take away."

"Nay, I need the routine."

"Mum, was it a friend of yours who died?" Liam watched as we exchanged glances.

"Aye, it was." I gazed into his grey eyes and tousled his hair.

His response was timid. "Someone I know?"

I inhaled and blew out a bushel of air. I'd held my breath too long. "Aye, it was, lad. We'll discuss it after supper."

"Do I need to stay wi' you, Bel?"

"Nay, go back to work. John will come by in a bit and I'll give him my statement. It helped to get everything written down before I overanalyzed the whole affair."

I tried to smile, but my eyes filled with tears again. I took a bite of food and concentrated on chewing, anything to forget the heap of lifeless form that two days earlier, lived, breathed, and hoped.

"I'll run in and check on progress then get back to you. How's tha'?"

Swallowing was difficult. "Aye, it'll be fine." I needed time by myself. I was accustomed to sorting my emotions out alone.

He scooped up a spoonful of rice, meat, and veggies, chewed and took a sip of wine. "Bel, it'll work out. We kent the risk."

"Yes, we did. But obviously he didn't or thought his relationship strong enough to bear the burden we gave him before he left." I hated being snippy with Cullum. He didn't make the problem; he couldn't fix it either.

"Nay, but we both warned him."

I sat back and crossed my arms over my nauseated abdomen, keeping my voice soft so as not to alarm either of my lads at table. "True, tha', but he couldn't ken everythin'."

***

The door opened to Inspector John Cooley. "Isabel, your friend at Minerva's cottage directed me to you. How are you?" He hung his coat, on a hook beside the door.

"I'm alright, still breathin'. Come into the kitchen. Kettle's on." I led the way to the back of the house.

"I need to get your statement." He took a seat on the bench.

The table was laid for tea.

"It's beside the tray." I poured hot water over tea leaves.

He read my version of the scene, verbatim, including the phone call to Bernie. "I see. It may become complicated."

"What isn't these days?" I sat and prepared my cup for tea.

"The techs are fingerprinting the cottage. Cullum's and yours are on file. We'll need your son's prints, if he's been inside lately."

"Aye, he was a few weeks ago." I smoothed back my hair, slipping from the braid I wore. It had been a long day. "No, it was more than three months, but I haven't had the cleaners in yet."

"I can take the prints here, so he doesn't have to go to the station."

"Thank you, that's appreciated. He's in the office on lessons. Cullum's at the pub. Do you need him? I want to tell you about our meeting with Bradley a few nights ago."

He leaned back and rested his still hands flat on the table. "That's best."

"Bradley told me he wanted to buy my father's company. He couldn't raise all the money, so he sought to bring in a partner. He'd become involved with someone almost a year ago. That someone was Damian Ferguson. Bradley didn't go into detail as to how they met or relationship issues. He was elated that he and his new partner were happy." I gazed into my teacup. "He was stunned, when I suggested that Damian may not be a reliable business associate, and was after the controlling interest in AIM

Enterprises. Cullum underscored the fact that Damian kept turning up in the oddest places, including the stolen rifle, which fired the shot that nearly killed him.

"Together we warned Bradley to step back and not tell Damian he didn't need his help. I offered him the company, for whatever cash he could raise, as long as he kept my covenant with labor." I stopped, sipped tea, and gazed out at Moray Firth. A large orange and white research ship sat at anchor in the distance.

The inspector's voice gentled. "How'd he respond?"

"He was shocked, disappointed, and uncertain. It wasn't that he didn't believe what we said. It was too unreal for him to navigate those waters, all at once. I thought he'd take the evening, mull it over, and get back to us the following day. As I didn't hear from him for two days, I called his mother, who was already alarmed, and his secretary. Neither had contact. It's highly unusual for them to not hear from Bradley more than twice daily. Even on holiday, he calls to check in with them." I tore my eyes away from the rain spitting against the window. Mist thickened.

"I spoke to his mother. She's on her way from London." He sipped tea. "Do you know where King lodged while in Nairn?"

"Wetherby House, the Forsyth's place. He said he booked the room before he arrived. Craig Forsyth is friends with Cullum...and me."

Liam entered the kitchen doorway. "Mum?"

I smiled. "Aye, love, come in." Motioning to him, I scooted along the bench, allowing him a place to perch. "This is Inspector Cooley."

Liam approached and offered his hand. "We met briefly at hospital." He's such a gentleman.

"Aye, we did, lad. How's it feel to be back in school?"

"I was away for nine weeks. It's strange, really. All the kids wanna know where I've been and why I've not been in class. The lessons are better than online and I tend to grasp a bit more." He parked on the seat beside me.

"Inspector Cooley needs to take your fingerprints."

"Cool! Will I have ink all over my hands?" His eyes brightened.

The inspector chuckled. "Nay, lad. These days it's done with a touchscreen pad."

I walked John Cooley to the front door, as Cullum opened it and stepped inside.

He offered his hand. "Inspector, how's the investigation going?" He glanced around the living room.

I pointed towards the office. "Liam's in there."

Cullum nodded.

"Early days yet. I came by to get Isabel's statement and Liam's fingerprints. The technicians are collecting evidence. Hopefully we'll turn up more than just Mr. King's killer. I'm sure it'd be welcome to bring closure to Minerva Banks' murder, as well."

"Tha' it would. The whole business is wearisome. But we'll stay put and fight it through. Did Bel tell you about the man Liam spotted out at the farm, watching the lads?"

"Nay, she didn't mention that."

"My brother put them off, sayin' it was probably a lost hiker. The man had binoculars, so the boys didn't get a good look at his face." Cullum sighed. "Same black garb as the shooter and the man Bel spotted here outside the window last night as well as the men Leah saw going into Min's."

I piped up. "Sounds like an invasion of ninjas, eh?"

"Or one very clever organization?" Cullum offered, glancing around. "The fact tha' Damian keeps poppin' up bothers me. He's either takin' a fall for someone or hiding in plain sight."

"I'm determined to find out which it is, Cullum." Inspector Cooley turned to the door. "Isabel, I'll let you know what the lab finds. If you can get within hearing of Constable Leighton's crew, let us know the scuttlebutt."

"I will, and thank you for coming by to take Liam's fingerprints." I crossed my arms.

"'Til tomorrow, then." He passed through and left us. Cullum and I stared at each other.

"How's inventory going?"

"Lads finished while I was away. Sorry it took so long to return. I was distracted with a customer for a while." He led out to the office.

Liam looked up. "Hullo, Da. Mum told me who she found—at Aunt Min's."

"And how are *you* doing with that?"

"I'm alright—really." His glance passed Cullum. "Mum, are you feeling better?"

I winked, nodded, and headed to the kitchen, wiping my eyes clear.

Cullum approached me quietly and wrapped his arms round me from behind. I lay my head back beside his face. "Hullo, handsome."

"Bel, I can't pretend to know what you're going through. But I'm here, if you need to talk, or just be. I don't wanna crowd you." He kissed my neck, released me, and left the room.

***

The following morning proved eventful. My phone chimed while I prepared breakfast.

"Isabel, good news!" Bernie sounded pleased with himself.

"What's good, Bernie?" So far, I'd been underwhelmed with Bernie Leighton.

"A man's fingerprints were found on the murder weapon. *And* we have an eyewitness who wasn't certain he saw what he did until he read about the murder."

"Who's your eyewitness?" I stirred porridge and fought nausea, just a normal morning on the shores of Moray Firth.

"My own brother-in-law, Damian." Bernie crowed.

Now he had my full attention. "What did Damian see?"

"The murderer struggling with the victim. Let me look at that name again...."

I spoke slowly, so he could keep up with me. "Bradley King was the murdered man found in Aunt Min's cottage, Bernie."

"Aye, tha's it, King. So there was a knife found at the scene, in the murdered man's belly and the fingerprints belong to...are you listening, *Ms.* Fielding?" His tone turned bitter.

I sat down after turning off the Aga. "Yes, Bernie, I'm listening."

"Your husband, the tavern keeper."

"Is that a fact?"

"Aye, it is. You'll be hearin' from your fine friend, the inspector today, *Ms.* Fielding." The phone disconnected.

Someone knocked on the front door. I leapt to answer, not wishing my son should open it to the inspector, come to arrest his da. I peeked out the spy hole and saw Kent grinning, waving a fresh baguette, from the bakery.

I swung the portal open and gestured him inside. "Coffee's on. I have to wake Cullum. Liam will be out in a moment. There may be chaos this morning, Kent. Brace yourself."

I hied down the hallway to our bedroom and eased inside. Cullum still slept. I rounded the bed and sat beside him, stroking his back, and exposed shoulder, gently. My gut churned at the thought of my fine, brave man in handcuffs. Whatever this was about, I was sure there was an explanation.

He stirred, mumbling. "Hmm? Bel, wha's wrong, darlin'?"

"Time to wake, my love. Shower, get yourself together. It'll be a circus today."

"Hmm? Wha', more circus than usual?" He opened those lovely pale grey eyes my direction.

"Bernie just called, squawking about fingerprints on a knife, lodged in—the murder victim. He said—they're yours. I'm sure the inspector will be here soon." I leaned down to kiss his cheek.

He froze, lips pursed, nothing moved except his eyes, checking every corner of the semi-dark room.

"Are you awake, my heart?" I fussed over him a moment and moved away to open the shade a bit.

He sat up in a rush, throwing back the covers in one sweep. "I'll shower."

"I'll fetch your coffee." I left for the kitchen.

Liam was at table with juice, a bowl of porridge, and Kent. "Where's Dad?"

"Showering. How about Kent takes you to school this mornin'?" I rushed to get Liam packed off.

"Does he no' feel well?"

"Nay, he's just, well…tired." I smiled and bent to kiss my lad.

Kent watched me closely, trying to make out the ruse. "Hey, lad, shovel it down and let's roll." He checked his watch. "I have to be back to report, in fifteen minutes." He hefted Liam's rucksack in one hand and headed out to the car.

Liam took two heaping bites of porridge and downed his juice. "Bye, Mum. I love you."

I kissed his forehead. "I love you more. Go!"

He dashed out the door, pulling it shut behind himself.

I carried black coffee to the master bath.

The door knocker sounded an hour later. Cullum showered, shaved, and wore denims with a pullover under a wool vest. He ate breakfast in silence, studying me carefully. He hadn't offered an explanation and I hadn't asked. I trust him with my life and our son's and—.

I was terrified.

The door swung open to Inspector Cooley. Kent propped on the glider out front with a thermos of coffee beside him, reading the newspaper.

"Isabel?" John Cooley bowed his head slightly. "Am I to suppose Constable Leighton called this mornin'?" His brows rose, as did his voice.

"Aye, he did. Said you found Cullum's prints on a knife lodged in the victim."

Kent dropped the paper, his mouth agape, watching us, bewildered.

"I'm sure there's a rational explanation."

"Come in and we'll see." I grimaced.

Kent returned to his newspaper and coffee.

I wished life had been that simple for the rest of us.

I led the way to the kitchen where my husband still sat in the banquette sipping coffee, studying the shore. The tide receded a little while earlier.

"John, will you have coffee?" Cullum turned a cool gaze on the inspector.

"Aye, sounds fine." He looked at me and I sat a mug in front of him.

Cullum glanced up. "Bel, leave us."

I was stunned.

I turned, feeling as though my legs were made of wood, and walked away from the man I love and the man who held our future in his hands.

In the office, I checked email on my laptop, thumbing through common trash that penetrated my filter. On a hunch, I checked an old address I still kept for trivial forms that sell information. It downloaded lots of junk and then a red flagged message popped up from three days earlier.

It was from Bradley.

Isabel, please forgive me for ignoring your advice, but I feel I must speak with Damian in person. It's so difficult to end a relationship by email or over the phone. If I see him, I'll be assured it's truly concluded. I won't share the information you revealed. This is purely a personal visit.

I called his office, here in Nairn, and ask for an appointment. I see him at 2:00 tomorrow afternoon. Afterwards, I will call you and arrange a time to meet to go over Cullum's contract. You're very lucky to finally have the love of your life back. I envy you the relationship and the commitment.

Take care, darling girl.

Bradley

I sat back and inhaled deeply, listening for any noise that might emanate from the kitchen. John and Cullum certainly took their time with my husband's reasonable explanation.

"Bel?" My husband ducked around the doorway. "Need to see you."

Leaping to my feet, I hurried to the foyer, where he'd returned. John Cooley stood there, his hands in the pockets of his tan trench coat, refusing to meet my eyes.

Cullum carried a leather rucksack.

"Where are you going?"

"With John. Remove Liam from school. Kent or Kevin will be here with you around the clock. Da's on his way in to run the pub.

I felt my knees giving way. Cullum grasped my arm and steadied me.

"Mam's comin' to stay here with you and Liam."

My voice came out a murmur. "Why? Wha's this?"

Cullum pulled me into his arms and whispered into my ear. "It's better this way."

Mumbling, I pushed him back to see his face. "Better than what?"

"Trust me, mo chroi?" His eyes gave nothing away.

I nodded. "I'll get an attorney and post bail." I crossed my arms, when he stepped back.

He shrugged. "No matter."

"Please, tell me you didn't do what they say." I begged, face wet, hands shaking.

He frowned, head tilted and reached for my chin, gently lifting my face. "My heart—you think I did this terrible thing?"

"Nay, I don't...but you act as though you're resigned to whatever they say happened." I covered my mouth to avoid screaming.

"It's just better for now, Bel." He studied me for a moment. "I'll understand if you need to leave Nairn. Go back to Edinburgh; take Liam and Mam with you."

"No, I'll be wherever you are."

"Alright then." He hefted his rucksack to his shoulder and turned away.

John opened the door and finally looked back. "I'm so sorry, Isabel." He closed the door behind them.

Dropping to the floor, I lost control of all that I held tightly battened down against the storms. There had finally been too many. Too much wind. Too much rain. Far too much heartache.

Liam, Genny, and Kent found me there an hour later, spent.

Chapter 14

"Well, let's see about you, lass." The elderly white-haired man, before me, placed his stethoscope into his ears with palsied hands. His bushy white brows rose when he rolled his eyes to a corner of the room and listened to my abdomen. "Hmm, the bairn's heartbeat's strong." He pulled the instrument away and draped it over his shoulder. Leaning across me, he smiled. "Now tell me how you're feeling."

"Where am I?" I glanced around the room and, for a moment, felt bewildered. When my memory returned in a flood, I began to shake uncontrollably.

"Well, there's my answer." He reached into his bag on the bedside table for help. Drawing clear liquid into a hypodermic needle, he held it up to the light.

I managed to squeak. "Wha's tha'?"

"Just a little somethin' to settle you down. It won't hurt the babe." He steadied my left arm and pierced flesh.

Genny spoke from the doorway of the master bedroom, her hand on Liam's shoulder. "I heard her voice, Henry. Is she awake?"

"Aye, she is, Gen. I'm giving her somethin' to help her nerves."

My voice sounded sluggish to my own ears. "I'm not hysterical."

"Perhaps not ordinarily, but today, it appears, is your day to get enough of bad situations, lass." He taped a plaster over the injection site and stowed his implements.

Genny and Liam came closer. My son had been crying; his face bright red and eyes nearly swollen shut. Genny's face paled in the brighter light near the windows. "We're here, Isabel. Everythin' will be fine, darlin'."

"Nooooo…!"

I slept.

When my eyes opened in the near dark, I stirred. Sitting upright on the side of the bed I eyed the master bedroom's toilet door and made a goal to reach it, while standing. My legs felt wobbly and my hands quaked with a life of their own. I leaned onto the bed and followed the edge until I could catch the corner of the Welsh dresser. From that point, the wall sufficed to keep me balanced.

I gratefully made the loo. I washed my hands, while seated, in the wash basin and dried them on my gown. I lifted the hem and wondered who undressed me. It didn't matter. Nothing did.

"Isabel?" Genny's voice neared.

"In the loo," I answered, sounding like a drunken sailor.

She appeared in the doorway. "I was only away for a moment, to check on Liam, darlin'." Her normal tone forced itself from her mouth.

"How's he?" I managed.

She glanced away. "Distraught, love. Let's get you back to bed." She reached out her hand for my arm.

I held out my palm to her, words muddling in my brain and mouth. "Give me a minute." Tears coursed down my face and neck. "Alright, I'm alright. I can rise from here…and get to the bed." I stood with help from the washstand. "Bring my lad to me, please." I took a deep breath, fighting to keep my eyes open long enough to make the journey.

"When you're safely tucked away, I will, lass. I just thought you'd both rest better in your own rooms. Liam's like Cullum. His heart's shattered, and there's nothin' said can offer him solace." She kept hold of my arm.

"Aye, he is…his dad's son." I wept, edging round the bureau to the end of the bed. Leaning my weight forward, I inched along the mattress to where my pillows beckoned. Finally, after what my body felt was hours, I collapsed.

Genny pulled the sheet over me and tucked the blanket at my hips. She laid her soft hand on my wet cheek. "I'll return in a flash with our fine lad." She left me.

The bed moved with Liam's weight. He crawled across to lie down at my side. We held hands and he cried, pressing his face into my shoulder. I passed out again, though struggling for a clear mind. I think I said something to him, but it failed logic.

I opened my eyes at another's presence. Caleigh hovered, watching a monitor. She must have noticed I was awake.

"Hello there, Isabel." Her voice was happy. "I'm here to keep you hydrated." She swept her soft hand over my hair, as a mother comforting a child.

She must not know my world shattered.

"Caleigh…." I dozed, but not before I felt her firm touch on my arm as she disconnected something.

I stirred again in a moment, as she packed her equipment. The curtain was slightly askew, casting a bright sliver of sunlight on her shimmering, straight blond hair.

She checked me again and smiled. "I'm goin' now. I love you. I'll check in later today with Genny." I felt her lips pressed on my cheek.

I think I nodded.

When my eyes opened again, a slice of sunlight shot through a crack in the curtain. Dust motes danced at the intrusion. I tried to remember who I was and where, but I knew for certain it didn't matter anymore.

Do I believe Cullum killed Bradley? 'I hoped never to hear his name, especially from your lips.' We were at Min's, on the settee. My first night back. But could he feel such jealousy and rage to kill a man who was as much a pawn as we had been, in my father's scheme?

I felt my son's heat, curled up at my side. I turned to glance down at his dark wavy hair. *No, Cullum would never risk losing Liam.*

The next step was legal assistance. I fought the fog in my brain to recollect who the criminal solicitors were here in the Northern provinces. A thought flitted through, barely leaving a contrail. Evan Mitchell, Leah's grandson. As soon as my mouth worked again, I'd ask Genny to call his office.

I slept.

Genny combed my hair back from my face with her fingers. "How're you feeling, darlin'?"

I opened my eyes, knew where and who I was, for the first time in…how long?

"What day is it?"

She rubbed my arm. "It's been three days, love. You need to eat and drink. We can't have you dehydrate. Caleigh's come by twice a day to give you fluids."

"I'll get up, then." I pushed myself up, leaned against the headboard, feeling the slight sting of an IV port in my left arm.

"Liam's in the shower."

"Right, that sounds wonderful."

"First we need to make sure you're steady on your feet. You've been sedated twice and it may leave you dizzy." She held out a tumbler with liquid. "Drink up. It's a glucose mixture that Caleigh left when she was here earlier."

I took a tiny sip. "Too sweet, but not bad." I tilted the glass again and let the liquid fill my arid mouth.

Genny smiled. She pulled a curtain back, so the light brightened both our prospects and the room. We sat and studied the temporary sunlight for a few moments in silence.

"Isabel, I've never understood your relationship with my son. To all but Minerva, it seemed—a bit strange." She kept one hand on me, as though I'd startle and vanish.

"How so?" I sipped more of the syrupy mixture.

A sad, nostalgic smile warmed her face. "Remember meeting at his sixth birthday party? He played with the boys. Min and David arrived, with you in tow, holding your hands on each side. Min introduced you to Robin and me. We talked for a moment, before Cullum noticed David was there. He left the lads and ran towards our cluster. He spotted you and stopped. I watched. I wanted to know how he'd react, when he saw Uncle David holding your hand. My brother was my son's favorite person in the whole world.

"He walked our way slowly, studying you. I supposed he was curious and bent down to introduce the two of you. Min knelt beside, to watch your interaction, and knew something rare was happening between you. Cullum took your hand and led you away to the swings, talking all the way. You climbed onboard and he pushed you until you were going very high and laughing. Then he took the one beside you and the two of you soared, as high as those swings would go."

We sat wordlessly for a moment, recalling that sunny day, filled with good things. I smiled. A strange feeling, that. "I remember. He always did tha'. When I learned his strategy, I laughed sooner. Then he could swing longer." My eyes filled, chin tremoring.

She rubbed her face and sighed. "When you left him, I thought he'd be alright after a while, recover his strength and get over your affair, your marriage. I always hoped he'd find someone he could love. But he was only half a man, there was no you to make him complete." She frowned my way.

"Gen, I existed on a different plain, being apart from Cullum. Liam became the motivating force in my life, until I realized my compulsion could damage him forever. After Daddy died, I decided to make an attempt to communicate with Cullum, if nothing else for Liam's sake. Aunt Min shushed me when I brought it up. I asked her for an address to mail a letter, so that if your son chose to ignore me I could pretend I'd never written. Much easier to accept the rejection in a fantasy world." I sipped the juice, feeling a bit refreshed physically but my heart was more forlorn.

Gen stirred. "After the first several years, he was prepared for you to come home. He and I attended Arthur's funeral together. I was concerned he might fall apart at the sight of you, so close but unable to touch. Later he told me of the many times he's watched you covertly in Edinburgh. I think he may have died had he not been able to see you."

"The man I was forced to marry was in odd circumstances. Bradley was not a woman lover. We were never intimate." I watched the sunlight for a moment. "He was in this house for dinner last week." I studied the ceiling a moment and choked back the tears. "Just to touch his fingertips, while Cullum blessed our meal, felt strange. He couldn't back away fast enough. That was our relationship. I revolted him. After meeting Bradley, my husband understood."

Genny patted my arm, scrutinizing dust particles navigating the transient sunshine. "Still, he's jealous for you, Isabel."

"The day we remarried, he reminded me we were made to be together, that neither can be whole without the other." I sipped the juice. "He's right. Away from him was like—being unplugged. My spirit was crushed. There was little laughter and the only love I knew was our son. Liam broke my heart with every smile, every tear, so like his dad. He was Cullum incarnate and I had to live with the memory of our love every waking moment." I looked away and fought the sorrow parked off to the left side of my mind. I turned up the glass and drained it, allowing the thick liquid to coat my throat.

"Well, then, other half of my son, how are we going to handle this newest development?" Genny rose from the bedside.

"We'll do the best we can, for now. Whatever transpires, we'll be alright. He didn't kill Bradley. I know him. He couldn't have done what they say. I don't understand what's happening, but I have to believe—it'll work out. There are ways—well, I'll not see him in prison—as long as there's breath in me." I slammed the door on sadness. Time to put my happy on and get to work.

Chapter 15

Liam and I sat at the kitchen banquette for a bite to eat. We faced one another, saying nothing, as Kent and Genny prepared food.

Kent had checked on Cullum. "He sends his love and says you both will be fine, as you've survived thus far. I thought I could reword the message but then, it doesn't seem fair to tell you somethin' he didn't actually say. He'd just returned from bein' interrogated. The inspector who was here has been removed from the case."

Kent laid a bowl of soup in front of each of us. I inhaled the aroma and felt queasy.

I must eat.

A glance at my son showed my sentiment reflected. We both took cautious sips of hot broth. It tasted good to my mouth, but my heart and stomach weren't ready for the assault. Still, for Liam and the tiny one I shared my body with, I must eat.

"Genny, did you call Evan Mitchell to see to Cullum?"

"He was going this morning." She turned a haggard look from the sink.

"You need to rest." I slid down on the banquette. "Come, sit. Kent, a bowl of soup for Genny, please."

"Aye, ma'am." He saluted, over a disarming smile.

As Genny sat beside me, Kent placed a bowl before her and returned in a moment with a loaf of Italian bread, torn into pieces. Liam dove for the crusty bread to dip into his soup and began making headway.

Patting my mother-in-law's thin thigh, I tried to offer encouragement. "Eat, we'll see what the next steps are for Cullum. Evan can request bail. If denied, we'll see what strings can be pulled for reconsideration."

She nodded and raked her hands through her greying dark hair. "It's been denied already."

"I'll make a few calls and see where the power players are located. If we can't get him out temporarily, we'll try another avenue."

She turned her tired eyes my way. "They denied bail for fear he'd flee the country, as you have the means to get him out if you decide to lam."

"Tha's true. I may have to freeze my assets to convince the court...." I sat back and turned my face to the shore of Moray Firth.

"What, Isabel?" She propped her hand on my shoulder.

I shook my head. *Bradley was killed, and Cullum implicated, because the dark queen pulled strings. By freeing himself of Bradley, Damian could still position his master, or mistress, to advantage.*

Mumbling, I shared my thoughts. "I think I see where this is going. I thought I understood what was happening, that if we just rid ourselves of AIM Enterprises, all would be well. It's more complicated. It's not Cullum they're destroying, it's me, one brick at a time. If I freeze the assets, they can stage a hostile takeover. If I fail to follow the game plan, they'll take another brick out of the foundation. Erode all that I hold dear."

How can I circumvent disaster with this game afoot? I must know their next move. Who can I trust?

"You speak of it as though it's sport." Genny took a small portion of bread.

"To them, it is. To us, it's life." I glanced back at Liam.

His eyes widened. "Mum, are we goin' to be alright?"

I nodded, sipping soup, and pondered an attack on their lair. I wasn't sure who was involved, other than Damian. I imagined the match far too complex for Naomi to mastermind. My guess was she was a pawn, as well. The possibilities narrowed to one source...Sir William Carmichael. He was the only other shareholder who stood to gain or lose control. Domination of AIM was worth billions, pound sterling.

Four years earlier I was smart enough to move my shares to a private agent, to give me a bit of leverage with the board and Sir William, in particular. I had no idea it would come to this unwieldy end.

I could loose my portion onto the open market and send the price into a tailspin. The next step was to find brokers who hadn't been pinned up by the power players in the UK. I considered my contacts, certainly limited, but there were two men and one woman who might take the bait. If the board caught on to the plot, a court injunction could stop me. Perhaps enough would be accomplished before they discovered my plan. Then there was an international estate agent who pestered me on a regular basis to sell property. I was about to make his dreams come true.

Daddy's money was finally going to a good cause…my sanity and welding my family back together.

"Genny, talk to Robin about selling the stock Min left you. I might have a way to get out of this mess. I might need it, or not."

"What're you going to do?"

I whispered. "Go public." I ruffled Liam's hair and sighed. *This may prove to be mildly entertaining, as well. I could use a bit of fun.* I kept my voice to a mumble. "Kent, I'm going to need a secure phone line. I'm not convinced anything here *is* secure. Do you have a friend, out of town, but nearby, who'd let me use their home, as an office for a few days?"

He pondered my request a moment. "Aye, think I may. I know someone in…."

I held up my hand and shook my head. "Not here."

Chapter 16

"Amaya Fumiko, please." I held the phone away from my ear as traditional Japanese music played on the speaker.

I ditched my personal cell phone in a dustbin in Inverness, before dropping Genny and Liam, and picked up new phones, taking the time to transfer necessary numbers. At least I could be sure they weren't bugged.

Conversations might still be monitored, if anyone could get within range—of a bothy—in a paddock in Wales.

I'd driven down in Min's beater as far as Blair Atholl and left it, key in the ignition. After taking the train back north, at the station in Aviemore, I caught a ride with a hired car headed back south. He dropped me near a bus terminal in Glasgow. From there I leased a car, driving to Kent's old girlfriend's grandmother's little cottage that her family kept for holidays.

"This is Amaya Fumiko." My old boarding school roommate's voice was welcome.

"Isabel Fielding, how are you?"

She squealed with delight. I held the phone away until her fit passed. "Girl! I'm fantastic, and you?" Her English was excellent, with a slight accent, but she could pass for a British subject.

"Worse for wear, at the moment. I need a huge favor."

"Anything."

"I want to sell my shares in AIM, covertly."

"Ooooh, that'll take a little work. How many?"

"All, everything. I don't care what the price becomes, start with current value, but if you must dive, do. Just flood the market."

"The value will tank if we push the controlling shares onto the public at one time."

"Exactly my plan. So, if you can share our secret with your partners....Small blocks to loads of individual clients. Do you know Sir William's agent in Japan?"

"I do."

"Avoid him. If you can sell everythin' in the next twenty hours, it would be good. After that, it's too dangerous."

"Are you secreting this information from a remote private island?" She giggled, another of her annoying habits.

"No such thing, Amaya. If I have a daughter this time, I'll name her after you, will tha' do?"

She squealed again. "You're expecting! Oh, I can't believe it. I just came back from maternity leave with my son. Really missed the rat race here. Okay, let me work on your request, quietly spread the word and I'll let you know when I have a solid plan."

I gave her my new cell numbers and rang off. Tokyo would activate while the players slept. I knew Sir William checked the market on rising, around five. Hopefully enough would be sold to tip the scale and make a difference in power structure. Next, South America and the US. I sighed and dialed the number, gazing out the speckled window, at lovely wildflowers blowing, sunshine beaming. I'd take a walk in a bit, completely alone.

"Tom Fenton."

"Tom, Isabel Fielding, I need a favor...."

An hour and a half later, I found myself on hold, waiting for Felix Mancura to come on the line. At least the Spanish music was lively. I stepped out a rhumba on the creaky oak floor and a cha-cha on the worn linoleum.

"Isabel, dahling!" Felix fancies himself a young version of Riccardo Montalbán.

"Felix, how good of you to take a moment to answer your phone. I'm ready to sell." I perused the list in front of me.

"Which properties, my love?"

A shiver passed over me at the term of endearment. No one has ever had that liberty, but Cullum. "Everything outside of Scotland."

"The market's slow in Spain and Greece for the villas. It may take a bit of time and...."

"Aye, well, I'll take half the appraised value. Will tha' help you move them?"

I smiled, imagining him barely dressed, an actress or model lounging in his pool, or his bed, purring, "Please, Felix, return to me."

His voice lowered. "I'll wire money for all four properties today. I will sell them over time, but there is no reason to let them go for *so* little, Isabel. If you really need the funds, consider this a loan on the balance those luxurious homes will bring."

"If you want them, you may have them for half the appraised value. I accept your offer. I'll fax you permission and a contract. You have my new address?"

"No, my sweet, let me get a pen."

I heard a soprano voice murmuring in the background, just as I suspected.

I gave him the address to Aunt Min's cottage in Nairn and disconnected. The money would go into trust in a numbered account in Switzerland, but might have to be the nest egg we'd need to start over—someplace else.

My jacket hung on a rusting hook, on back of the painted door with its green-tinted skin shed in chunks. I grabbed my coat and slipped out, walking briskly across the paddock avoiding piles of poo on my merry way to nowhere. I inhaled the sun-crisped air and realized it had been three weeks since I'd been for a run on the shore.

I wondered about my lover, how he fared, what he felt and ached for our temporary separation.

At least our son was safe, at a b&b in Inverness, with his gram. My concern for Cullum was that the long arm of the players could reach inside a cell.

Slowing my steps, I surveyed the area. The scenery was breathtaking. Autumn on this isle is stunning. The burnt orange, carnelian, and gold leaves riot against deep, dark green fir trees. Chilled breezes pushed me along in haste for a few moments, before my invaded warmth became immune.

I trod the crest of the hill up to the summit and studied the surrounding countryside. The roar of the burn in the valley below echoed in the silence of the meadow. Late blooming wildflowers grew in clumps. Hearty stuff, that, to avoid the sheep and the fierce, harsh weather.

Carefully, I scaled down the hill to the water and followed along the embankment, back towards my little hideaway. October was upon us, with its promise of winter biting my cheeks. It felt wonderful to be outside stirring, with no point to my journey.

I kept along the mossy edge, peering into the crystal clear roiling water, skirting boulders and felled trees. Inhaling the fragrance of rotted leaves and a whiff of distant peat fires made me smile.

Clearing my mind of troubles, I spread my arms and embraced, in a figurative sense, God's resplendent creation.

He made this moment for me to enjoy. So, I did.

***

Propped in the soft feather bed, I opened one of Min's diaries. In 1986, I was five. Her handwriting brought familiar warmth to my, otherwise, disrupted existence.

Mrs. MacDougle phoned today. Arthur left yesterday for the continent, on business. Naomi has locked Isabel in the cellar again. I called Arthur's office to get a message to him, but received no reply, as yet. David offered to go by and see to it, but Naomi will only take her wrath out upon her cook and my baby.

We'll wait for Arthur to deal with his wife. In the meantime, I pray my child is not frightened. The last time I was in the cellar was more than two decades past, before Arthur installed the wine vault. There were cobwebs everywhere.

Oh! I'm beside myself with worry. God, please let there be working lights. She's a smart lass and will find the switches easily enough. She's so afraid of dark!

I pondered the incident. Three more years of her terror were ahead for me, before making my escape to private school.

The dark was impenetrable, the chill and damp soaked through my thin dress. I found light switches and turned them all on, parking myself on the bottom step to survey the cellar. I had convinced myself that it was a new place to explore, on a previous visit. I searched through old magazines for anything to read.

An ancient trunk yielded its treasure of a moth bitten wool blanket and a musty satin pillow. I found an old stuffed chair under boxes and pushed it towards a light fixture suspended from the ceiling. I fluffed the pillow and covered myself. In moments, my chilliness dissipated and I read a *National Geographic Magazine*, sorting through words I didn't know.

At tea time, Mrs. MacDougle opened the cellar door with her handful of keys on a chain she wore at her plump waist. She found me in the dusty, worn chair.

She spoke, barely above a whisper. "There, there, wee one. I brought yer tea, now."

She leaned over me, raking my wild hair away from my face with her rough fingers.

"Yer mam don't ken I'm down here. Are ye alright?"

I nodded and stretched. The tray was filled with goodies. Naomi would be disappointed thinking she punished me by banishing me from her presence.

"I called yer auntie. She said to tell ye she loves ye and she'll try to get ye outta here."

"I'm fine, really. Though there's no bath. I can sleep here and the lights are on. If you bring me food, there's no need for anyone to worry."

Tears filled her eyes. "Poor bairn, ye haven't any idea how wrong this is, do ye? Darlin', God intended children for sunlight and playin', not sittin' in a dungeon, tryin' to survive a maniac."

I smiled. "She *is* loony, eh? I just wish Aunt Min could've been my mam." I ate my favorite tiny sandwiches, filled with prawn mayo and crisp sliced cucumbers from the hothouse.

She listened intently for a moment. "I better scoot back up, the missus will be lookin' fer me and tha' won't do. I'll be back to check on ye in a couple of hours. I'll leave the door unlocked, fer yer escape, if needs be." She lifted the hem of her long black dress and hied up the steps.

Listening for the lock to snap into place, she held true. I wasn't trapped in this miserable place. I'd stay put, as it would cost her job and I'd lose an ally on premises. Aunt Min couldn't be everywhere.

After eating all the goodies on the tea tray, I closed my eyes and dreamed she'd been my mum and Daddy my da and we lived happily ever after.

I opened Min's diary again, to the following entry:

Arthur finally called late last evening and told me he was on his way home. Pray, God, he doesn't find Naomi with one of her lovers. She usually meets her men away from our family home, but I found her poolside with one, earlier this summer.

David, Isabel, and I returned from an outing, to discover Naomi and a studly lad skinny-dipping. Isabel and David waited in the foyer, for my return, so thank God; the child wasn't witness to my sister's debauchery.

A thousand times daily, I repent for giving my innocent lass over to Naomi. A thousand times daily, I squelch the longing to be Isabel's mother, in more than the biological sense.

I told David, after he proposed, that Isabel was my child. He shares my concern for her and realizes I have no recourse, but Arthur's favor. How I hate our circumstances, but David's a gift from my heavenly Father. Finally, someone shares my secret.

I closed the book and thought about that hateful time. *So Naomi had already taken lovers.* That explained why she wanted me out of the way. Mrs. MacDougle lost her job at the mansion, a few years later, but Daddy kept her on payroll, to open his homes, when we traveled. She retired the year before his passing.

I snuggled into the feather bed, pulling the down comforter over my chilly frame. The peat fire had burned out in the hearth and the damp cold began to settle inside. I took small comfort that, perhaps, the dark queen received justice that day.

I slept.

Chapter 17

I drove a rental, secured from a friend, into town for a few necessary items for the second time in ten days. I pulled a woven hat low on my brow and ducked into a market, snagging a basket. The veg aisle offered seasonal carrots, beets, broccoli, and greens. I loaded the cart and located almond milk, almond oil, rice vinegar and sea salt. The only things I brought from home were tea and biscuits. I fetched a fresh loaf of whole grain bread and a bottle of juice.

The clerk smiled as I handed over cash. "Have a good day, miss."

"Thank you kindly, you as well." I returned the pleasant look and departed. The village of Cwm in Gwent County is home to almost 3,000 people. Small enough to elude much interest from the busy world, large enough for a stranger staying nearby to evade notice.

Cranking the older model Ford Escort, I drove slowly through the village, taking in the shops and reveling in a moment of almost human contact.

I stopped at a crossing to allow a tiny, bent figure to push her rolling walker across the lane, grocery bag tied to the front. I could practically smell her attar of rose parfum and the moth balls from her hall closet. She waved a wrinkled hand my way and I returned the favor, with a smile.

After a week, more than two-thirds of my stock in AIM Enterprises traded, at an extreme loss. Deposits from the sales and Felix, made into a numbered account, had cleared. All was quiet. Liam was safe. Cullum communicated through Kent daily. Still, no word came from a judge, reconsidering bail.

The trail up to the bothy was fraught with holes and ruts. I drove slowly, dodging all in my power. Parking in front, I unloaded the back seat of the small car and carried my provision inside. There was no lock on the doorway, disconcerting at first, but I was almost accustomed to the insecurity. After all, who would want in but sheep?

My purchases covered the small wood table in the kitchen.

I longed to go home, but knew the house was still bugged and I was still a person of interest in the near downfall of AIM. Sir William now held power. I wish I could've handed him the reins years ago. But there were clauses in the trust to adhere to, besides I wanted the money to go to the rightful heir...Scotland.

Stirring a few drops of rice vinegar into my medley of veggies, I relished the simple act of being in a world gone mad with greed. I was finally an ordinary woman, with limited means. Unfortunately, my limited means was sitting in a cell in Inverness.

My phone rang. "Hullo, Kent."

"No' Kent, Bel." Cullum's voice made my heart yearn for his touch.

"How are you, my love?"

"Well, and you?" He sounded strong.

"Good, safe for now. My part in the family business was sold, at least enough, I no longer have controlling interest. I've dumped the foreign property. I'm exploring avenues of getting bail approved."

"Ah, the judge denied tha' again."

"I see. Well, is there anythin' I *can* do?" I sat at the small table in a rigid, folding chair.

"No' much at this point." He sounded so near.

I closed my eyes and breathed deeply. "I'm returning in three days. The furor is dying and I'll have to face Sir William soon."

"Tha' was brilliant, by the way. I'm sure he's in a stupor over the stock losing momentum so quickly."

"Well, serves him right. At least, we're no longer the target. He is, and how he deals with the dark queen is between himself and his maker."

He chuckled. "Aye, lass."

Silence fell between us. Was this all we had left?

He cleared his throat. "I'll let you be. Rest. There's still a long road ahead of us, Bel. It won't be easy."

"Has it ever been?"

He growled his answer. "Nay, but I canna stand for you to be bored."

"Life with you is anything but dull, Sinclair."

"Glad you feel that way. I'd better go, mo chroi."

My heart sank, and with it hope. "Right, take care and call me again? Or may I see you?"

"No need, Bel. I love you with all my heart." He ended the call before I could respond.

I checked my watch. The call lasted less than three minutes. Not time enough to trace. I sat there until after dark, my supper cold on the stove. I watched shadows play across the room when the wind picked up, bringing rain. Lightning fractured the gathering gloom and thunder echoed in response. Windows rattled. I rose and donned pajamas, ignoring lights, shuffling about in the murkiness complemented my mood...dismal.

Sleep came swiftly to the big soft bed I lay in, wrapped in a warm blanket and the fluffy comforter.

Morning dawned too soon. Chill ruled, as I failed to build a fire the previous evening. I wrapped in the blanket and hied to the other room, crouching before the cold hearth. I piled dry peat onto the grate and lit it with a long match. It sputtered for a moment then caught. Running back to the comfort of bed, I bundled back into the bit of heat left behind, warming my toes.

A half hour later, the entry door opened. Creak of rusty hinges gave away someone else's presence in the dank cottage. The floorboards squeaked beneath weight greater than my own. I reached below the pillow, beside the one I slept upon, for Uncle David's Glock. My hand encircled the familiar grip and the heft assured me I was safe. I sat straight up and waited for the culprit to show his face.

A hooded figure rounded the short wall of the bothy. He reached to push the damp covering off his head and glanced towards me, framed by the bedroom doorway. He paused to back up to the fire.

"I hope you don't need that, mo chroi." Beloved winked at me.

"Cullum? What're you doing here?" I bailed, leaving the weapon in its hiding place.

"Thought you sounded lonely last night. Figure it'd be better to put in an appearance." He turned to spread his hands in front of the small fire then reached for another batch of peat. "It's wet out there this mornin'."

My mouth must have hung open, because he extended his cold hand to my chin and pushed it closed.

"How're you out of jail?"

He scratched his unshaven neck. "I never was actually locked up. John just took me from Nairn and we finished our plan to push things into motion." He cut his eyes at me. "I'm sorry I couldn't tell you, love. It was better that everyone believes what they do. Even Da could give our secret away, without intending." He glanced around. "So, do you have food? What's for breakfast?"

I went back to the bedroom, slipped into clogs, pulled a wool jumper over my pajamas, and hied to the kitchen to light the stove. "My supper. I forgot to eat after we talked. Where'd you stay?"

He motioned towards the door. "Camped down next to the burn. The storm almost flooded me out. Slept damp, then woke to a roaring stream beside me. Decided you were up, when smoke from your fire became visible."

I crossed my arms. "Why'd you not come in last night?"

"Didn't get here before your lights were off. I didn't wanna startle you."

"Well you did." I flung a tea towel at him.

He caught it and chuckled. "Are you angry?"

"Am I angry? I believe the love of my life is rotting away in jail, worried sick you'd take a shiv in the ribs from a passing prisoner owned by the dark queen's cohorts. Am I angry?"

He took two steps and enclosed me in the shelter of his arms. "Sorry, love, it had to be this way. We couldn't take the risks or endanger you and Liam more than we had already."

"What about the knife, Cullum? You've never told me how they got a knife with your fingerprints on it." I pulled away in a pout and stirred the food in the pan.

"Teachin' Liam to cut fruit and veg, mo chroi. Anyone could've picked up a knife I'd used at the pub, like they were takin' it to the dishwasher. Somehow it wound up in Bradley's belly. It wasn't what killed him, though. He was strangled."

"So the knife was planted? Who works for you that would take a knife with your prints on it and give it to *them*?"

"Kent's on it, love. He and John're checkin' bank accounts now, to see who's makin' unusual deposits."

"I thought Inspector Cooley was off the case."

"Officially he is, so Bernie doesn't ken wha's happenin'."

"Please, start at the beginning." I scooped up warmed veggies and sat a plate in front of my husband.

"Well, it's long and tedious." He filled his fork and then his mouth.

"I have nothin' but time." I picked at broccoli and peppers on my own plate.

"You're more than annoyed?" He almost smiled, but stopped himself.

"Aye, and hurt tha' you feel you canna trust me with the truth."

He lowered his fork and sat back. "Love, it's never been about trust. How could you act to Liam, as though this awful thing happened and his dad was in jail?" He studied me a moment. "Could you've convinced him that I was charged with murder? I didn't ken it would affect you like it did. I apologize for the three days you had to be sedated. But I saw no other way around our problem. The house is bugged, our every breath, recorded." He glared at me and grasped my arms. "Talk to me."

"How'd you convince John that the knife was planted?"

"I didn't, it was too pat. Had it been the murder weapon, we'd have been in a fix. I took pictures with my phone each time I returned to a job and the knife I'd used disappeared. It happened a dozen times or more, in the past four months. Occasionally, it was carried to the dishwasher. I recorded those events, as well. Each photo was date and time stamped. John saw them. He came by the pub twice a week to check my phone."

"You've known you were bein' positioned to take the fall for this?"

"Not this in particular, just somethin'. I didn't tell you because…I couldn't."

Chapter 18

"Couldn't? As in, my mouth didn't work tha' way, my mind went blank at your beauty, I haven't found the right time...?" I became louder, as my indignation grew.

"Aye, all those." His cool grey eyes studied me. "Part of me doesn't ken how to separate life with you from the rest." He sighed. "Bel, some things are in the works, with the election looming. Scotland *must* be able to provide her own security, with no weakness evident to England's Prime Minister. You ken?"

"Makes sense, it'd be to our failing to leave England with the idea we can't function without their oversight." I crossed my arms and relaxed a tiny bit.

"Well, a group of us, having been trained in military intelligence and security measures, have formed a cohesive unit. We educate and train young men and women. We'll act as home guard in case of emergencies. We're to back up the men and women in police and military units." He paused, gazing past me, out the specked window, at the paddock. A small herd of sheep grazed just beyond the rental car.

I lowered my voice. "I ken it would be difficult to discuss, in light of the house under surveillance and the press of people coming and going. It's hard to have a few moments alone that aren't spent...well, otherwise."

He grinned. "Aye, I like the otherwise just fine, prefer it to what I'm saying now. I joined the group reluctantly, hoping you'd come back to me. Now that you're home, it's hard to get excited about a project that endangers you and Liam. I'm tryin' to back away from the responsibility."

We sat in silence for a few minutes. He fingered his fork, balancing the handle on the rim of the plate. It rocked precariously then settled, while Cullum found the words he needed.

"So, tha's where it is, without going into details." He glanced around for something missing. "Where's your weapon?"

"In the bedroom. Why?" I rose to fetch the Glock 17 from under my pillow.

191

"Keep it handy. We're about to merge our difficulties, lass. Have a weapon nearby until this is over."

I scurried to the bedroom, in obedience, grasped the pistol, and was on my way back to the kitchen. "Is Kent part of your organization?"

"Aye, he and his brother are invaluable—bein' identical twins."

My steps froze. "I didn't know they were." I pondered my lack of knowledge, returning to the hard chair.

"Impossible to tell them apart, unless you pay close attention." He smiled.

"How often did they change shifts while watchin' me?"

"About every two hours or so, unless you were on the road."

"Wish you'd told me."

"They didn't want you to know. Said it gave them good practice imitating each other."

"So, what happens next?"

"You've burned your bridges with the company?"

"For the most part. I didn't sell your parents' shares. The price dropped too sharply. I now own less than Genny and Robin. It puts the ball in Sir William's court." I left my chair. "The money's hiding in a numbered account in Switzerland, along with the dismal proceeds of the property sales."

"Why've you kept it?"

"Liam." I settled my hand on my mound of belly. "And this one. What'd I do if you were wrongly imprisoned?"

"I apologize for tha', lass. You may rid yourself of the burden, now."

I smirked at his arrogant remark. "Thank you kindly, sir, for permission."

He threw back his head and laughed. "You're welcome." He glanced around the bothy and back to me. "I need to bathe, shave, and brush my teeth. Have you a privy in this place?"

"Aye, come along I'll show you. You'll wanna build a fire before undressing." I led the way through the bedroom to an enclosed porch with a hearth at one end, beside an incinerating toilet. A rickety shower enclosure stood to one side.

He grinned and kissed my forehead. "Ta, Bel. I'll rejoin you in a bit. Be kind, darlin'. Get over your ire. I'm makin' love to you in that bed, within the hour."

He closed the door and left me standing there in my pajamas, still smoldering.

***

I lay against Cullum's side, spent. We'd sated ourselves with each other most of the morning, but I needed to move about. Our child awoke, kicking.

"Wha's this?" He laid his hand against my tummy, smiling.

"Our bairn."

"When did it begin?" His smile dissolved.

I dropped my gaze. "I woke to activity the third day after you left us." I tried to roll away but he reached out and held me back.

"Talk to me, Bel." He sighed. "I'm sorry I wasn't there."

"Liam joined me late, on the second day. I woke to movement the following day. I was well enough to walk to the kitchen and we had soup. Genny sat with us and Kent hovered nearby and I made a plan, in my mind at least." I met his eyes, honestly. The pain was still real, a chamber of my heart rent.

The hurt and regret in his voice brought tears to my eyes. "Mo chroi, I am sorry. I wanted to celebrate that day with you. I promised myself and you that everythin' about this pregnancy would repay all I missed with Liam. Now I'm missing this child as well."

"Life's a tradeoff at this point. You can't abandon Scotland and be a father and husband round the clock." My voice sharpened. "I need the loo, may I move now?"

He released me from his grasp, but followed me with his eyes as I rolled off the bed and strolled past, making for the toilet.

We walked in the afternoon's hazy sunshine. The valleys held onto their dense fog through the day. It would burn off by nightfall. Cullum held onto my looped arm, my hand stuffed in my jacket pocket.

193

"When do you leave?" I hated the answer, no matter how long our Utopia lasted.

With a sidelong glance, he answered curtly. "I can stay with you, Bel. We'll just have to work remotely."

"I need to fetch Liam, let Genny go home to Robin and the farm. What of our son?"

Cullum glanced behind us. "I can't guarantee safety. Would he not fair better with Mam and Da?"

"You can't guarantee safety there either, my love." I pulled my hat lower over my eyes, as a shield from the brightening light.

"Alright then. I'll situate the two of you in an isolated place and work from there. You don't need to confront Carmichael, Bel. Let the sleeping dog lie in his mess for now. The repercussions'll come soon enough."

"Liam also needs to be part of our pregnancy, so that he feels he's not bein' excluded and abandoned."

He raked his free hand over his well-trimmed beard. "Aye, he does." He sighed into the crisp breeze.

"Cullum, we're a family. If we don't come out of this mess, we go down together. If one or another is left behind, the loss is greater because of time we failed to spend together." I shrugged my shoulders and rolled them back. The soft bed was ruining me.

Squinting, he locked gazes with me. "You've convinced me, lass. We'll pack and leave from here today. I have a safe house we can take shelter in for now."

I nodded.

We walked on in silence for another hour across the paddock. At the crest, we enjoyed the view of the farmhouse in the valley, then returned to the bothy by skirting the burn and climbing the hill.

We arrived cautiously. Cullum went a few paces ahead to scout the path. He nodded the all clear and we entered quietly. I took a few steps inside and shed my coat. He stayed clad and started to the back for his dried rucksack and bedroll.

He carried all our gear to the Ford Escort, loading through the hatch. "Where'd you rent the car?"

"Glasgow, from a friend of a friend who trades used vehicles."

"You can drive us back then. Deposit me at Queen's Park Railway and I'll pick up another hired car while you're away. I can fetch you from your drop-off."

"He's only two blocks from the station, on Victoria Road. I can walk." I gathered the remainder of our supplies and left for the car.

His manner shifted. "Become accustomed to hearing this, mo chroi: no." He opened my door and shooed me inside, rounding the vehicle to the passenger side. "Don't fight me, Bel. It'll make these next few weeks much harder."

"I wasn't fighting, only attempting to make things easier for you."

"I'll determine ease. You get us to Glasgow. You'll head to Inverness for Liam and have Kent accompany Mam home. Hopefully, we'll make our hideout by nightfall." He watched me for a response.

"Aye, aye, sir." I tossed a salute into the mix.

He burst out laughing. "I love you, lass." He glanced out the window. "Bel, I've never had the choice of lovin' you. It just was—has always been. Almost like being born into it, as much a part of me as my eyes." He quietened for a time. "I'm sorry for draggin' you into all this. I'd do anythin' to make it different."

"What'll your organization do if we don't win our freedom from England? I'm sure you heard the Queen's address to Parliament on May 8th ...though we haven't discussed it." I swerved each pothole and rut, trying to stay on the track.

"I won't entertain the thought, love. However, bein' a realist is a difficult thing. We'll go on as we've done for 700 years, but with a spot more pride in who we are. The days of apologizin' for bein' Scottish are past."

Chapter 19

Once we arrived in Glasgow, the swap of rented vehicles proceeded smoothly. My phone chirped and I left the vestibule of John's building for the street, where Cullum double parked in a Ford Taurus.

We found a room for the night on the outskirts of the city. Traffic was lighter the following morning.

We drove to Inverness, making a stop outside city limits. We entered a pub, my hand tucked in beloved's bent arm. He held the door for me to step inside. It took a moment for my eyes to adjust to the dim light. I heard the smack of balls on the snooker table before I could make out where the players were standing.

The noise that was evident when we entered, lessened as the natives looked us over.

Cullum's deep voice boomed. "Hayo!" He steered me to the bar, his hand in the small of my back.

The publican leaned forward, squinting. "Cullum!"

"Aye, Benjie, how're you then?" He seated me and shook hands with the barkeep. "This is my wife, Isabel. Benjie's an old chum, mo chroi."

I extended my hand. Benjie, a lady's man at first glance, beamed a toothy grin and took it in his large paw. "I had no clue this man could land such a dish."

"Yah, yah. What'll you have, love?" Cullum perched on the stool beside me.

"Um, might you keep juice?"

My husband grinned, keeping his gaze on me. "She's drinkin' for two, ol' man. Pour us up a glass of your finest pomegranate, if you keep a jug."

"And you?"

"House ale, please."

"You would, since it's your own."

"Only the best will do."

My lover turned away and studied the snooker game, which had resumed. His chin rose twice, so I assumed he kenned the lads at play.

The pub was newer by several hundred years than Jacobite's Folly. The bar's thick wooden counter was gullied in places from the many thousands of bent elbows resting upon it over the centuries. Likewise, shallow trenches were evident on the other side. The gloss had faded long ago.

Cullum laid his hand on my arm and leaned to my ear. "You'll go on from here and fetch Liam. Tell Mam I'm alright and don't worry. Kent has instructions to take her home." He pulled out his wallet and handed me a roll of bills. "Pay Tom and Nancy and bring our son back here, then we'll go to a safe house."

"Alright." I tipped my glass of juice and sat the empty on the bar.

"Be careful, mo chroi. Eilidh is probably under surveillance. Tom may not even realize they're bein' observed. It'll be a professional unit handling the watch." He brushed a wisp of hair away from my cheek. "We'll switch vehicles on your return. Call my phone when you're near and I'll be waiting in the parkin' lot."

"What's your new number?"

He smiled indulgently. "In your phone. I replaced it while you were in the privy. Any other questions?" His hand worked its way from my knee to my thigh.

"Alright, we're only twenty minutes from the inn." I inhaled and leaned to his lips for a kiss.

He's very obliging in the way he makes it easy to meet him less than halfway. Once begun, it's hard to stop, with only one brief peck. Withdrawing, the look in his eyes was anything but wary.

I slipped off the stool and kissed him again then whispered, "I love you."

"And I you, my heart. Be cautious and alert." He slid down behind me and followed me to the door.

He stood, in the glaring light, until I pulled away.

The drive into Inverness was uneventful. The two lanes curve sensuously, round the mountains, alongside Loch Ness.

I parked in the pea gravel lot, in front of Eilidh Bed and Breakfast, on Glenurquhart Road. Cullum and I stayed with my friends, Tom and Nancy, two months earlier, returning to hospital for his final examination. We'd gone to dinner and dancing to celebrate his release from medical care.

Tom answered Eilidh's buzzer at the door. "Hullo, Isabel. Didn't know you were comin'."

"Aye, here to fetch my lad." I stepped into the tiny foyer. "Thank you for watchin' over them, Tom. You have no idea how much it's meant to me."

Nancy stepped out of their cozy apartment. "Isabel!" She hugged me briefly and patted my belly. "Hullo, you."

Liam poked his head through a doorway, opposite. "Mum!"

I opened my arms and received my boy. "Oh, Liam, I've missed you so much."

Genny followed, slipping into a cardigan. "Are you here for us, then?"

"Just Liam, Mam. I have a message for you, though." I couldn't keep the smile from my face.

"Come inside." Tom motioned for us to head into the rented room. "Get straight and I'll help you carry luggage outside. You shouldn't be liftin' anythin' in your state." Tom and Nancy ducked back into their apartment, leaving the door ajar.

"Then I shan't." I'd moved twice, while expecting Liam, but hadn't strained a muscle since.

I stepped inside the spacious room that Genny and Liam lived in for two weeks.

Genny packed and talked at the same time. "You're takin' Liam?"

"Aye, Kent's takin' you home."

She nodded, watching me expectantly. "And...?"

I whispered into her ear. "Cullum's fine. He's safe and said to tell you not to worry."

When I stepped back, she wiped her eyes and sniffed. "Thank God!"

I kept my voice low. "Yes. We're going to a safe house from here."

"Good, we'll have news of you?" Genny looked tired. It couldn't have been easy, being cooped up with Liam, though Tom or Nancy had taken them, daily, on jaunts and tours, to pass the time.

Almost whispering, I sought to offer her comfort. "I'll see to tha', but you have to remember, surveillance equipment is sophisticated these days. *They* could be listenin' right now." *Whoever they are.*

"Oh, aye, I'm sorry, I forget." She appeared harried.

"Not a problem." I patted her back with a smile. "Everythin' will work out soon." *I hope.*

I felt a heel lodge against my lower rib and reached for Genny's hand. She turned and followed to my belly.

Her mouth opened. Her eyes teared when she felt our bairn kick. "Another like his da." She glanced at Liam, shouldering his rucksack.

"Wha's going on?" He hurried around the end of the bed.

I took his hand and replaced Genny's, while she held his shoulders and whispered into his ear. "It's your brother, lettin' us know he's awake."

Liam's face split into a grin, as beguiling as Cullum's. "Mum tha's incredible!" He stilled and quietened, as though he could hear something from the wee one.

"I couldn't wait to share it with you." I squeezed him into my other side. "Now, le's get the two of you on your way. I'll tell Tom we're ready. Liam, take another look, especially under the bed for stray socks and such." I stepped through and across the hall to peek inside the open door.

Tom grasped three reusable bags, prepared for a trip to market. "'Lo, lass. How can I help? Ready to leave, then?"

"Aye, we are. I want to thank you both for all the care you've given Liam and Genny in my absence." Nancy stepped into the vestibule. I reached for her arm. "I ken you don't normally take children, but I thank you for takin' Liam. There was no other place that I could feel he'd be as safe as here with the two of you."

"Ah, well, you know, he's a good lad and much more mature than most twelve-year-olds, these days." Tom nodded, his chin set. "We've had teenagers now and again. They're messy, but they know to be quiet and respectful."

"Thank you, dear friends. I'll fetch them home now." I turned, Tom on my heels to carry bags. "Well, let's be off, shall we?" I hefted Genny's knitting tote and led the way.

Outside, Kent, who waited for us, left his car to help Genny settle. We placed her case in the back seat and Liam took his to Cullum's rental. He ran back to give Genny a big hug. I followed and hugged her again.

I whispered to her. "You can trust Kent. Hopefully, we'll see you soon."

Genny whispered back. "Give my son my love. I'll tell his da and brother."

"But they must keep up the charade." I chided her gently.

"Aye, tha' too. You take care of yourself and our baby, Isabel. You're in my prayers daily." She slid into the passenger's seat and Kent closed the door.

"Tell the boss I'll see you before dark."

I nodded and glanced around, heading back to the rental.

Keeping an eye on the rearview mirror, while navigating sharp curves on the carriageway, was a challenge.

"Why're you lookin' back, Mum? Is someone following us?" My lad turned his frown my way.

"Perhaps. I just wanna ken for sure."

I pulled over at the first layby and allowed traffic to flow past, until twelve cars passed us by. I pulled back onto the macadam and studied the vehicles ahead and behind. None looked as though our car held any interest for them. No one glanced back or turned in their seat.

"Are we safe?" Liam still scowled.

I reached for his thigh and squeezed, making light of the nuisance. "Of course, we're safe. We're going to meet your dad."

"Why didn't you tell me before now?" His face brightened.

"He's waiting for us ahead with another car. We'll switch off and go to a secret place."

"Tha' *you* don't even know about?" He was on board with the plan.

"I don't even know about it. I think it's a surprise your dad's planned for a while."

"So, he's no' really in jail?"

"No, he isn't."

"When did the police let him leave?"

"You'll need to speak to him about tha', lad." I snagged the phone and scrolled to the number Cullum entered and pushed call. It rang once before he answered. "We're near, eta five minutes."

"I'll be waitin'."

We rang off.

The car handled well. By that time, I was accustomed to its habits and how hard to brake. The steering pulled a little to the left.

I'm glad I had the time to learn its idiosyncrasies. When we rounded the next curve, there was a traffic backup. I slammed on brakes and automatically reached out to catch Liam, buckled snuggly into his seat. I sat back and loosened my grip on the steering wheel. We crept along two lanes for four minutes. I watched time ticking past and reached for the phone again.

"Look out!" Liam screamed, focusing beyond me.

I twisted away, as the driver's side window exploded.

Rough hands grabbed at me. I wrenched myself free and slammed on the petrol pedal, lurching forwards.

One of the two men, attempting to open my door, swore. "Damn!"

I caught a glance in the side view mirror, blood spurted from his arm. I reversed, at an acute angle, and pulled forward again, the car my only weapon. Uncle David's Glock was in the boot, safely inside my case.

The second man was about to round the front of the car, headed for Liam's door. I hit the petrol, snagging him with the front mudguard. A car, moving the opposite direction barreled down upon us, the driver's eyes widened as she braced for impact.

Bam!

The assailant was sandwiched between the mudguards of each car.

He screamed, "Aah!"

He pounded his fist on her vehicle.

The other driver reversed enough that the man dropped to the ground; he flinched and twitched as spasms dispersed through his crushed lower body.

Grabbing Liam's face I pulled him into my shoulder, now free of the harness. "Don't look!"

The man with the bleeding arm backed away quickly, turning to run towards his vehicle pulled off a layby behind us. I watched him move and thought there was something familiar about him. He sped past the wreck in the wrong direction. I failed to read his registration plate.

My bonnie boy shook and wept. It felt as though an eternity passed. I glanced at the dashboard clock to find we were three minutes late meeting Cullum. I reached for the phone again and rang.

"We're in a crash. Two men attacked us. The rental's wrecked. I don't know how badly."

Liam pulled away and stared dumbly out the front window, in shock.

"I'm almost to you, love. Take a deep breath. Are the bad guys gone?"

"In a sense. One's injured in the motorway. The other man's arm was cut open. It appeared to be an artery the way it gushed. He might make it into hospital."

Beloved's voice cooed, "Where's your weapon, Bel?"

"Boot—suitcase. I was with you, what could possibly happen I'd need it?" My hands were shaking so badly, I could barely hold the phone. "I must tend Liam."

"I'm parkin' nearby now." He responded.

I laid the phone down and held my son's chin. I spoke sharply. "Are you alright, Liam?"

He blinked and looked up. Tears flowed down his cheeks. "Mum?"

"Aye, lad?"

"I wanna go home." He pressed his face against my arm. "Please."

Cullum dashed into view making for us, straightaway.

"Here's your dad."

Sirens blasted in the distance.

Cullum opened the door and scooped Liam out, standing him on his feet. "Lad, look a' me."

Liam glanced up and wrapped his arms around his dad's neck. "It was *so* scary! They broke Mum's window. The man grabbed her. That man in the road was pinned between the cars!"

Cullum held our son, ducked and looked past, at me. "Bel, you alright?" A frown did nothing to brighten his paleness. He bit his lower lip.

"Aye, fine." I held my hands flat against my thighs to stop them shaking.

"Get outta the car, or do you need a checkover?" He straightened and pushed Liam back. "Let's see to Mum." Cullum slid into Liam's seat, keeping an arm around our son and reached for me. His voice gentled. "You have glass in your hair, lass."

I felt him pluck out shards and rested my cheek on his shoulder.

The sirens became a solid roar around us.

"So, they knew where Liam was all along and didn't snatch him. Who are they after, me?"

He whispered into my ear. "In their eyes you're more valuable, love."

I looked up. "And yours?"

"You're my heart, Bel. I can't keep breathin' without you." He didn't bother to wipe his eyes.

A paramedic approached. "Is anyone injured?"

Liam pointed to the man still in the middle of the carriageway. "He is." He looked back at me. "Are you alright, Mum? This man wants to know." He was through the worst of the shock, but each time he looked at the bundle of man in the road, he wrapped his arms around himself and shivered.

"What about the bairn?" Cullum placed his hand on my belly.

"Sleeping, I think." I wiped my face with my gritty hand and thought better of touching too near my eyes. "Ask the medic to check us, please. To be certain."

"Tha's best...to be assured. "Cullum climbed out and approached the second paramedic. "Please, take a look at my wife. She's about six months with child."

A young woman loped round the car to my side. She reached through. "Ma'am, are you feeling unwell?"

"No, but shaken. If you could just listen, be sure the bairn's heartbeat is strong?" I turned to Cullum. "Go. Hurry. Take Liam."

"I canna leave you, Bel."

"You must. I'll be fine."

"Randy's on his way. When he arrives I'll hand off Liam…."

"Go, Cullum. Your presence cannot be explained."

He nodded and gathered our lad to his side.

The paramedic spoke. "I'm opening the door. Give us a moment. Turn your head, please."

I looked left, across the car to my two men outside, Cullum kneeling to watch the process.

The door opened slowly, with a groan. The sound of glass slivers, pecking the pavement, followed.

I hissed. "Go, please!"

"I'll go. Come on, lad, we must leave now." He held Liam's shoulder.

"But we can't leave Mum."

"Liam, go with Dad, I'll see you in a bit."

"But, Mum…."

"Now!" I snapped.

Cullum steered our lad from the scene. They rushed towards his vehicle.

I watched them move away, stop, and turn back to me. I waved and put on a brave face.

"You may relax, ma'am." I glanced up at a lovely brunette wearing dark-rimmed glasses. She smiled. "Hi, I'm Jamie."

"Isabel Sinclair. I think everything's fine, but I need to be sure. I wasn't hurt in the impact. The airbag deployed and my belt locked, but I'm sure I'm alright." I babbled on until I ran out of breath.

"I'll lay your seat back and check on your bairn." She worked the lever and lowered the seat.

I stretched, once I relaxed. "This feels good. I ken you have an injured man out in the road but…."

"Shh," She shushed me quietly and listened.

Even in the midst of all the noise, you can hear a babe's heartbeat. I listened to Liam's every day. He was all I had, my only family, except for Aunt Min and she betrayed me.

Chapter 20

Following orders, I waited for police inside the car. Pounding footsteps approached the hired car at a lope. I glanced in the rearview mirror, recognizing the lanky figure of Randy Ross. He stopped to speak to the paramedics. Jamie assured him my scratches and scrapes were tended and the bairn fine.

He slid into the passenger seat, speaking loudly. "Well, sis, you did a great job this time."

"I'm not deaf." I watched him fold his long legs to fit in the seat beside me.

"Aye, Isabel. I'll stay with you and get you where you need to be, as soon as you're finished. You are my sister, after all." He patted my hand, resting on my thigh.

I noticed his puffy black eye and cut on his lip. "What happened to you? Run into a door?"

"You're husband's fist, actually." Randy glanced down. "Cullum didn't tell you?"

"No, what?"

"We had a run in over you." He brushed the front of his denims off, avoiding my eyes.

"Why?"

"Kent passed on the information about your collapse when Cullum left with the inspector the day of his arrest. I didn't feel he needed to hear it, so I didn't tell him until two days ago. I couldn't. Strategically we were committed. It would have foiled the plan, if he ran home to hold your hand." He cut a sidelong glance at my frown

I considered the new information for a moment. "You didn't tell him in order to protect him from my reaction?"

"Aye, tha's the way I saw it. He obviously didn't agree." He gingerly touched the cut on his swollen mouth.

I nodded after pondering his confession. "You did well, Randy. I should've trusted him and not lost hope. You made the right choice."

He smiled, a little lopsided near the puffy lip. "Ta, I thought so, too. Well, now I have my orders and it was stressed I'd better follow them to the letter. Tha' lass take care of you?" He jerked his thumb behind us.

"Jamie is her name, and yes, she did. Gentle touch, tha' one, sweet nature."

He nodded, short jerky movements. "I wanna ask her out. Am I too grubby?"

We both glanced over his denims and jumper. "I don't think so. When did you brush your teeth last?"

He blushed and straightened. "Rather personal, don't you think?"

"Wee brother, ladies prefer fresh breath to stale and have no desire to suppose you had onions at lunch."

He slipped out of the seat, kneeling outside, peering in, with a frown. "You're difficult, aren't you?"

"Look in my handbag, there in the floor. In the side pocket, you'll see Altoids and gum. You need 'em."

He dug around until he found the gum. "Thanks, sis. We'll name our first daughter after you. Wish me luck." He rolled the stick of gum and stuck it into his mouth, rising to his feet.

A policewoman waited outside the car to join me next. "Mrs. Sinclair?"

"That's me." I handed over my wallet with my police credentials and driving license, as she seated herself on the passenger's side.

"I'm Sergeant Bess Rogers. How're you today?"

"I've been better. Haven't killed anyone—ever before." I tried sarcasm to keep from erupting into tears.

She patted my arm. "It appears to be an accident. Don't shoulder that burden ." She glanced over my identification. "Ah, you're with Edinburgh Police?"

"Aye, I'm a scientist in the forensics division."

"Welcome to the Highlands."

"I'm from Nairn, so all this beauty is home to me." I smiled and inhaled the salt air.

"Can you tell me what happened?" She concentrated on her tablet and made notes.

"We stopped when traffic jammed. I was almost over the shock of braking quickly, to avoid a crash, when a man smashed my window. He grabbed at me. I goosed the petrol and shot forwards. He cut his arm on broken glass. The man with him headed towards my son. I reversed the car then drove headlong, striking him. Another vehicle slammed into mine, pinning him—between the two. Is he dead? I merely presume he died." I tightened my hands into fists.

Her voice softly coaxed responses. "Aye, did you know who these men were, love?"

"Never seen them before." I rummaged in my handbag for a hankie. *But the one who ran away....*

"Who was with you?" She took notes on an electronic pad.

"My son. A friend took him away, to his dad. He was too shaken, what with a dying man in the road in front of us. My brother's back there," I jabbed my thumb towards Randy. "He came immediately and is caring for me until he takes me home. That is, supposing he remembers."

She grinned. "Handsome lad, that one."

"Don't say it loudly, he may hear."

"What do you think those men wanted?"

"I can't imagine. Neither wasted time introducing themselves or their intentions. But it was evident they meant to do us...or me, harm."

She sighed and smiled. "Are you well enough to go with your brother, or do feel the need to go to hospital, so they can check you over?"

"Safety devises deployed. I'm fine. The paramedic examined me. I just need a loo and a tall cold glass of milk."

"I'll get out of your way, then. I have your phone number, if we have questions."

"Thank you." I turned to climb from the car.

Randy was at my side in a tick. "Well, sis, let's get you home and check on Liam, shall we?" He smiled at Jamie, winked, and patted his pocket. If I remembered right, that indicated she gave him her number.

Chapter 21

Randy turned off the carriageway onto a long uphill private road. We were still in the Highlands; it's all I knew for sure. A mile or so through rough terrain, we arrived in front of a log house. Cullum and Liam waited, blocking a splendid view of further mountains.

Beloved was at my door before Randy's Jeep stopped rolling. He unlatched the handle and offered his hand to help me out. I took it and curled up in his arms.

"You alright, Bel?" He kissed my hair and my neck.

"Aye, fine. The bairn's fine, too."

I felt Liam's arms around me from the back. "Mum, did that man die?"

Reaching behind, I grasped his arm. Cullum loosened his hold on me to tend our lad. I gazed into Liam's dark grey eyes, cupping his face, and nodded. "He did, the policewoman told me, on the way to hospital." I failed to keep the incident filed in its compartment under the label *deal with that when you have the time*. My eyes were wet again, my lower lip trembling.

Tears spilled down his cheeks. His voice dropped. "I wanna go home, Mum. Why can't we be home, just you and Dad and me?"

"Because, apparently, the calm part of our lives are on hold, Liam. One thing I'm certain will happen…the violence *will* end. Good men and women are working on the problem. They'll find a solution soon." I glanced up at his father, then back to our lad. "We must be brave and stand firm. Our place is with your dad. Whatever happens includes us all."

Cullum nodded, taking my arm again and steered me up a few steps across a deep porch, with lounging furniture that I promised myself to test, and inside. A cavernous room opened to a kitchen.

"Whose house is this?" I turned to my husband.

"It's the place I wanted to show you a while back. We've not had a chance to come up here." He absently scratched his forearm with his thumb. "Come, I'll give you the tour, if you're up to a look around." He led out, toward the back, to three familiarly furnished bedrooms and a staircase.

At the top of the stairs, a large open space, the length and breadth of the lower level, greeted us. The ceiling, walls, and floor were fir plank lined. The lack of furnishing made the views accessible from every angle.

"It's beautiful." I turned in the middle of the room. "When did you have time to build this?"

"Been workin' on it for ten years. Good therapy. I just laid this floor before you came home." He jammed his fingertips into the pockets of his denims and surveyed his handiwork. "It came together as I had money and time to spend up here. The land was a gift from Uncle David, when I left S6 for university. We had the lower level blacked in the week before he passed. I never told you because I wanted it to be a surprise, Bel. I didn't wanna bring you up here 'til the house was finished." A sad smile touched his lips.

"It's incredible." I watched him process my pleasure. "I like your house in Nairn a lot, but may we live here? Would it be an awful drive in to the pub?"

"We'll see. When all the havoc plays out, we'll see." He started for the stairs to descend. I followed with Liam behind.

"Dad, may I go down to the waterfall now?"

"Aye, fetch Kent to go with you though."

When we reached the lower floor, Liam left us at a sprint and Cullum started for the kitchen. A folded newspaper lay on the granite covered breakfast bar. He handed it to me. "Page two."

I opened the newspaper and scanned for the article he obviously wanted me to discover on my own.

"Sir William Carmichael Dies of Natural Causes"
Edinburgh Evening News
Sir William Carmichael, Chief Financial Officer of AIM Enterprises, was found dead this morning, in the predawn hours, by his wife.

Inverness Police say there is no reason to suspect foul play. Sir William, known to suffer a heart condition, apparently experienced an attack sometime during the night. The Sheriff's office reports that medication for his condition was found spilled from its container on the nightstand.

Lady Carmichael declined comment. Her solicitor assured the press that her ladyship deeply grieves her husband's loss. She and Sir William married less than a year ago.

I glanced up at Cullum. "I wonder the identity of her ladyship. I had no clue Sir William married. He's always been acclaimed a most desirable bachelor."

He shrugged. "It changes things, Bel. It *will* be interesting to see who landed the big fish since he became the majority shareholder in the company."

"It will, at that." I refolded the paper and returned it to the bar. "I need to make a few calls. Is it safe to do so from here or should I…."

"No." He didn't snap, but was forceful.

"I need to ken when the funeral will be held. If I can be there, perhaps I can identify Lady Carmichael."

"I'll get the information for you, but you'll go, under heavy guard, if at all. An even better idea is that some of the lads can attend, with hidden cameras, and bring back the footage."

"That's fine if they can get past the old guards, Cullum. I can walk into the building or the funeral, without questions."

"Aye, but at this moment you're far too valuable to risk. They want you, Bel, and I intend to see they don't get you." He stretched his hand out for me. "Now, let's sit on the veranda and enjoy the outlook. We need to discuss strategy."

"I could do that best with tea in hand."

Cullum glanced back at Randy. "Lad, put the kettle on, please."

"Where's the waterfall that our son's run off to see?"

"It's best viewed from the basin," he pointed off to his right, to the south.

"I look forward to seeing it myself."

"I'll arrange it, then." He tucked my hand into his arm and we stepped out the door to the panorama.

Mountains in the distance, shrouded in mist, and a meadow of lambs and ewes, at pasture in the valley, gave me great pleasure after the turmoil of the day.

Strange, I hadn't felt as cozy in Cullum's other house. This one spoke my secret name. Here's where I would raise our children and grow old with my handsome man at my side.

Oh, the things we daydream! Looking back now, it seems infantile to think life could be so simple.

"There's been a meeting called by SSP." Cullum leaned back, closing his eyes.

"You're going?"

"Aye, *we're* goin', as in you and I."

"What'll we do with Liam?" I watched as he settled. *He's relaxing, good. Wish I could.*

"The lads'll keep an eye on him. It's in two days, Bel, in Aviemore." He sighed, his shoulders loosening. "I have a room booked at Ard Na Coille, in Newtonmore."

"Thank you. Would you care to tell me why you socked Randy?"

He opened his eyes and turned a narrowed gaze my direction. "Not your concern."

"I beg to differ with you, Cullum. He did the right thing. I was alright after a few days. Returning would have snuffed your plans." Watching him is like watching our son. It makes me want to smile, so I did, even though he scowled.

"Nothin' comes before you, Bel. Never again. The party can go to hell. I'll leave our home behind for foreign lands, but nothing ever comes between us again." He crossed his arms.

"Well, I believe he made the right choice, though it may not have appeared so at the time." I continued to study the fine line of his jaw.

"I concede that events turned around, but I'll never trust...."

Randy appeared with a tray full of tea cups, the pot, and a few pastries. "Here you are then." He placed the tray on the table before us and bowed.

I clapped my hands twice and grinned. "Well done!"

Cullum nodded and mumbled, "Aye, well done, lad."

Randy glanced my way then back to beloved. "Cullum, I apologize for failing to be forthright with you about Isabel's situation. I promise to never make tha' kind of decision again. I should've told you everythin' and let you make the choice."

My husband shrugged. "It's done. I'm sorry I popped you. I should have better control of myself—and do, but for her." He turned to meet my eyes and sighed.

It was my turn. "I apologize to you both. I lose heart easily, on occasion, when the situation involves my husband. As in the past, I tend to respond as though all is lost." I locked eyes with my lover. "I resolve to trust you more and stay strong, even in the face of losing you." My eyes teared. I inhaled a shaky breath.

"I resolve to not let you out of my sight again." He dropped a kiss on my mouth.

When we looked up, Randy had gone.

In the middle of the night, I left our bed for the loo. As I trod softly towards the open door, I remembered where I'd seen the man with the gashed arm, from the accident scene. He was at Min's cottage after Bradley's body was found. He was one of the men that Bernie sent to secure the premises. Constable Bernie Leighton was involved deeply in the whole affair.

Chapter 22

Kent...or Kevin wore a hidden camera into the Inverness Cathedral, also known as the Cathedral Church of Saint Andrew. Sir William Carmichael's body lay interned inside. The funeral was about to commence.

I wiggled uncomfortably in my seat on the passenger's side of Randy's Jeep.

"Wha's wrong?" Cullum shot a sour look at my discomfort. "Are you ill, Bel?"

"Nay, I need a loo." I looked around the area. "There's a shop down the way, or I could duck inside this magnificent edifice and around the corner to the toilet."

He gave me his best *really?* look. "Not happenin'. I'll walk you to the shop, or take you over to Eilidh to wait out the surveillance. What'll it be?"

I had no hope of my idea working on him. "I can probably wait a few minutes, then I'll need to go to the shop. This is all recording, isn't it?"

"Aye, we'll have a second camera inside in...," he checked his watch, "five minutes."

"Where?"

"Balcony."

"Might catch her leavin', but with the paraphernalia one wears to a funeral these days, she's no doubt well-covered." I thought of Naomi's elaborate headgear at Minerva's funeral. *Had I not known it was her, by the way she moved...that's it then. If the new Lady Carmichael is someone we know, we may identify her by her gait. Hopefully, she won't be a newcomer to the gruesome games.*

I settled myself as it would be at least an hour before the procession began. I dozed, missing the fireworks, until they were well under way.

"Bel!" Cullum's voice startled me from sleep.

"What?" I opened my eyes to overcast skies and my husband's smile.

"Look!" He indicated the monitor we'd watched when Kent and Kevin entered the nave. Cullum turned the volume off. He doesn't care for organ music.

A free-for-all had broken out at the head of the procession.

I glanced at the entry doors of the Cathedral as Sir William's casket was carried out on the shoulders of six honor guards from his former regiment. The guards proceeded to load the casket into a waiting horse-drawn hearse.

Checking the monitor, two women haggled. Both wore large brimmed hats with long black veils attached. The most enjoyable moment came when one reached beyond a referee to snatch the hat off the other. At that point, the referees managed, with considerable help, to pin the woman's arms to her side.

Cullum cackled. "Bet the old man had no idea the pain and pleasure his departure would bring, eh?" He threw back his head and laughed.

I hadn't heard that wondrous sound from him often enough since I'd come home. I enjoyed his pleasure as much as he did, finally wiping both eyes free of tears, before he caught me.

"Well, who are they, love?" He blew his nose into his hankie and continued to study the women.

In the tangle, both hats became dislodged. Dignity was lost to each party. They had to turn to their respective comforters.

The papers won't touch this, and we'll never have the joy of cutting out articles for a scrapbook.

"Do you ken them, Bel?" My husband insisted.

"The one on the right is Naomi."

He studied the monitor. "The other?"

"I believe that's Annmarie, Sir William's private secretary."

"So which do you think is the newly revealed Lady Carmichael?"

"My money's on the serious blonde. I don't think Naomi has the intelligence needed to plot so complex an operation. Annmarie, on the other hand, has exactly what it takes and she's been in his employ a quarter of a century. She knows everything about him and the company."

We were looking at the dark queen.

Finally!

215

"So, now what?" I asked my husband.

"At least we know who we're dealing with, mo chroi." He sobered.

"We'll see," I muttered, unconvinced.

Chapter 23

At breakfast, with Jacquie, at Ard na Coille Bed and Breakfast, we feasted on her marvelous, light version of Eggs Benedict. Afterwards, we departed for The MacDonald Highland Conference Center, nineteen miles away, in Aviemore.

Our shoes crunched in the pebble driveway. "Why did we not stay at the conference center? They have an abundance of rooms."

"Aye, but this way, we're apart from the mass. I prefer we come and go on our own. Stayin' in the midst of the muddle, everyone wants a moment of our time. There's little to spare. I want the event done so we may be on our way home."

"I like that. It would be inconvenient to divide your time with others."

He opened the door to the Jeep, tucking the hem of my cloak out of the way. He placed a kiss on my mouth and followed with his usual, "Mmm." He closed the door.

"My thoughts exactly."

He climbed in and cranked the beast. We proceeded down through the car park, turning left at the gate. We took the motorway through Kingussie and headed to Aviemore on A-9.

***

Cullum and I stood at the back of the auditorium, having arrived a few minutes late. There were close to a thousand people in attendance at Scotland's Socialist Party gathering. I looked over the milling crowd and my stomach felt fluttery.

"I need the loo. I'll be a few minutes." I patted my husband's hand and he released me.

David Ferrell approached the podium, as I passed through the doors. "Good morning, members. We come together today to celebrate our freedom. I ken it's still only a dream, however...."

After I washed my hands, I dashed to the side entrance and told the usher where I was expected.

He offered his arm and we commenced the journey to the platform. In a few minutes, after clearing security three times, we arrived at an open side door, stage left.

I watched the back of the room from my niche. Beloved checked his watch twice, while David droned on about the possibilities and probabilities facing our country.

The president glanced back at me and I made a rolling motion with my right hand. He needed to move along before Cullum became suspicious.

I made sure there was no tissue stuck to my shoes and my loose dress hung straight when David began the introduction.

"If I say Cullum Sinclair's name...."

Cullum had almost passed clear of the door to exit. At the sound of his name he turned to face the podium.

"...most everyone in this room kens the man." David scanned the hundreds of raised hands in the auditorium.

"But if I say Isabel Sinclair, only a handful knows I'm speaking of Cullum's wife. Isabel is not center stage, as few of us are, but behind the scenes. She operates outside the limelight, but don't make a mistake and discount her contribution to our organization." David droned on with his introduction.

Cullum's attention fixated on stage. He waved an usher over and leaned to her ear. She pushed through the double doors and reappeared a few moments later, shaking her head.

Please, God, let him understand why I couldn't tell him.

He turned and strode through the doorway with resolve.

Please, God, keep him from leaving!

I glanced down at my notes. Tears obscured the words. *Ah, to have come this far, back into my husband's life, another child on the way. Please, please don't let him be so angry over money that he abandons us.*

David held out his hand to me, as light applause spread across the room. *I have eyes and ears for only one's approval and*—I scanned the crowd—*he's not returned.*

The microphone on the podium had to be lowered. I waited, while David made the adjustment and stepped up to spread my transcript. I leaned toward the instrument, frightened my voice would break.

I've always hated public speaking.

I could face the devil, one on one, but put me before a crowd of more than ten and I freeze.

"My name is Isabel Sinclair. I'm Cullum's wife and the mother of his children, our son, Liam and another on the way." *Where is he?* I tried to see the notations I'd spent hours compiling.

David retreated to the side doorway, where I stood earlier. Peripherally, I noticed movement round him, supposing his bodyguards moved into place.

"I've never intended that you know who I am or what I contribute, but it seems I have no choice. Speculation has exceeded limitation. The time is now, to come forward, that I may offer assurance to members of SSP." I gulped air into my dry throat before continuing.

"I have no aspirations for parliament. No intention of seeking the Prime Minister's position. There's no time, with a twelve-year-old and a baby coming, to be involved more than I have, these past fourteen years. I do not attend meetings, although I basically agree with the tenets of Scotland's Socialist Party." A quick scan revealed Cullum still missing. "I participate the only way I'm able, funding projects." I glanced down again.

"There are rumors about that there should be a split in SSP, because of a dark queen in the background." I raised my hand. "That would be me. Ladies and gentlemen, I'm not a threat to anyone here with political careers, concerns, or ambitions. I've only been a purveyor of funds. David and I discussed my role and the fracture that's widening as fear grips laypeople. I'm no menace! Please take your positions and stand firm."

I felt eyes upon me. You could hear the proverbial pin drop in that room. Scanning the chamber, to be certain I hadn't missed Cullum, proved futile.

"In closing, I'd like to read a poem very near my heart. It was penned by a dear friend after visiting our historic battle site of Culloden.

"It's called "Blàr Chùil Lodair" or "The Battle of Culloden.""

"Heart clenched, I survey
distant mist shrouded
mountains. Moray Firth churns

beneath majestic spires,
crowned by last night's snow.

April 16th, 1746–reputed
as a beacon, to all who hold liberty,
precious and fragile in their sturdy hands.
Scanning the historical clash,
Jacobite blue flags mark our lines,
red marks England's. I stand at the junction.

The Macgillivray led the charge that fateful
day when no orders came from command.
Clan Chattan's finest were consumed,
when the enemy closed ranks.
Annihilated in a flash.

British cannon roared, rupturing
our defenses, standing fixed. Still no order
delivered to the warriors. To the right and left
Highlander's fell, valiantly
spilling lives into sacred ground
for one man's dreams of a crown.

Exhausted, they'd pushed through long,
cold nights, no food, no rest.
Still, no edict to charge the British,
as Bonnie Prince Charlie
wrestled conflicting demons.

Bleeding to death at that seam of hell,
kilts held fast, glancing down
upon writhing comrades. A son?
A brother? A cousin? No matter,
death became certain that day.
There was no escape.

The few surviving
the massacre fled to their lands.

Redcoats hotly pursuing
to murder them in their homes.
With wives and children—
burnt to death.

But the dreamer fled to safety, posing
in maid's attire, serving tea to guests,
in Flora MacDonald's shelter,
'til he safely returned to France,
from whence he sailed.

His effrontery cost Scotland, dearly.
Lives lost, dreams shattered.
The Young Pretender died an old man
 with no legacy, but folly.

Two thousand fearless men's blood soaked
into your hallowed earth, Culloden.
Buried together, in mass graves
beneath my feet,
some fought with England, others,
Alba and independence, as *they* elected,
 at no English king's command."

Rumbling swept over the crowd, a call for liberty. I looked up
to see hundreds on their feet. Arms hoisted clenched fists. I leaned
closer to the microphone as I neared my favorite part and shouted
above the roar:

"Hail, Scotland, brave and bold!
Never forget that day, though you've fed
your sons to bleaker conflicts.
The opportunity now is your choice
to claim your land and freedom.

No longer shedding costly blood
but rather, shed the cloak
of oppression for your children

and theirs to come."
The final line rang out, with all my strength.
"Culloden, you were not the end of our struggle!"

I looked up, amazed to see the house front packed. The orchestra box was filled with non-musicians, clambering over one another. Only when I stopped reading and dared glance up, did I spy the cheering throng. Strong hands gripped me from behind. I turned to find my husband holding fast as people joined us on the dais.

His grip became firmer, with the press of flesh into our space and I had trouble breathing, as I could see no clear way out. Cullum steered us toward an exit sign. I followed his guidance, unable to fathom anything before or behind us. We were only a few feet from the lectern.

And then….

A shot rang out!

Over all the riotous noise, the report of a handgun quietened the crowd for an instant, before they began to flee, a large number shouting.

I felt my body falling, in spite of the packed mass of humanity. Cullum pushed me down, riding the retreating crowd to the floor.

Another explosion resounded, nearly at hand.

Piercing screams echoed!

The throng earnestly shoved towards exits.

Voices yelled above the melee. "Subdue him!"

Others yelled back. "We have him!"

A hard object smacked against the side of my head when, finally, we tumbled to the floor.

"Bel!" Beloved cried.

I lost consciousness.

Chapter 24

"Bel!" Cullum's voice resonated in the near silence.

"What?" I squinted at the surrounding fuzzy brightness.

"Bel, can you hear me?"

"Aye, not deaf. Wha' happened?" I tried to determine our location.

Relieved, he chuckled. "Your head hit the base of the podium, mo chroi. You scared the life outta me."

"Shooting?" I could make out his outline, shadowed by a halo.

"Aye, a young man with a pistol fired into the crowd. I think he was aimin' for you, though. He looks like the chap you photographed the day you went to the estate *without permission.*" He cradled my head and shoulders, sighing in relief.

The doorways, off stage, began to take shape in my field of vision. "My head aches. I need to sit up. Will you help me?"

"The physician wants you to lie still. Obey." He raked his hand over my hair. "You could have told me, you ken?"

I tried to see him, without the glow softening his features. "Nay, I couldn't. I'd sworn David to silence five years ago, when he took control. I required the same from myself. If I'd told you, it would've added more fuel to the fire of abhorrence that you carry against wealth. I hate feeling like your enemy."

Cullum's lips pursed as he considered my admission. "You're right. I wasn't ready to listen. I apologize, Isabel." He brushed wispy hair from my face. "Thankfully no one's dead or wounded this time. You're going to have a knot on your head, though." He leaned down and planted a fine kiss on my lips.

"How's my patient?" An elderly man stooped over me to place his bag beside my head before he knelt. His white hair glistened in the bright light.

"She's awake, Doc. Mo chroi, this is Doctor Henry Campbell."

I only knew him as Henry, from Genny's reference, when I was sedated those three days. "Pleased to finally meet you in person."

He lifted my wrist in his wrinkled hand, winked and checked his watch. "Mmm, pulse is normal. Shall I listen to the bairn, darlin'?" He studied me over the rim of his half-moon glasses.

"I believe we're fine, sir. But may we sit up now?"

He nodded. "Let's try it, then."

Cullum lifted my shoulders and I sat, legs widened, making room for my belly. I stretched. "That's better, I think."

A policeman worked at the wall, behind the doctor. I hadn't seen him when prone on the floor. "What's he doing, Cullum?"

"Digging the bullets out of the plaster, love." He glanced up. "That's where we were standing a half hour ago. I don't ken how he missed us either time he pulled the trigger."

I glanced around. It didn't make sense to me either. We were no more than two feet from the lectern in direct alignment with the damaged plaster.

The policeman shouted out towards the auditorium. "Found them both, sir."

Chief Inspector John Cooley made the steps to the stage and stopped to nod my direction before he met the sergeant. "Fine work, lad." He whirled back to face me as Cullum helped me to my feet. "Isabel, good to see you."

"John, it's fine to see you, as well. What do we owe the visit on this important occasion and how did you get here so fast?" My husband kept me propped into his strength.

"I was in the neighborhood, keeping an eye on you." He pointed his long, elegant forefinger my direction.

"Am I suspect then?" I beamed my best smile, though half concussed.

"Now, now, play fair. Cullum's informed you what our circumstances were the day I took him in; they couldn't be changed, lass."

"I ken that, but why me, now?"

Cullum grasped the back of my neck and answered. "We're sortin' out the bad guys, love." He kissed my forehead. "I was concerned that they'd make a move here in the crowd."

"So they did. Do you have an idea who the lad is, Inspector?" I leaned into my husband's hold.

"He says his name is Ronny Pearl. There was no identification on him, when we arrived."

"Ronny Pearl...," Cullum mused, with a smile. "Sounds like a gigolo. Any connection with Damian Ferguson?"

John Cooley grinned. "I'm betting we'll find the handgun he used is from Ferguson's collection."

"If it's the same lad I photographed at the estate, he's certain to be tied in with Naomi and Damian. That's too obvious a connection, though, isn't it?"

"Sometimes bad guys hide in view and a cigar is just a cigar." John stuffed his hands in his trench coat's pockets. "Well, I'm off to see what the man has to say for himself. Isabel, may I use the photographs you gave to me?"

"Aye, whatever you need, do. It's not as though they threaten my relationship with Naomi." I stretched again and thought I felt well enough to walk to the Jeep. "We'll need a stop at the loo."

Cullum grinned. "I expected no less. But I'm waitin' for you outside the door this time."

Chapter 25

The lads left for home and jobs when we arrived at the lovely house in the Highlands. Liam waited with Kevin, or Kent, when we parked.

He practically bounced on his feet, waiting for Cullum to park. When we opened our doors, his news spilled over. "Mum! Dad! Lachlan came to visit. He and Gramps stayed the night and we had a fire and roasted mallows over it, just like at home, Mum. They left only moments ago."

Aghast, I checked with Cullum.

He grinned. "Good, Gramps said he'd try to get here. I'm glad you saw Lachlan." He hefted our luggage and strode towards the veranda. He laid the case down and turned to our son as Liam launched into his arms. They wrestle-hugged and laughed together. One might think they'd been acting that way for years instead of months.

I waited for a kiss and an explanation. Cullum released the lad.

Liam remembered I was present, and reached his hand out for my small bag, laying a kiss on my cheek. "Did you have a good time, Mum?"

"Aye, I think we did." I draped my arm across his shoulder. At 5'8", he was my height. Nairn had been good for his growth, more than two inches taller thus far.

Cullum watched me, a smile in place. "Lad, your mum's an amazing woman."

"I kenned tha' for a long time." Liam held the door for my entrance.

Cullum caught my arm. "I called and asked Da to come up while we were away. The lads, but Kent, all had commitments. I'm happy the boys saw each other. Liam's missed bein' at the farm. I ken it's worth the risk. Da's careful to not be followed."

"Oh, you could've told me."

"Don't want you worried." He rubbed my belly. "You've plenty to tend to without concern over the rest of our world."

"May we start supper, then?" I headed to the kitchen, turned, and enjoyed the view through the front room's large windows. "Incredible."

Cullum followed my gaze. "It is lovely in sunshine. When the clouds lower on top of us, it's like we're cut off from the world." He glanced back at me. "I wouldn't mind bein' cut off from the world with you awhile, Bel." His grey eyes were wistful.

"The feeling's mutual."

Liam joined us, sighing.

"You sound like an old man, lad."

"I like it here, but I miss my friends, Dad. When are we goin' home?"

I leaned into my husband. "We need to find a midwife, unless you're up to birthin' a bairn in the wilderness."

"Ah, well, Caleigh will know who to contact, I imagine. If no' couldn't you just use a hospital?"

"I did with Liam, but I was totally alone. A midwife at home suits me, lover."

He nodded. "Alright, you two, we'll head back to Nairn in a few days, then."

Chapter 26

"You haven't told me how our clothes came to be here?" I dressed for bed, slowly, as my husband helped.

He glanced up, while his hands were busy at various fasteners on my garments. "Kent and I parked at one of the golf courses, outside town, and ran in around one in the mornin' two weeks ago. We packed cartons he delivered the night before. The next day a delivery van loaded our belongings. One of the neighbors accosted the driver and asked where we were going. 'To auction' he said, as that's what he was told. His instructions changed when he neared Inverness. He was relieved and one of our men took over to bring our belongings to our new nest."

"Tell me you packed for me."

"I packed for you, love." He chuckled. "I wanted to be assured you'd have a bra."

"Aye, Randy did his best for us the day you were shot but he's clueless."

"I'm comin' to realize most unmarried men are, when it comes to a woman." He gathered my gown, and slipping it over my head, followed its progress with kisses. "Between you and Mam, I think I'm well trained."

I turned to the painting of sailboats harnessing Atlantic winds off the coast of America. It hung on the wall opposite the bed. "I see you decided to keep it?"

"Aye, reminds me of Uncle David. He loved Winslow Homer."

"Did you have it appraised?"

"Aye, but I'm not even tempted to sell. Min knew I loved it when it hung over the mantle at their country home. I wasn't astonished she left it to me."

Hefty knuckles rapped on the bedroom door.

Cullum shook his head, mumbling. "Damn communal livin', anyway." He narrowly opened the door, stepping through.

He was away for more than ten minutes. I'd settled on my side of the bed with one of Min's diaries.

228

The spine read, 'Summer 1992'. Cullum and I were eleven that year. I opened to the beginning:

David and I had the most splendid picnic today. I resolved there and then to picnic at least once a week. We become so enchanted with worry and tedious little things in our lives, we forget to breathe.

We took a blanket and basket to the glen on the estate and chilled a bottle of wine in the burn. Once we stilled, the birds came calling. Those magnificent creatures, in their bright plumage, are a wonder of God's hands. I think He may have made so many tiny birds, so very brilliant, just because He can. In the doing, He reminds us that He pays attention to every detail. No part of life is so unimportant that He overlooks the need.

Having said that, what completed our outing was a visit from the children. It seems that Isabel and Cullum have found the glen by the burn, as well. They shared their secret meeting place with us today. We laughed as David told tales of his youth and what Genny was like as a child. He's almost twenty years her senior, but a doting brother.

When we parted, I was so refreshed, sharing my girl's happiness, for those few short hours. Seeing her and Cullum together, I'll never forget the moment they first laid eyes upon each other. Speaking of enchantment resurrected the memory of the way they interact. I've only ever known one other couple so devoted to each other and they were friends, when children, as well.

Ah, someday we'll all be together for picnics and watch their little ones scampering among the rocks, slipping into the burn, and collecting every manner of leaf and twig stuffed into their wee pockets. I do long for those days. I shall indulge every whim my daughter has while carrying her bairns, making chocolates daily, if it suits her desires.

I closed the book without finishing the entry. I could no longer see the words. Reaching for a tissue, I heard the door open and my husband returned. He wore a smile.

"You were gone too long. Is something wrong?"

"No, mo chroí, something's finally right. John called. He says the Ronny bird's singing. They just came from interrogation. They have the whole sordid mess recorded. He sent for Naomi and Damian. It may almost be over." He crawled across the bed to me and lowered himself, face to my belly. He nuzzled my side. "Wake up, lad. It's time to play." He glanced up at me and winked.

Our son stirred at the sound of Cullum's voice so near.

Chapter 27

I sat across a grey metal table from Naomi. She made the jail issue jumps look stylish, in the posh way she carries herself. She tucked a strand of fashionably colored and styled hair behind her ear and I wondered how she'd handle the prison facilities.

"I didn't know who else to call, with William gone." She looked nervous and uncertain.

My voice stayed neutral and gentle at the same time. "Wha' do you need?"

She gazed at her well-manicured fingertips. "Everything, Isabel. I realize I'm at your mercy." She finally met my eyes.

"That must be difficult for you." I glanced away. "You can't call Bernie or some of Damian's relatives to make bail for you, then?" Leaning back in my chair, I released a sigh.

"No, there's no one. I have men friends whom I might phone but…." She leaned back as well. "This is embarrassing. Well, I must apologize for the…*things* that happened when you lived in my home, Isabel. I never wanted you, or any child. I had three abortions, you know." She fingered her hair into place and tucked it behind her ears. "To have Arthur and Minerva hand you over, the great symbol of their love, for me to rear as my own, was revolting." She waved away any objections I might make. "I know, they thought they did some noble deed, but I didn't want you. Minerva could've had her dream but Arthur wouldn't allow me to return you to her care. He always said a child should grow up in her father's house. To me you were just an albatross."

"Neither of us was happy. I prayed every night that I'd wake up and Aunt Min would be my mum and Daddy would be my daddy and you had only been a vague nightmare. But since our dreams never came to fruition, let's talk reality."

"Yes, well, fine. I did *not* kill my sister. I did *not* kill Bradley. Damian did the dirty deed both times. He thought he was doing me a favor by removing obstacles to the executorship of AIM enterprises. My only desire was to see it all destroyed." She lost control and giggled, a jarring, shrill sound that always gave me chills.

I waited for her hysteria to pass.

She wiped her eyes carefully to protect her makeup. I wondered how long that perk would last.

I kept my voice low. "Well, it *was* nearly lost, but for Sir William. Did you not know he and Annmarie married?"

"He never told me, even though he entertained himself with me, as she was in the next room." She absently scratched her forearm. "He left me a little money. Arthur left me a little money. Between them, I'll survive, but barely."

"What part did Ronnie Pearl play in all this mayhem?"

She smiled, gazing at the floor. "He's hot, that one. He was supposed to have *killed* Cullum the first time."

A shiver passed through me at her cavalier statement. Cullum thought I had been the target.

"He gave up his future to attempt it a second time." I tried to hide my desire to flee.

"Serves us right for employing a cocaine addict. Damian met him at a gay nightclub in Glasgow and brought him home to play with. We shared him for a while. But then I lost interest and he had to do something spectacular to get my attention again." She locked her fingers together and stretched, still amused at the turn of circumstances.

"So you threw him to the wolves?"

She nodded her head and appeared bored. "He was just so— needy, that one."

Naomi was made to be pampered. Aunt Min was right about a number of things concerning her sister, but I wondered if she realized the depths of depravity Naomi could reach.

"I'm taking over the estate. If it comes to pass, I'll give you a flat in Edinburgh."

"Why not the villa in Spain? I like it a great deal, even though Minerva gave birth to you there. It suits me." She dared meet my eyes.

"You're about to be on trial for helping a murderer, lying to police, hindering an ongoing investigation. I'm not worried about what suits you. Besides, I sold all the property, but what I wanted, in Scotland."

She brightened. "But you're getting me out of here?"

"Have you told your story?"

"I tried, but the inspector acts as though I'm lying. He smugly watches every breath I take." She shook her head, too violently for the scene she played. She tried to drag her eyes back to mine.

"Really? Well, I'll speak to him about that before I leave. I'll not post bail, because I'm sure the judge will consider you a flight risk."

"Oh, but I'm not, Isabel. I promise I'll be available." She reached her hand towards my arm, but failed to touch me. I couldn't recall a single time she touched me tenderly. She was never anything like Min.

"Mmm, we'll see. You understand I owe you nothing. I survived, in spite of your mental illness and refusal to maintain medication." I gave her a moment to consider her plight. "Why did Aunt Min have to die? Cullum was in process of doing your bidding. He was about to approach me in Edinburgh to ask me to come home."

She glared at me stupidly. "Well, I...I didn't know that. He refused my offer...." She quickly added, "of money."

I had to smile. "And everything else. He told me."

Her face flamed; she looked away. "I would never have...well, I wouldn't have done something so perverse as having relations with my daughter's husband."

"Come now, don't act proper, Naomi. I'm not your daughter and you don't give a hang who you bed. They must only be breathing to qualify." I sighed and glanced around at the prison Naomi had chosen. "Why Min? She stepped aside from her inheritance, gave you everything, even a child she'd rather have kept and you killed her. Even you should have some limit of depravity."

"I did not kill my sister." She mustered tears.

"You did, Naomi. I know it but I can't prove the truth—yet." I crossed my arms and looked away.

She laughed, then clamped her hand over her mouth. "Sorry." She leaned forward, as though sharing a secret. "I tricked her out of her inheritance. I told her I'd leave Arthur alone if she'd sign over the estate and title to me." She wagged her finger at me. "I know you think I'm not terribly bright but I fooled her—and your father."

"The button off one of your blouses was ripped away in the struggle with her. It broke almost cleanly in half. Perhaps you stepped on it while wrestling Aunt Min. She had you in weight."

She gasped. Her face paled.

"She had boundaries. You have none." I slapped the table between us. "That's it…you lost the little control you maintain, without narcotics, and murdered her. Did you intend to kill her? Was it an accident?"

She clasped her hands in her lap and stared at a corner of the grey room. "I don't have to answer your questions."

"Nay, you don't. Fine then. God knows the truth and one way or another you'll pay a dear price for all the pain you've caused." I stood, pushing the chair beneath the table's apron.

She came to life, standing with her hand on her hip, spitting her words. "I've never understood what you see in Cullum. You could've had any man you wanted, but you always returned to a *publican's* son."

I needn't have answered and had to consider her accusation for a moment. "We were made for each other, as though God's own hand fashioned us together and separated us into our mothers' wombs." I searched for words she might grasp. "We have an extraordinary love. There was never anyone for me but Cullum. The years apart melted into insignificance when we reunited."

She shook her head, slower that time. "Still I don't see why you threw everything away: your money, your education. You're reasonably attractive. With all that you inherited from Arthur, you could've had anyone."

"I only wanted Cullum Sinclair. You and Daddy saw to it that I couldn't have him." I sighed, realizing she was hopeless, our conversation, pointless. "It's best to end our interview on a positive note." I turned for the door and thought of another question. "How did you lure Daddy from Min?"

A sly look skimmed over her face. "I seduced him and told him I was pregnant, which I was." She grinned and checked the upper corner of the dull blue-grey ceiling. "It wasn't his, of course."

"And you aborted the child?" I had trouble grasping the nonchalance, even pride, she displayed.

"I had no choice, considering who I'd been with, it would've been obvious at birth." She chuckled, at my naiveté I assumed.

"I'll never understand you." Grasping the handle on the door, I pushed as a guard approached from the other end, for Naomi.

"Will you visit?" She tucked her hair behind her ears again, the little girl seeking approval, or having a go at manipulation.

"Why? You've never cared for my company, remember?" I considered all the hours, sometimes days, I spent locked in the cellar. It gave me motivation to pass through the door without waiting for her answer.

Inspector Cooley loitered in the hallway. "Isabel, how did you fare?" He straightened at my approach.

Digging into my jacket pocket I produced the recorder I'd carried inside for my visit. "Hear for yourself." I followed him to his office and took a seat.

Cullum met us after a few minutes. He bent and kissed me. "How'd it go, mo chroi?"

I nodded and shrugged.

Inspector Cooley cranked the volume and we listened to the interview replay.

I felt a heel lodge in my ribcage and stretched. I found our son's foot and pushed back. He retreated a bit and I relaxed.

Glancing at the frown my husband wore, I grimaced. *How can I feel sorry for her when she's spent my entire life trying to destroy me? And yet....*

Cullum propped his arm on the back of my chair and lightly rubbed my shoulder. He turned a sidelong look my way.

Only one glance, yet I knew he felt my angst. He squeezed my arm. "I know, my love."

John Cooley switched off the recorder. "Damian tells the story differently. He says Naomi killed Minerva and begged him to take care of her body. He also swears he didn't see Bradley King the night he was murdered. Yet, your friend Craig said Bradley left the b&b around nine that evening. We can corroborate his whereabouts by the timestamp on the email sent to your old account."

Cullum regarded me. "What do you think, Bel?"

"I know she killed her sister. But, John, you'll have to work it out. I don't think I have anythin' left to give." I stood, my legs feeling shaky. My voice began to break. "The past seven months I've been shot at on two occasions, had the wits scared outta me on two more and nearly kidnapped. I'm over the whole affair."

Cullum followed me, a hand on my elbow. "Let's go home, Bel." He glanced back at the inspector. "John, let me know how things progress. We won't post bail for Naomi and we probably won't attempt to keep up with the trials. My bride needs rest and a change of focus."

"I understand, Cullum. Thank you both for your help. I'll call you with any news from our front."

Beloved and I left the station for the garage and climbed into the Jeep for the rough ride up to the fine house in the midst of the Highlands. The one he built with his own hands, for his family.

Chapter 28

Caleigh, Becca and I met in the café beside the harbor. My sister-in-law handled ordering tea and cakes for us before Becca and I arrived. The table was in process of being laid when I entered. I stopped to savor the smell of sweets and several types of tea brewing, catching a glimpse of a cake I have an affinity for these days.

Caleigh met me for a hug. "You look marvelous." She patted my belly. "How is he?"

"Great, considering the roller coaster ride we've been on for the past few months."

Becca stepped out of the tiny restroom, drying her hands. She is a very pretty petite brunette with luminous hazel eyes and a perfect complexion. She smiled and offered her damp hand. I took it in mine.

"I've always wanted to meet you, Isabel." Her head tilted to one side and I had an eerie feeling there was more to her statement.

"Thank you, I suppose. Let's sit. I'm starved. My men are manning the pub so I have an hour of freedom."

Caleigh looked over at Becca. "Isabel needs a midwife, Becca, she's due in about seven weeks. Do you have room on your calendar for us?"

"Us? Are you her doula?"

"Yes, but I'd be there anyway. I have the baby itch right now and can't wait for this one to arrive." Caleigh served us a sampler of cakes.

I took two to be polite, though I could have cleared the platter.

"Sure, I can work you in, though this is a busy time for me. Lambin' season seems to bring the bairns, too." She opened a leather appointment book and checked our dates. "I only have four due that week and three are in the village." She closed it and studied me again.

I sort of hated being the center of her attention. "Do you stay busy?"

"Aye, I dash up and down the coast and over to Inverness almost every day. I have good references, if you want them." She reached for her briefcase.

"I'm fine with Caleigh's approval. We won't have a difficult time, I hope. If so, we'll pop over to hospital." I sipped a good spiced tea. "We were at our home in the mountains but my husband wanted to be nearer medical facilities." At the mention of Cullum her eyes flashed, ever so slightly. *Aha!*

"Well, we have a deal then." She smiled and picked at the food on her plate, almost pouting.

Caleigh checked the time. "I must leave the two of you on your own. Lachlan and I have an appointment with a teacher." She gathered her bag. "Tea is on me today, ladies." She passed quick kisses around and disappeared.

Becca studied me for a moment and glanced at the current patrons. "Have you enjoyed being back?"

"In Nairn? Yes. With my husband? Absolutely. There's somethin' you want to tell me. You may say whatever's on your mind." I leaned forwards on the table, as Ana had cleared the dishes.

"Cullum and I had a bit of a...thing. Well, it was more me than him. Caleigh doesn't know and I'd prefer she didn't." She looked away.

"Alright, she won't hear it from me. Will you be uncomfortable delivering our son?"

"No, it's just that...we saw each other a few times. Alright, truth told, I chased him like I was on fire. He finally took notice, after a year or so, and asked me to dinner. Then we went to Inverness to theatre and had a nightcap. On the last date, after dancing and a couple of drinks, I made it clear I wanted more than the evening had offered to that point. He politely declined and walked away. After two weeks and no phone call, I wrote a sappy letter him and told him it was time to move on, you weren't comin' back and if he accidentally called me Bel instead of Becca I wouldn't kick him out of bed."

"I see." I tried to keep the jealousy and amusement under control. I suppose some women would be angry by that time.

"You need to know I thought I was in love with him and would have no problem replacing you, once I had his attention."

"Now I know. Do your feelings for him still run in that direction?"

She sat back. "He called me on the phone, said thanks for the note and the time I spent with him, but he wasn't in the market to replace you." She studied me a moment, expecting more than I offered. "You aren't upset?"

I pondered her question before answering. "Becca, there is no one else on earth for Cullum but me. There's no one else on earth for me but Cullum. Circumstances kept us separate for years. But, now Liam and I are home, where we belong, and all is well. What happened while I was away is not my concern. But bringing our son into the world, with the least amount of drama possible, is our main consideration just now. Caleigh says you're the best midwife in the area. I trust her. I must also trust you. Can you keep from throwing yourself at my husband long enough to get the bairn delivered?"

She laughed, kind of a braying donkey noise that made me want to join her. I smiled and waited for her to calm herself.

"Cullum said you were one of a kind and there'd never be another. He said if he couldn't have you, he'd remain celibate the remainder of his life. I've tried to keep in touch with him, but he'll cross the street to avoid me." She folded her arms and waited for a response.

I lied to save her dignity. "If it makes you feel better, he would do that because he can't trust himself with you. In his view, he isn't avoiding you, he's saving himself the trouble of having to turn away from you again. That's the way he thinks."

In reality he'd be shocked and appalled she'd settle for so little. He'd dodge her to save his reputation and quell gossip. Then there's the matter of my name tattooed on his chest. What woman would *want* to wake up to that every morning?

"And you just know him that well?" Her mouth tightened.

"Aye, and he understands me the same way. One look or touch and we identify what the other is thinking and feeling. Becca, we've been friends since we were six-years-old. You get to know someone you love quite well...when your life and breath is arranged around them." I sat back and sipped my cooled tea. It was just as good cold as hot.

She smiled and shook his head. "The relationship you two share is very odd."

I nodded. "I prefer to think of it as unique and eternal."

She chuckled. "Well, Mrs. Sinclair, I hope to have that someday with the man of *my* dreams. You're on my calendar for the first week of March." She stood with her green leather briefcase in hand. "Let me know if your due date changes, or you just want to chat. I'll call you when I'm in the area and swing by to measure you so I'll have my kit prepared."

"Thank you."

She left me alone to ponder her revelation.

The tea in the pot on the table was barely warm, though covered with a cozy, but I poured and drank it watching the inhabitants of the scenic village come and go.

A lorry driver stopped in for tea and asked Ana, "How do you say the name of this place?"

She smiled and laid his place at table. "Like it's spelled, but the i makes a soft eh sound. Is it your first time here?"

"Aye, it is. I'm up from Edinburgh with a load of furniture to deliver to a shop. I'll have a cheese and tomato sandwich, toasted, and a slice of the Victoria sponge cake." He left his table for the loo.

I snagged my handbag and left Ana a ridiculously generous tip and departed for the pub and the company of my husband and our firstborn. Life was good and I could still walk a mile or so a day, but I went home for my car.

At the pub, Liam cleaned the remnants of tea from a table. He glanced up and smiled when he saw me. I made a pass towards him and kissed his cheek.

"Good day?" I asked.

"Excellent day, Mum. Dad's in the office." He nodded to the back.

"I'll see to him then." I headed past the bar into the small back room, crowded with a large desk, three chairs and two file cabinets. Beloved was attached, by a cord, to the landline.

He looked up and broke into a grin, rose and met me as far as the cord reached. "On hold. How was your meeting with the midwife?"

"Very good, she's one of your old girlfriends." I shed my coat and draped it over a chair, turning back to his deep frown.

"Who?" His voice sharpened.

"Becca, she said you had a thing once or she had a thing for you once, somethin' like tha'."

He stepped back around the desk and hung up the phone, dropping into his leather chair.

"You've lost your place in the queue." I pointed at the receiver.

"Why'd you choose her?" His brow wrinkled.

"Caleigh says she's the best."

"You can go to hospital."

"Do you not trust her?"

"It isn't that, Bel." He ran his hands through his hair, obviously irritated.

"She told me her story, Cullum. It's the past. Now and our future are what matter."

He leaned his elbows on the desk. "She tried to be more than I *ever* intended her to be. I only wanted to go out to dinner with female company once in a great while. It went too far. I was a fool to think I could have a woman as a friend with no consequences. I missed your softness, mo chroi." He searched for words for a moment, his gaze locked with mine. "In the company of the lads all the time, I'd become brash. Hardness was settlin' into my soul."

"I understand, lover." I reached over the expanse of oak between us. "Really I do. I was so focused on Liam, there was only work and our son. I needed to balance my life. I went out to dinner with a man from work. It was wasted. I compared every move, phrase, even his laughter to you. Felt so guilty, I picked up the tab." I rubbed his hand. "All that's history. The day we wed erased the board clean."

He took my hand and kissed it, lingering. "Aye, we're set right, now."

"I need to make a dash by Min's. Mrs. Peterson called, Liam's au pair? Her husband retired last month and they're taking a driving holiday, headed our way. She misses Liam fiercely. I offered Min's cottage as a base of operations for them, while in the Highlands."

"No liftin'. Take our lad with you and I'll be along as soon as I settle things here. We'll dine out this evenin'. You've had a full day already."

"The cleaners are at the cottage now. I'm just going to check the place over and drop off a few staples and a map of the village. Shall I return Liam?"

"Nay, I won't be long."

I met him at the back of his desk and leaned over to kiss him.

He held my face with one hand. "I'll never love anyone but you, Bel."

"That's good because I'll never love anyone but you." I kissed him again and left him to fetch Liam from the kitchen and head to Min's.

"Hullo!" I called out when we entered, considering two dead bodies had been found there within the past seven months.

"In the kitchen, Isabel." Alice answered.

Alice and her teenage daughter, Marion, were finishing up in the kitchen when we arrived. Marion is a grade ahead of Liam in school and very bright. Like Liam, she's on the rector's list every term without fail. She danced with him at the pub on his first night home in Nairn.

We rounded the corner to find her completing stock in the tea cupboard.

She offered me an envelope. "I found this slipped down from the top shelf against the wall of the hutch. Since it has your name on it, I thought you may want to take it with you. I've cleaned out the drawers and cupboards and packed everything you listed for the benevolence fundraiser next month."

"Thank you kindly." I turned the envelope over to my name, written in Min's hand, while touring the cottage. I slit the top, with a letter opener from her desk, and peeked inside. It was dated the night she died.

My dearest Isabel, if you're reading this, I'm dead. I must warn you that Naomi and I are at odds. Just this evening she visited, turning what had been a lovely day into a nightmare. The confrontation became physical, at one point. She ripped a handful of hair off my head, to the point of blood. I have no idea when she last took medication but she's raving mad.

She returned with Damian Ferguson in tow. His job was to convince me to change my will, leaving Naomi in charge of my finances. I've refused. She's after what little I have left to me from David's estate. I relinquished my birthright to her, under false pretenses. I surrendered you, my darling to her, at Arthur's plea. I'll not give her another bloody thing.

I've hidden this note in the tea cupboard because she'll not search for it there. She never darkens a kitchen door so I'm assured it'll be safe for you to find.

The latest debacle arose when I declared I would tell you the truth about your parentage and how you were subject to her care, or lack thereof. I had no idea she would take it as she did, and melt down. I just wanted my daughter to know she belongs to me before I pass from this world. I want my grandson to be able to name me as his own and enjoy him as such.

She's terrified you'll evict her from the estate and take her allowance, which you so liberally provide. I meant no harm in that quarter, honestly. I was surprised at her reaction. She's never cared for you or Liam so I thought to warn her only as a matter of politeness. Now I can't back away from my declaration.

This one thing I know for sure: she is not beyond killing me to shut me up. She's never stopped at anything, no matter how drastic, to get whatever she wants. I have little, but I've resolved to dictate who'll receive what I own and not give her an inch in this battle.

Isabel, in case you don't read through my journals, know this, dear heart; I love you with every fiber of my being, as I loved your father and I believe, he loved me.

Do whatever you must to find the truth and recapture your love with Cullum. He needs you like never before and I know you need him as much, not to mention my grandson. Have a houseful of wee ones and know I'll be with you if I can. If not, set a place for me at every picnic and family gathering, for I shall surely be there in spirit.

Your mother and friend, Minerva Banks

Someone spoke. I needed to turn my attention in that direction. I looked up at him, before me, a frown on his face. He knelt at my feet. At some point I seated myself on Min's bed in her room.

"Are you alright, Bel? What's this you're reading?" He reached for the letter.

I surrendered it to him as it concerned him as much as me and whispered, "It's from my mother."

He took the letter and read it, his hand resting on my knee. He sat back on his heels and let out a sigh. "Still not enough proof to convict Naomi though, eh?"

I shook my head. "I think not, but we might send a copy to John Cooley. The one thing I do know is she'll never see light again if I have my way."

"I'll call John from home. Alice is ready to leave. I paid her, but she needs to know if you have instructions other than weekly cleanings."

"Nay, tell her I'll call her if necessary. I just need a moment."

He rose, patting my knee, then my hair. "Take your time, mo chroi." He left me to myself for about ten minutes before I looked up to find him propped in the doorway.

I glanced up at the man I love more than life and smiled. "Where are we dining, sir?" I stood, not nearly as wobbly on my feet as I felt inside.

"It's Liam's turn to choose, I think." He met me and took my arm. "And if you're up to a walk on the shore, we'll take a turn before bedtime."

"When the tide's out?" I smiled at the prospect of a treasure hunt for beach glass. Red rocks and certain mollusk shells, amethyst in color, are also favorites, when discovered intact. Few survive the scourging of the fierce surf.

"Aye, and the Northern Lights spilling their brilliance across the sky."

We left my mother's home for the evening.

Chapter 29

Two months later:

I switched on telly, as there was little else I could manage, on bed rest. I'd read everything that interested me in the mansion's library and the public library in Nairn.

My pregnancy had not been difficult, but the stress of events, for nine months had been more than enough to cause my blood pressure to rise. To avoid problems, I rested, reclined, and was generally lazy those last weeks.

We moved back into Nairn shortly after I met with Naomi at the prison, for a little while. I believed Cullum was concerned we'd be too far from hospital, should I require a doctor.

Switching on telly was an act of sheer boredom.

Commercials droned for four minutes before the well-coiffed blonde BBC Scotland news anchor reappeared. "In other news tonight, from Inverness, a local solicitor awaiting trial for murder was found hanged in his cell.

"Damian Ferguson, a solicitor with offices in Inverness and Nairn, committed suicide, according to the sheriff's spokesperson. His accomplice in the crimes, Naomi Rose-Fielding, had no comment from her confinement in Inverness Prison's Women's Division.

"Ferguson is survived by his mother, his sister, and his brother-in-law, Constable Bernie Leighton. Constable Leighton is also under investigation for related matters."

I left the settee and walked to the French doors to consider the receding tide. Forty weeks past, I stood beside my lover, at this portal, studying the snow-peaked mountains of Black Isle. We'd been reunited for ten months.

Though conflict, confusion, and chaos ruled our lives for the majority of those months, I'll cherish the good things they birthed.

Recalling the night Liam and Cullum met, I'd live through it all again for that single beautiful moment.

My phone chimed. I left the scene I never tire of watching, to answer. "Hullo?" I hadn't bothered with call identification.

"Isabel?" A familiar voice inquired.

"Aye, it's me, Annmarie." I massaged the cramp in my lower back.

"I only just heard that your mother was sentenced to five years in prison. Is that true?" Her tone transmitted concern.

"Naomi was found guilty of conspiracy to murder, yes. We employed a psychiatrist, who confirmed that she's schizophrenic and has bipolar disorder. It helped to keep her sentence light, but she'll always be institutionalized. While incarcerated, she'll be forced to remain on medication." I returned to the settee to lie flat and prop my feet on the rolled arm.

"I'm so sorry, dear. I had no idea she was ill. Is there anythin' I can do to assist you?"

"I have no need of help, Annmarie. I have a husband who adores me and our second son is about to be born, any day. Tell me, how do you find the chairman's seat at AIM Enterprises?"

"I've run the company, from the background, for years, Isabel. William and I married twenty years ago. He had a need to wander, so it was better to not advertise our personal life. I wanted to touch base and thank you for opening the door to my entrance into the public sector. In appreciation, I assure you that I will keep your covenant with labor. I know that it's important and you've proven the programs work."

"Thank you very much. In all the tumult, it was my primary concern." The cramp migrated to my side and the front of my belly. I stretched, trying to find a comfortable position.

"Well, I'll leave you to your hearth and home, dear one. Do give your husband my best wishes."

"I shall, Annmarie, and good luck on all your ventures." *So the dark queen threw me a bone to be sure I wouldn't raise suspicion about Sir William's timely demise. I've waited for this call for three months.*

I pulled myself into sitting position as we rang off and dashed to the loo.

Doctor Henry Campbell held the stethoscope to my belly while I panted with pain. His faded eyes rolled to the corner of the bedroom, as he mumbled. "I believe it's time to birth this one, lass."

Caleigh stood at the end of the bed, donning scrubs, and watched. She and Kyle arrived two minutes behind Cullum after I called the pub.

"Caleigh's my doula. The midwife should be here momentarily." Another spasm struck. I inhaled deeply.

"I'll stand by with the lads and Father Ralph, then." Dr. Campbell left us, his old leather bag tucked beneath his arm. "The Petersons arrived with a pot o' soup. I think I heard its chowder. I'll be back if you need me."

Caleigh, pulling her dark blonde hair into a clasp, left the end of the bed to sit beside me holding my hand. "Robin and Genny should be here any moment now."

"Someday soon it'll be my turn to hold your hand." I took a deep breath and panted.

She smiled. "We've decided to adopt."

I realized what Min must have felt, or nearly. Watching this lovely woman, her heart's desire to birth another child, I knew I'd carry that child for her if she wished.

I love Caleigh like a sister. We bonded immediately, sixteen years ago, loving brothers and their family who took us both under their roof and into their hearts.

"We've had interviews, the investigations are under way, and then we'll find our child. Though we've come to realize, he might not be a baby—or a son, this time. We'll know when we meet, I think."

She rubbed my belly as another cramp gripped my body. I panted and tried to relax.

"I hope Becca arrives in time." I managed to squeak, as I panted into the next pain.

Caleigh laughed. "You're in good hands, though. I think between Dr. Campbell, who could deliver a bairn in his sleep, and me, we can take care of you two."

The door opened to Becca, my midwife, with Cullum following. "How's our patient?" She grinned, with a strained undercurrent of sadness.

Caleigh moved aside and reached for my husband, whose pale countenance suggested he might not make it through without help. She squeezed his shoulder. "Go, sit nearby, or climb on the bed with her. You can coach until we get close enough she needs me, alright?"

He just nodded and wiped his hand over his trim beard. "Mo chroi, is it bad?"

I shook my head and panted. "I think we're almost ready." Perspiration tracked from my forehead, into my hair and onto my neck.

He took note and dashed to the bath for a cool cloth. Climbing across the bed, he parked beside me, dabbing my face. "I love you, Bel."

"I love you too, my heart." I inhaled and panted. "I need to sit up when this cramp passes."

He propped pillows against the headboard and assisted me pushing into an upright position.

"Better?" He looked hopeful.

I smiled. "Aye." Another spasm gripped my abdomen. I pushed forward. Sitting is so much easier than lying flat during all that melee.

Becca checked me. "Cullum, are you catchin' at this end?" She was still smiling as she climbed on the foot of the bed.

He closed his eyes. "Um...."

"I'm just askin' because I can see the top of his noggin'." She braced herself against the footboard and studied my beloved with amusement.

"I suppose I must, eh? I've dreamed of this moment for almost thirteen years." He left my side and rounded the bed for the chair at the end. "I feel torn between holding your hand and being the first to see our lad."

Caleigh was at my side. "Breathe, both o' you."

I panted as my body convulsed. My knees brushed my ears as I pushed our new life into the cruel injustice of this world.

I squeezed Caleigh's hand and inhaled.

"One more time." Becca called out.

I pushed with all my might.

Cullum had his hands full of newborn boy. I watched from my position, as Becca tied and cut his lifeline to me and his da turned to show off the newest Sinclair.

Becca swaddled our son and Cullum rose to lay him to my breast.

A final cramp caused me to press forward. I smiled with relief.

Caleigh helped me unbutton my gown.

Enjoying every moment of Cullum's delight, I allowed him to lay our new lad to his first meal, only moving my hands into place as his receded.

My husband beamed. "My God, he's beautiful."

I studied half the wee face exposed to my vision. "He looks like Liam."

"He does tha'." Cullum wiped his hands clean with a damp rag that our sister-in-law handed over and watched our lad's every breath, while Becca finished.

Caleigh hovered, waiting her turn a bit impatiently. She decided to take the route across the bed. Suddenly, she was perched beside me, stroking the newborn fuzz on our lad's head. "I don't know anythin' more precious than this moment." She whipped her phone from her pocket and shot a few pictures.

"You can't go showing those around without exposing me too. He'll be finished in a moment and we'll have a good head-on look at him." I smiled down at our son and wondered what his dad would name him. "Have you a name ready for him, my love?"

His dad grinned, staring down at the marvel of life. "As a matter of fact, I do." He ran his thick forefinger along our lad's hairline. "Welcome to our family, Leith Robin Micheil Sinclair." He checked with me, one brow raised.

"I like it…Leith."

Caleigh chuckled. "Keepin' our lads in the ell tradition." She bent low and placed a kiss on Leith's fuzzy cheek.

Leith smiled. Angel sighs, Min would've said. I felt a huge gulf of longing to have known her as my mother, for her to share this joyous moment she'd dreamed of for years.

Oh, to have her here, by our sides to relish this lovely, tiny marvel of God's handiwork.

A tear slipped, unnoticed, until Cullum lifted my chin. "I miss her, too, mo chroi." He kissed me. "If she could've only been here."

Chapter 30

2014

September is upon us. Leith has been the sweetest baby ever born. He's held almost constantly between all his loving relatives and his dad. Cullum can't get enough of him. Liam is a grand brother, changing nappies like he's done it his entire life.

Caleigh and Kyle adopted a baby girl, Lily, two months ago, so Genny and Robin play their parts well, splitting their time between Leith and Lily.

The Petersons decided to stay in Nairn but I could not bear to part with Min's cottage permanently so they rent. Mrs. Peterson helps me with Leith as we prepare for another addition. Our daughter is due to be born in four months. Genevieve Minerva Lucille Sinclair will be her name. Cullum chose names from our families, to the delight of his mother. We call her Lucy.

While a palatable tension surges throughout our fair land, in our home peace reigns.

Our political climate quakes with tension. Households divide over the vote for independence. I've heard the new constable has his hands full of domestic disagreements this week past.

The English make speeches against our liberation, with a few Scottish agreeing. Phrases like: We're stronger united with England, and, How will we cope without the Queen? are whispered at every turn.

We cannot approach this historic opportunity through a curtain of fear. The future is unknown, as we've been at England's mercy for more than seven centuries. Still, a lot of us hold out hope that the fearful will venture towards freedom rather than bondage. We're familiar with bondage; the future, with liberty, is uncertain.

Cullum and I hold hands as we walk to the polls, greeting neighbors and pub regulars as we pass. A few pat my expanding belly. How I long to tell my children of the day Scotland *won* her freedom, not through might but through the courage of casting a ballot. I'd written down my thoughts on the subject when I carried

Liam, then again when expecting Leith. I continue the Freedom Journal through this pregnancy.

The next generation needs to weigh the cost, for liberty will never be free.

We take our places in the queue, huddling closely in the damp, frigid morning mist. I lower my hood for a moment and turn my face upwards, for the haze to moisten my skin. Inhaling the salty air, I meet beloved's eyes with a smile.

He brushes his hand over his cleanly shaven chin. His deep voice falls flat in the soggy atmosphere. "What do you think, Bel?"

"It's out of our hands and into the hands of the people of Scotland."

A loud cry rings out over the area, when a hearty pronouncement begins:

"For as long as one hundred of us shall remain alive, we shall never *in any wise* consent submit to the rule of the English, for it is not for glory we fight, nor riches, or for honor, but for freedom alone, which no good man loses, but with his life."

Reverential silence follows, a few sobs break through, more trail.

The commanding voice continues.

"Those words were uttered, by Robert the Bruce 700 years ago today. He was one of the greatest heroes this land has known, and *there have been many*. Stand with us, united, and do not allow your heart to fail. We hold, within our hands, the key that opens the door to the prison. *Do— not— lose—heart*."

A glimpse beyond the crowd reveals the speaker. Straightening, he stands a head higher than those around him. Father Ralph's lecture carries on the wind, blowing inland, to nearby polling places in Nairn.

Weeping begins in earnest as he prays over our town. His huge white-haired head thrown back, arms extended, he speaks directly into the sky above.

"Great God of heaven, hear the cry of poor, impoverished wretches, standin' before Ye, askin' fer the courage to meet our duty this day. Give us the fortitude we need to put our fears behind us and move forward, into the glorious future of this land."

He takes a huge breath, the few hundred people nearby waiting expectantly. He bellows, "Ye are the God of deliverance, the God of liberty and Ye'd have none of us, as slaves to any man, nor any fear. Ye'd have none of us cowerin' in dread of the unknown. Ye hold our tomorrows as securely as Ye held our yesterdays. We trust Ye to lead us out of our Egypt and into the promised land."

Applause becomes a roar of approval. Everyone within reach slaps the old man's back in encouragement, as shouts of *Amen*, beginning with Vicar Angus MacBride, are heard from blocks away.

I spot Leah Mabry-Mitchell, Hazel at her knee, near Father Ralph's elbow. Her eyes narrow, her lips purse, as she offers her hand to him. The old man bends double to lay a delicate kiss on her wrinkled fingers.

I wipe my cheeks free of tears with my gloved hand and search out a hankie in my pocket. I glance up at Cullum, the concern faded from his eyes, his face turn towards me, smiling.

"Bel, I ken it'll be a fine day today."

Looping my arm through his, I lean in for a kiss from his luscious mouth. "I think I agree with you, my love. Tonight we'll stay up until all the ballots are counted and we can go to bed knowing today's battle is won."

He kisses me again. "Aye, lass, today's battle is won forever."

Dedication

This novel is dedicated to the people of Scotland.

Should you ever have need of two expats with the fervor of Wallace, the fire of Burns, and the resources of Rob Roy, let us hear from you.

Our prayers are with you in 2014, a year of decision and conflict.

Hopefully, this modest work will touch an unsure or timid heart for the better result.

Acknowledgements

Thank you for the use of your information and assistance grounding this book.

The Forsyth family of Wetherby House Bed and Breakfast Nairn, Scotland

Tom and Nancy Tomlin of Eilidh Bed and Breakfast Inverness, Scotland

Jacquie and Mike of Ard Na Coille Bed and Breakfast Newtonmore, Scotland

The staff of The MacDonald Highland Conference Center of Aviemore, Scotland

Thank you, Judy Kemper for your persistence in editing. You are a blessing, dear lady.

In lieu of a Bonafide glossary, I used a few forms of Gaelic endearments.

- Mo chroi (muh khree) means my heart.
- Cuisle mo chroi (Kush luh muh khree) means pulse of my heart.